Slings
and
Arrows

NICK McLOUGHLIN

The Book Guild Ltd

First published in Great Britain in 2024 by
The Book Guild Ltd
Unit E2 Airfield Business Park,
Harrison Road, Market Harborough,
Leicestershire. LE16 7UL
Tel: 0116 2792299
www.bookguild.co.uk
Email: info@bookguild.co.uk
Twitter: @bookguild

Typeset in 11pt Minion Pro

Printed on FSC accredited paper
Printed and bound in Great Britain by 4edge Limited

ISBN 978 1916668 317

British Library Cataloguing in Publication Data.
A catalogue record for this book is available from the British Library.

To Mum, for making me a reader.

PROLOGUE

Terry knew what was coming. He'd heard the rumours of course, talk amongst the lads on the shop floor and in the pub after work, but it was their faces that confirmed the truth. The faces of those who went in before him, as they came out, unstrung, already wondering how they were going to make the next month's mortgage payment. Terry was luckier than most in that regard, he would at least get a bit of a pay-off; thirty years' service surely counted for something. But he doubted it would get him much past Christmas.

The door opened and another shattered figure appeared through it. Terry tried to catch his eye, wanting to show sympathy, solidarity, but the man walked on in a trance. Terry knew him only vaguely; he'd been at the same table at the canteen a couple of weeks back passing around a picture of his wife with their newborn baby. Terry had looked at the photograph out of politeness rather than curiosity; he could see how proud the man was. He was new to the firm, less than three months, he would get nothing.

Terry got to his feet, walked into the room and shut the door behind him. As he turned to face the men behind the polished wood table, he saw Phil. And saw him look quickly down at the pile of papers arranged neatly in front of him, unable to meet Terry's eye.

The man at the centre of the table cleared his throat. 'Ah, Terry,' he said, 'sit down. I think you probably know everybody: John from HR and Bill from the Union. And, er, I asked Phil to be here too, as your immediate line manager. I know you two go back a long way.'

Phil looked up and nodded his head. Terry could see that Phil would rather have not been asked to be there. They'd been friends long enough for that to be blatantly obvious.

'Yes, well, I think you've probably worked out why we're here, and I'm terribly sorry, we all are, but...'

Terry wasn't really listening. Through the window, the leaves were just beginning to change. A gust of wind blew some to the ground, and the low sun caught their colours as they fell.

'So, yes, as I said, I know this is difficult, and we really are awfully sorry.' He paused, aware seemingly that Terry was paying him little attention. 'Have you got any questions?'

Terry turned to Phil. 'How long have you known?'

'Well,' said the man at the centre of the table, 'we've been doing all we can to avoid this, but in the end, redundancies were inevitable and—'

'How long have you known I was on the list?' said Terry, still looking at Phil.

Phil tugged at the cuff of his shirt and shook his head. 'I, well they only—'

The man cut Phil off again, 'Things... names, were only finalised very recently. As you can imagine, it was very difficult.'

Terry nodded. He pushed back his chair and stood up. 'I'll see ya,' he said to Phil and walked out of the room.

Outside, the wind had picked up, and it had started to rain. Terry opened his mouth and inhaled an enormous breath of damp air. *What am I going to tell Pat?* he thought.

ONE

Saturday, 9 January 1982

Terry stuffed the T-shirts he was holding back into the drawer and stood up with a groan, catching the back of his leg on the edge of the bed. As he snatched open the wardrobe doors, the dry-cleaning bag containing his work suit stirred in the disturbed air, as though to mock him, the ticket showing the date when he'd dropped it off still visible through the clear plastic. Three months. Terry pushed it aside and unhooked the pink polo shirt he was looking for from the rail. He walked through to the living room without putting it on. Pat sat one leg crossed over the other in the armchair ready for work in her pale blue uniform and light tan tights, watching *Jim'll Fix It* on the television.

'Right, I'm ready,' said Terry.

'Well, put your shirt on then, you'll frighten the neighbours. I see enough of that at work.'

Terry slapped his large gut. 'I bet you don't see many bodies like this though, eh?'

'Not still breathing I don't, no. Come on.'

Pat turned the television off and stood up from the sofa, poking her finger into Terry's pale belly as he pulled the shirt over his head. On the left breast, embroidered in white cotton,

1

was the profile of a stag's head with "The White Hart" sewn beneath it. On the back, in four-inch-high iron-on letters, were the words "BALD EAGLE" in capitals.

'You'll look a right set of pillocks turning up at The Swan in those. You'll be lucky to get out alive.'

'It's not that rough,' said Terry. 'Tom had them done at work, reckons it's good advertising.'

'Well, you're definitely advertising something,' said Pat, laughing.

Pat drove, though she spent most of the short journey fiddling with the heating in the car and wiping the condensation off the inside of the windscreen with an old tissue, which quickly fell apart in her hands, leaving bits stuck to the smeared glass.

'What time does your match start?' she said, stopping the car outside the front of the pub.

'Half past.'

'You're a bit early, but I start at seven, so I'll have to drop you. See if you can get one of the lads to give you a lift home. I've left you some of that pie we had for tea in case you're peckish when you get in.'

Terry cleared the side window with the back of his hand, wiping it dry on his jeans. 'The curtains are still drawn. I don't think they're open yet, I'll freeze.'

'Well, it's a good job you brought a jacket then. Go on, it's five-to; they'll open in a minute. I'll see you in the morning.'

Terry got out of the car. Laughter echoed from inside the pub, and a chink of light seeped from the bottom corner of the curtained window. He tried the door, but it was locked. He stepped back and looked up and down the row of dark brick buildings, wondering whether or not to try one of the other pubs that stood on either end of the narrow street. Before he could make a decision, he heard the bolt slam back on the pub door and a sign above it flickered on, appealing to him to "Try Worthington's Bitter".

Terry pushed open the door, and the laughter increased in volume, spilling out into the dimly lit street. Inside, the heat of the small room struck Terry in the chest, wrapping him in a cloak of stagnant air thick with beery sweat and nicotine. A group of half a dozen or so men were sat drinking at a couple of tables pushed together in one corner of the room. Judging by the debris in front of them, they had obviously been there all afternoon. Terry had been in the pub once before, ten years ago or more, and as far as he remembered, little of the layout or decor appeared to have changed. It was a one-room pub with the bar occupying the centre of the back wall, facing the door. Beyond it, a narrow passage led through to the toilets; the dartboard was tucked into an alcove on the other side. Five or six small round tables, their surface varnish stripped with wear, filled the remaining space. The once red, patterned carpet was worn smooth and black from years of spillages and dirty boots.

As he entered, the men turned to look at Terry. One of them threw back what remained of his pint, picked up a further seven empty glasses from the table and got to his feet. The man was tall, six–four at least, with a massive chest and shoulders and hands that made the pint glasses look like halves. He had grey-white hair shaved short to his head and a deeply lined face, with a great flat nose that looked to Terry like it had been broken more than once.

'How do,' said the man, as he and Terry crossed paths on their way to the bar. 'What can I get you?'

'Pint please.'

'You here for the darts?'

'Yes,' said Terry, 'just waiting for the rest of the team. Thanks.'

Terry picked up his pint from the bar and took it to a table against the side wall, away from where the others were sitting. He unzipped his jacket and went to remove it completely but remembered the shirt and thought better of it. The group in the

3

corner were still talking and laughing loudly. He overheard one of them, a small wiry man with a hollowed-out face, say to the others in a thick Scottish accent, 'I told him to fuck off or I'd chin 'em.'

Terry took the top off his pint and glanced at his watch. The door opened, but it was only another local. By the way he staggered in, he looked like he'd been preparing hard at home for the session in the pub. Terry was two thirds of the way down his pint before Phil arrived.

'Do you want another?' Phil asked on his way to the bar.

'No thanks,' said Terry, picking up his glass but then putting it down again without taking a drink.

'They look like they've had a few,' said Phil, when he got back to the table with his pint. 'Landlord seems a sweetheart though.'

Terry glanced towards the bar, but fortunately the landlord was occupied with restocking a low fridge with bottles of Gold Label and had not heard Phil's comment. Phil sat down and took off his coat, throwing it onto the seat next to him.

'You haven't got your team shirt on,' said Terry.

'No, I forgot.'

'You'll look an idiot, the only one without it.'

Phil eyed the room. 'I think I'll need to do more than that to look an idiot in here,' he said, louder than Terry would have liked. The group around the table in the corner bellowed over one another, cackling like hyenas at a watering hole.

'How've you been?' asked Phil, lowering his head to suck the froth of his pint. 'Busy?'

'Oh yeah,' said Terry, 'what with washing my hair and tidying my sock drawer, I've been run off my feet.'

'Yeah, sorry,' said Phil. 'I just wondered – well, you know, it's been three months and—'

'I know how long it's been,' said Terry. He took a pull on his pint and turned as the pub door opened. Tom and Dave came in.

'Alright, fellas,' said Dave, as the pair sat down and began removing their coats.

'Bloody hell, where's your shirts? I'm going to look a right prat, the only one,' moaned Terry.

'Yeah sorry,' said Tom, scanning the room, 'we thought it might not be the best idea in here. Thought we'd save them for the next round.'

'If we survive,' said Dave with a grin. 'Look on the bright side, you can be team captain for the night, take on the landlord. Though I'd go easy on him if I were you.' The three men laughed.

'Bastards,' said Terry.

The landlord came out from behind the bar and made his way over to the dartboard. He flicked on a spotlight fixed to the ceiling that was angled to light up the board.

'Right, gents,' he said, 'shall we get started?'

Dave and Tom were already putting their darts together on the table, screwing the shafts into the pointed tungsten barrels and inserting the flights. Terry stood and finally took off his jacket, dropping it onto the chair.

'Nice shirt,' shouted one of the men at the other table, and the rest of the group laughed.

'Right,' said the landlord, 'split your team into two pairs – each pair plays two matches, one point for a win. Then we'll play three singles, so leave out your weakest man, point for a win again. Seven matches total, max, first team to four points, OK? Each match best of three legs.'

'OK,' said Phil to the others, 'let's see how it goes in the doubles before we decide who drops out in the singles – if it comes to that. Tom, you're the strongest, you play first with Dave. I'll play with Terry.'

'I should play the singles, I'm the only one in the shirt,' said Terry.

From the start, Terry could see that the landlord was a decent player. And his height and reach made the board look two feet closer for him than for everyone else. But the Scotsman, clearly the worse for wear, was a liability. Tom and Dave won the match two legs to nil.

'Cunt,' said the landlord to the Scotsman.

Terry, paired with Phil, played next and won easily. One of their opponents, his arms a mess of blue ink, was so drunk that he missed the board entirely with at least half of his darts, while the other, an old man in a flat cap and thick glasses, was no better. Terry and Phil stayed on to play their other match but lost to the landlord and the Scotsman, much to the latter's delight. Tom and Dave, though, won again to make the score 3-1 after the doubles.

'You boys want a drink?' said the landlord. 'Take a break for five minutes?'

'I'm just nipping to the gents,' said Terry.

He pushed open the toilet door and was hit by the acrid tang of disinfectant. Hockey puck disks of lurid pink and blue lined the base of the metal urinal that ran the full width of the bare brick toilet. Terry placed his feet to avoid the puddles of urine on the torn lino and unzipped his fly. He looked down and then ahead at the flaking white paint covering the bricks six inches from his face. Eventually, a weak, intermittent flow splashed into the urinal. A cigarette butt bobbed and drifted in the direction of the central drain but stuck in a dam of sanitiser cakes. Running over the glossy blocks, his pee picked up their colour, turning blue and then pink. The door behind him slammed open against the toilet wall. Terry shook his penis and stuffed it back inside his pants, wetting his fingers in the process.

'Hey, bald eagle,' said a slurred voice, and a hand slapped him between the shoulder blades. Terry managed to free his arms just quickly enough to prevent his forehead from colliding with the brick wall. He turned and hurried out of the toilet, rejoining the others at the table.

'Nice one, boys,' said Phil, bringing over the last two pints and sitting down. 'We only need one more from the singles, and they'll play the landlord up first. You should take him on, Tom, then, if needed, you go next, Dave – you're playing well tonight. I'll sit out.'

'What about me?' said Terry. 'I might not get another game.'

'The quicker we get out of here, the better,' said Tom, picking up his darts.

At five foot five, Tom was dwarfed by his giant opponent, whose colossal build gave the impression that he could throw Tom at the board as easily as he could a dart. Physically, at least, this was a mismatch, and Terry wondered whether Tom might be as well doing them all a favour by not winning. But it was not necessary. It was obvious immediately that Tom felt intimidated by the landlord, who appeared to deliberately stand in his eyeline each time it was Tom's turn to throw. He lost the match two legs to nil; a result that looked in no doubt from the start.

'Sorry,' said Tom dejectedly as he joined the others at the bar.

The Scotsman threw back a short and leaped up to play the next match.

'George,' said the landlord, and the Scotsman sat down again.

Dave made short work of the old man, who was back in his chair sipping from his pint of mild almost before the last dart had landed.

'Flippin' 'eck,' said Terry, 'I hardly played.'

'Never mind,' laughed Dave, 'at least you looked the part.'

'Good game,' said Phil, extending his hand over the bar.

Terry was surprised to see the landlord take it.

'Jesus,' said Phil, when they got back to the table, 'he nearly broke my fingers.'

'Serves you right,' said Terry, 'he probably thought you were taking the piss.'

'Anybody want another drink?' said Dave.

'No thanks,' said Tom, looking around the room, which had gained another half-dozen locals while they'd been playing darts, most of whom, Terry noticed, appeared to share the same barber as the landlord. 'I think we should get out of here before there's any trouble.'

'Speaking of which,' said Dave.

They all looked around to see the Scotsman weaving his way towards their table.

'Any o' you lucky bastards wannae drink?' he spat, smacking his hand down on the table.

'No thanks,' said Tom, picking up his jacket, 'we were just leaving actually.'

'Agh fuck off and have a drink wi' me, you wee shite.'

Terry saw the landlord glance up in their direction and then begin making his way out from behind the bar. 'Shit,' Terry said and got quickly to his feet. But the Scotsman slapped a hand on his shoulder and pushed him back down into his seat.

'Sit down, baldie, and have a drink wi' me.'

As Terry half turned and went to stand up again, the landlord appeared behind the Scotsman and lifted him off his feet, carrying him upright across the room before depositing him back onto his chair. The landlord then took a few strides over to the door and pulled it open.

'Good night, fellas,' he said, 'good luck in the next round.'

The four of them were already heading for the exit, snatching up their darts and cases from the table and throwing on their jackets. They filed past the landlord, and he closed the door behind them.

'Nice place,' said Dave, 'remind me to pop in again sometime.'

'Yeah cosy,' said Tom.

Before Terry could ask either of them for a ride home, Phil shook his keys. 'Pat working, Terry? I'll run you if you like.'

There was less than eighteen months between Terry and Phil, but it looked like more. Phil was six foot and lean, with a full head of dark hair and a moustache he was proud of to match. On a Sunday, when he wasn't fishing, he cycled with a local club, sometimes as much as sixty or seventy miles out into the country around Ashbourne and the southern parts of the Peak District. Terry, on the other hand, was short and significantly overweight. His gut, all bought and paid for as he liked to say, overhung the belt on his jeans, and but for an inch or so of thin, blondish hair above his ears, he was bald. A thick roll of flesh at the back of his head rested snug against his shirt collar. Walking to the car, Terry had to scamper to match Phil's stride, and though the distance was less than forty yards, he was breathing heavily when they reached it.

It was cold in the car. Terry sat hunched low in his seat with his head on his chest, his hands deep in his jacket pockets. The roads were slick and greasy with rain, and it looked like it was trying to snow. Neither of them spoke. They had spent years travelling to and from work together, but this was the first time that they had been alone since Terry's redundancy. In his heart, he knew Phil had had nothing to do with it, but he was still finding it hard to forgive him. The last three months had been the worst of his life.

'What the hell is that?' said Phil, as they pulled up in front of Terry's house.

'What?'

'That sign, you can't sell the house; you've always lived there. What does Pat think?'

Terry turned his head to look at Phil. 'It was her idea, mate. And we've had an offer already. If it goes through, Pat reckons we'll come out with a few grand and be able to buy a place on Langley's, no mortgage.'

'A caravan, Jesus you're joking?'

'Mobile home,' said Terry, 'static.'

Phil blew out his cheeks. 'Shit, I didn't realise things were that bad.'

'Yeah, well maybe you should tell your mates on the redundancy committee,' said Terry, pushing open the car door, 'I'm sure they'd be really upset.'

'I didn't know any more about that than you did,' said Phil. 'I tried to get them to take your name off the list.'

Terry bent to look at Phil. 'Well, which of those was it, because it can't be both.' Without waiting for an answer, he turned and set off up the path.

Fumbling with his front door key, Terry realised that Phil had not yet pulled away. He was probably still staring, shocked, at the large "For Sale" sign in front of the house. Inside, Terry slung his jacket over the banister post at the bottom of the stairs and walked through to the kitchen. Dennis, their fat black tomcat, whined at the back door, and Terry let him in.

'Hello, matey,' said Terry, 'looks like it's just the two of us tonight.'

A note lay on the worktop alongside a plate covered by a tea towel and a small jug of gravy with a thin skin on top. Beneath the tea towel was a large portion of meat pie, a mound of mashed potato and what looked like a whole tin's worth of peas and baby carrots. Terry took a teaspoon from the drawer and stirred the gravy while he read the note.

There's more pie in the oven if Martin gets back. Stick yours in the microwave for 3 or 4 minutes. The gravy might need a stir.

See you in the morning. P x.
PS Hope you won!

Terry poured the dark gravy over his meal and put it in the microwave. He fed the cat while he waited for it to heat up and took a beer from the fridge. When the microwave pinged, he transferred the plate onto a tray, carried it through to the living room and began flicking through the television channels for something to watch. He'd missed *The Two Ronnies* but settled on *Match of the Day* and cut into his pie, releasing a cloud of pungent steam.

The following morning, Terry sat slouched at the kitchen table in his dressing gown, drinking tea from a huge Derby County mug, when he heard the key in the front door and then Pat taking off her coat and shoes in the entrance hall at the bottom of the stairs. A moment later, she came through into the kitchen. She kissed Terry on top of the head and slumped into her seat at the end of the table.

'God, I'm knackered,' she said, getting up again to flick the switch on the kettle.

'I know love, I'm sorry—'

'No, no,' Pat said, cutting him off, 'it's not your fault, Terry. It's just I've been on my feet all night; I've not sat down. Martin OK?'

'I've not seen him this morning. He's still in his pit, the lazy sod. It'd help if he got himself a job; it should be easier at his age.'

Pat spooned a sugar into her tea, stirred it and sat back down. 'Oh well,' she said, 'you won't have to worry about it much longer. He told me yesterday he's not moving to the caravan with us. Pete's offered him a room at his place.'

'What? You're joking. How's he going to pay his way?'

Pat sat back in her chair, clutching her mug to her chest, her face drawn and pale but for half-moon patches of grey beneath her eyes. 'I don't know, but he's twenty, Terry. He needs his independence; he can't stay under our feet forever. And anyway, it'll mean we only need a one-bedroom caravan, cheaper.' She paused and took a sip from her tea. 'The agent called yesterday as well. Apparently, that couple that came round last week has offered the full price for this place, cash, so the agent reckons the sale might go through in a couple of weeks or so.'

Terry exhaled. 'Flippin' 'eck, I never thought it would come to this.'

Pat put down her mug and placed her hand over Terry's. 'Don't worry, love, we'll be fine,' she said.

She got up and took two slices of bread from the loaf in the bread bin and dropped them into the toaster. When they popped, she removed them and spread a thick layer of margarine on each. 'I'm going to take these up, love, and get a couple of hours' kip; I'll see you in a bit.'

TWO

Terry shut the back door behind him, turned the key and left it in the lock. 'Any idea where the cat is?' he shouted, walking through to the hall.

'I don't know, Terry, we'll find him later,' replied Pat, making her way down the stairs with a cardboard box in her arms. 'Come and give me a hand; there's still a couple of things to bring down.'

Terry stepped aside to allow Pat to pass him before heading up the stairs himself. He stopped for a moment at the top and then slipped into Martin's room at the back of the house. It was empty. Remnants of Blu Tack dotted the walls, and a rectangle of carpet, less faded than the rest, revealed where the bed had stood for the last eighteen years. Terry closed his eyes, and the room was furnished: bright and busy with toys and books and children's paintings. Martin was sat cross-legged on a rug beside the bed, pushing a yellow lorry backwards and forwards across the floor. He turned and looked up as Terry came into the room, and smiled.

'I've finished in there, but there's a couple of boxes left in our room.'

Pat's voice broke Terry's reverie, and he followed her across the landing. Stripped of furniture and curtains, and without the usual scattering of clothes and magazines on every surface, their bedroom appeared somehow smaller to Terry. Only the bed remained, marooned in the centre of the room, the aged mattress saggy with the contrasting impressions of its long-term occupants.

'Looks like Phil's here,' said Pat, picking up a box from beneath the window. 'Where did he get that van?'

Terry looked down and saw his friend getting out of a battered Bedford van that was probably once white.

'It's his brother's,' he replied. 'He's a musician.'

Across the street, old Mrs Thompson opened her front door to take in the bottle of milk from her doorstep. She paused for a minute to check up on what was happening opposite, pulling her dressing gown more tightly around her skinny frame, and then closed the door behind her. A few seconds later, she reappeared in her usual spot between the gap in the net curtains.

'Well, I won't miss that nosy so-and-so,' Terry said to himself.

When he got downstairs with the final box, Phil and Pat were in the living room surrounded by containers of crockery, suitcases, lamps, plants and bin bags stuffed with blankets, pillows and cushions.

'Is this it then?' Phil asked, looking around.

'Yeah, not much really, is it?' replied Terry.

'We've got rid of a lot of stuff, and Martin's taken a few things with him,' said Pat, 'and we've managed to get quite a bit in the Allegro.'

'Martin not giving you a hand?' said Phil.

'No, he's playing football this morning.'

'Football my arse,' said Terry. 'He's just bone idle. The thought of grafting for a few hours brings him out in a cold sweat.'

'Right,' said Phil, 'let's start with the big stuff first. We might manage it all in one run with a squeeze.'

An hour or so later, the living room had been cleared and the van stuffed to the back doors.

'Well,' said Pat, her voice echoey in the empty room, 'I suppose that's it then.'

Terry surveyed the room. The sofa and chairs had left indents like mini crop circles in the carpet, and rectangles of clean paint marked where pictures had hung on the walls. He glanced at Pat, who seemed close to tears, and reached across to give her hand a squeeze.

'Dennis,' he said, as the cat strolled into the room and rubbed himself against their legs, 'you didn't think we'd leave without you, did you?' He bent and scooped the cat up into his arms. 'You jump in with Phil, Pat, and I'll put Dennis in the footwell and follow in the car.'

The caravan site was located in a field on the outskirts of town, between a bend in the river Derwent and a new housing development of thirty or so small red-brick semis. Terry knew it from his childhood. Back then, the whole area had been a farm, before the Langleys had started selling off the land to developers as the town expanded ever outwards into the countryside. Now, the section of the site closest to the river was used as a place to park up towable caravans when the owners weren't using them. The larger, more permanent, homes were laid out in two neat rows either side of a gravel track, at the end of which, backing onto the new builds, stood the original farmhouse, in which the current Mr Langley still lived.

A sheet of plywood hung from the gate with a hand-painted sign.

Langley's Mobile and Residential Caravan Park
No Trespassing

Driving slowly along the track, Terry counted a dozen static caravans, each one beige, with a thick, brown stripe running horizontally all the way around. They stood two feet off the ground on breezeblocks, a set of metal steps leading to the door, situated in the centre of one of the long sides of each unit. A large window, split into two panes, filled most of the upper half of the ends facing the track, below which *Langley's* had been written in the shape of an upturned mouth, so that the windows became eyes in a smiley face, the painted brown stripe a thick moustache.

A few of the caravans had potted plants either side of the entrance steps, but a couple, Terry thought, encircled by miniature white picket fences, were definitely trying to outdo the rest. Within the perimeter of the fence, one owner had positioned a dozen or so terracotta figures: gnomes, hedgehogs, rabbits and a small winged child on its knees with his head in his hands. Terry knew exactly how he felt.

Terry stopped the Allegro a few feet behind the van, outside the last but one caravan. At the end of the track, a Land Rover was parked up in the drive of the farmhouse, alongside a shiny X-reg. Ford Granada.

He's doing OK for himself, thought Terry.

Phil and Pat were stood on the grass beneath the broad front window of the caravan, Phil with his forehead against the glass and his hands cupped around his face, peering in. Terry passed them, took a key from his jacket pocket and let himself in. In the centre of the wall opposite the door, a window above the kitchen sink gave a view of the next caravan in the row. Melamine kitchen cupboards, cream with a brown trim, lined the wall either side of the window and the sink. A white gas cooker with a high grill stood in the corner. Terry had seen the bottles on paving slabs outside the back of each unit on the drive in.

'It needs airing a bit,' said Pat, coming up the steps behind Terry. 'It'll be better when we get some heating on.'

Terry moved through an archway to his left into the living room, which occupied the full width of the caravan at the front, overlooking the track. It was empty, save for a thick brown carpet patterned with orange and mustard-coloured circles within squares and a set of chocolate-brown curtains. Through the window, a woman in a pair of pink, fluffy slippers and a Union Jack apron come out of the home opposite to shout at a boy, who was racing a bike up and down the track, to come and put a coat on. She was pale and scrawny, with inky-black hair like the feathers of a crow scraped back from her weary face in a tight ponytail. *Irish*, Terry thought, *and probably younger than she looks.* Her son skidded to a stop in front of her, spraying her slippered feet with loose stones, and then took off again laughing, showing little inclination to heed his mother's advice on the need for a coat. She noticed Terry at the window, shrugged and smiled.

The light faded quickly as they worked, and it was completely dark by the time they had moved everything out of the vehicles into the caravan.

'Shall we have a cuppa?' said Terry, removing a box of crockery from a chair to sit down. 'I'm parched.'

'I'll have to find the teabags and milk first,' said Pat, rummaging through a carton of food. 'Just give me a minute.'

Phil pulled a kettle from the box on Terry's lap and handed it to Pat. 'That reminds me,' he said to Terry, 'what you doing tomorrow?'

'Well, apart from sorting this place out,' Terry replied, waving his arms at the chaos around him, 'and painting my nails, nothing, as usual, why?'

'You remember Mike, my brother-in-law? He's looking for someone to give him a hand with his milk round next week, cash in hand.'

'I don't know,' said Terry, 'there's a lot to do around here. What do you think, love?'

'Rubbish,' said Pat, filling the kettle. 'It'll do you good to be working again, even if it is only for a few days. This won't take us long.'

'Great,' said Phil. 'You'll have to meet him at the dairy on Mill Hill Road at three to load up. I think he's usually done by about half-eight, nine-ish.'

'Bloody hell, three in the morning, never mind unpacking, I may as well go to bed now,' said Terry. 'Who needs milk in the middle of the night anyway?'

'Babies?' said Phil, with a grin.

'Yeah,' said Terry, 'but they've usually got their own supply.'

'Welcome to my world,' said Pat, putting her hand on Terry's shoulder. 'At least you won't be wiping old men's backsides and emptying bedpans.'

'On that note,' said Phil, passing Pat a couple of mugs, 'I'm going to get off. Good luck tomorrow, Terry, don't forget to set the alarm.'

'You not stopping for a cuppa?' asked Pat.

'No,' said Phil, pushing open the caravan door, 'Julie's been a bit strange lately; I don't want to be late for tea.'

Pat closed the door. Terry picked up a bag of ornaments and pictures and took them into the living room. He put the bag down on the sofa and began fiddling with the controls on the electric fire until the three bars began to glow orange, light at first and then darker as the heat increased. A couple of minutes later, Pat came through carrying two mugs of tea. Terry turned the backs of his legs and his palms to the heat. 'Just me and you,' he said.

Pat handed him a mug. 'Martin would have helped if he could. You know he would. And he's better off at his mate's, it might push him to look for a job.'

'Yeah, I suppose,' said Terry. 'I just want him to make something of himself. Do better than...' he looked around the room, 'better than this.'

Pat took Terry's mug and placed it on a box next to her own. Then she smiled and put her arms around his waist. 'We'll be fine,' she said, 'as long as we've got each other, we'll be just fine.'

Terry pulled her in close to him. He felt her chest rise against his as she breathed in deeply and then her breath, warm on his neck, when she exhaled.

THREE

Phil hung up his coat, untied his shoes and lined them up on the mat inside the front door. He sat down in the chair beside the coat stand and eased on his slippers, sighing quietly as the woollen lining enveloped his feet. He looked at his watch: teatime.

In the living room, he stood for a moment in front of *Songs of Praise* but didn't recognise the hymn and turned it off. The dining table, its surface gleaming under the overhead light, was laid for two. Phil sat down and poured himself a small glass of Bordeaux. One of his nice bottles, he noticed. Julie came in carrying two plates and sat down opposite him.

'Oh, chops,' said Phil, 'white might have been better with these.'

'I fancied something with a bit more oomph,' said Julie, filling her glass.

Phil made a little noise in the back of his throat and took a sip. 'Terry sends his regards,' he said, 'and Pat.'

Julie raised her eyebrows at him over the rim of her glass and swallowed a mouthful of wine. 'How did it go?' she asked.

'God, you should see the place,' said Phil, shaking his head. 'It's tiny – and damp. And it's got these awful brown curtains and a carpet that looks like it came out of a working men's club. I feel so sorry for them.'

'Well, you've got your lovely Mrs Thatcher to thank for that.'

'What's she got to do with it?'

'It's her fault he got laid off,' said Julie, 'him and about three million others.'

'That's the unions,' said Phil. 'If anyone's to blame, it's them.'

'I quite envy them actually,' said Julie. 'At least it's a bit of excitement, moving house, a chance to start afresh.'

'What do you mean?' asked Phil.

Julie shrugged. 'Oh I don't know. Just something different, I suppose.'

They ate on in silence, under the relentless tick of the carriage clock on the mantlepiece. Phil watched Julie as he ate, but she appeared more interested in the wine than the food. 'I told Terry about the milk round with Mike,' he said, picking up his chop and gnawing at the remains of the meat on the bone.

'I really wish you wouldn't do that,' said Julie.

Phil dropped the bone onto his plate and sucked at his fingertips. 'I thought it would do him good, you know, for his self-esteem. I think he'll thank me for it.'

Julie poured herself another glass of wine. 'Very noble of you, I'm sure,' she said. She picked up Phil's plate and took a step towards the kitchen.

Phil sat back in his chair, his hands in his lap. 'Have you done something to your hair?' he said.

'Washed it,' replied Julie, over her shoulder.

FOUR

Terry tiptoed to the toilet and back to bed in an attempt not to wake Pat. But still unfamiliar with the layout of the caravan, he collided with the kitchen table in both directions, hard enough on the way back to nudge it across the floor, causing him to let out a sharp moan at the sudden pain in his thigh.

'Is it that time already?' Pat said to him as he got back into bed, her voice slow and thick with sleep.

'No, it's only just gone twelve. I needed a pee. Go back to sleep.'

Two hours later, when the bedside alarm sounded, Terry, who had slept fitfully since his midnight visit to the toilet, reached over to turn it off but, in his haste, succeeded only in knocking the clock to the floor.

'It's OK, I'm awake now anyway,' said Pat. 'I'll make you a flask.'

Terry fumbled for the bedside light while Pat slipped out of bed, threw on her dressing gown and went through to the kitchen to put the kettle on.

'There's some sandwiches there,' she said to him when he stumbled into the kitchen, still pulling his jumper over his head and yawning loudly. 'Corned beef, I made them last night. Here you go.' She placed a flask down on the table in front of him and handed him a mug of tea. 'I'm on seven 'til seven today, so I won't be here when you get back. You'll be able to get some more sleep. I'll take the bus; you can have the car.'

'OK, love,' said Terry. 'Thanks.'

Outside, a thin frost had whitened the ground around the caravans and coated the windscreens of the cars. Terry used the box of his Rod Stewart cassette to scrape the ice from the glass, his breath fogging the air in front of his face. It felt as cold inside the car as out, and Terry cranked the heating control up to the maximum in a vain attempt to raise the temperature.

Lights in the roof of the loading bay lit up the yard as Terry pulled into the dairy. A small group of men, wrapped in thick coats, scarves and hats, were loading crates of milk onto four blue and white floats, each with "WestPark Dairies" written across the front. He recognised one of the men as Phil's brother-in-law Mike, grabbed his bag from the passenger seat and scurried over.

'Alright, Terry? Chuck your bag in the cab. These are all our crates. Start loading from the front with the full fat, that's the silvers, then work your way back with the reds, then the gold tops and the red and white stripes. There should be a few green tops as well, stick them at the back.'

Terry had met Mike on a few occasions, social things mainly – the odd barbecue and a couple of times at the pub with Phil – and had not taken to him. He'd always found him just a bit too slick, too fond of himself. The kind of bloke, Pat had once said, that if he'd been chocolate, he'd have happily eaten himself.

'Right,' said Mike, once they had finished loading all of the crates, 'let's get this wagon rollin'.'

There were no doors on the milk float, so Terry just slid onto the bench seat in the cab alongside Mike, who handed him a clipboard with lists of names and addresses, grouped into streets, detailing what each house was expecting to be delivered that day. 'OK, that's the list of victims. It's a piece of piss. I'll drive – obviously, still my pony – then when I stop, you take the left-hand side of the street, and I'll take the right. If you use the bottle carriers, you can usually do two or three houses per stop depending on what they've ordered, *comprende?*'

Mike put the milk float in gear and pulled out of the dairy yard onto Mill Hill Road. Terry flicked through the papers on the clipboard, scanning the lists of customers. He recognised the names of many of the streets and knew some of them intimately as the places he had played as a kid growing up. He had gone to primary school on Percy Street, walking there each day on his own from a small terraced house just around the corner. His first proper girlfriend, Gail Mathews, had lived in a 1930's semi across the park on Bramfield Avenue where they'd shared their first kiss in the upstairs back bedroom. *Back when I had hair,* he thought to himself.

He put the clipboard down on the seat between them, pulled his hat further down over his ears and shoved his hands deep into the pockets of his jacket. The cold was already working its way through his jeans, and he made a mental note to get himself some thermals for the rest of the week, as well as a pair of fingerless gloves like the ones Mike was wearing.

'Okey dokey,' said Mike, pulling the milk float to a stop, 'let's get this party started. You're on the odds; I'm the evens, see?' He picked up the clipboard and leant over towards Terry. 'You've got two full fat at number forty-one, three at thirty-nine and then two gold and a stripe at number thirty-seven. Pick up the empties as you go, and if there's a note, check there's no change for today, otherwise just bring it back to me, OK? You take the list, photographic memory me.' He tapped his index finger against his temple and winked at Terry.

The street was narrow and lined with red-brick terraced houses. Between every second house was an unlit alley, which Terry knew led to the tiny backyards, some of which would still contain the outhouse that had once been the house's only toilet. Cars were parked along the kerb on either side of the street, leaving Mike no option but to stop the float right in the centre. But there was no other traffic. The street was still, each of the houses in darkness. Cloud covered the half-moon visible earlier so that, other than the weak headlights of the milk float, the only illumination came from a half-dozen street lamps casting a bleary orange glow onto the damp ground below.

Terry took another quick look at the list and then got out of the milk float to fill up the bottle carrier from the crates behind. As he retrieved the clipboard from the seat of the cab, he saw that Mike was already on his way back to the float, his bottle carrier in one hand and two empty bottles pinched in the fingers of the other.

'I'll move the wagon along; you can catch me up on foot,' he said, as Terry set off to deliver his first bottles.

This pattern repeated itself for several streets, each of which looked identical to the last. It seemed to Terry as though every time he turned around, after placing his bottles on the doorstep, the milk float had moved on again so that he never managed to actually ride in it. Instead, he was forced to scurry the length of each street at a brisk trot.

Eventually, though, he did succeed in quickening his pace or, more likely, he thought, Mike had slowed his a bit. He began to remember better what the next few houses had ordered without having to look at the list two or three times, and he learned that he could safely jump out of the float before it came to a complete standstill, gaining him vital seconds. This meant that he could finally get to sit in the milk float occasionally, albeit only for short periods, and rest his feet. He was relieved when they moved into an area of semi-detached council houses where the roads were wider, adding precious time to Mike's back and forth journeys to the far side of each street.

After a while, when he was able to forget about his cold fingers, and numb toes, and the dull ache in his calves, Terry began to realise that he was actually quite enjoying himself. There was a certain rhythm to it that he liked: the stop start of the milk float, the in and out, the walk to the doorsteps with full bottles of milk and the walk back with the empties, the low hum of the float's electric motor and the chink of the bottles when the road was anything other than billiard table smooth. And it felt in some way secretive, illicit even: moving through the streets in the dark, up and down garden paths, stooping in doorways as the occupants slept undisturbed in their curtained houses. But it felt important to Terry too. Like those sleeping people were relying on him.

By the time the sky began to pale to the east of the city, only a few full bottles remained. Lights began to appear in upstairs windows, followed by more in kitchens and living rooms, as the morning broke further. Curtains were pulled open, and people inched out into the streets, wrapped and hunched against the February chill.

Though it ought to have been fully light when Mike and Terry arrived back at the dairy, grey cloud across the rooftops smothered the sky. The lights in the bay had been left on in an attempt to cut through the gloom. Mike pulled the milk float to a stop and the two men got out and began to unload, adding their own crates to the stacked rows already there.

'Well, what do you think?' said Mike, when they'd finished piling up their crates.

Terry leaned into the cab to retrieve his bag and slung it over his shoulder. 'Yeah, thanks. Knackering, but I enjoyed it. Just need to thaw my hands and feet out and get myself some thermals. Same time tomorrow?'

'Yeah same time. No, I mean what do you think about taking it on, buying it off me? We can talk about it later on in the week, but Phil reckoned you'd be dead keen, what with you being out of work and sitting on your jacksie all day.'

Terry adjusted the strap on his bag and walked around the back of the milk float to where Mike was standing, peeling off his fingerless gloves.

'What?' said Terry. 'What are you talking about? Why would I… are you selling it then? Not that I've got any money anyway.'

'I'm leaving, going to Australia, mate. I thought Phil had talked to you about it. He said he'd give me the money and you'd pay him back once you got the round going.'

'Oh yeah, he did, did he?' Terry felt his neck and face begin to flush. 'Right, OK. I'll have a little chat with him about that. I'll see you tomorrow.'

Terry marched across the yard to his car, shaking his head, his heart beating hard in his chest. He threw his bag onto the passenger seat and sat for a few moments without starting the car, his hands gripping the steering wheel.

'The cheeky bastard,' he said aloud. 'Who does he think he is?' He looked at his watch. *I might just catch him before he goes to work*, he thought. He started the car and set off for Phil's house, still chuntering away to himself, rehearsing what he was going to say when he got there.

As Terry pulled up in front of the house, Phil was coming up the front path in a dark navy suit with a small rucksack over one shoulder. He looked surprised to see Terry.

'Hello, mate, what are you doing here?' he said, pausing on the pavement alongside his car as Terry came around to confront him.

'Never mind that, who do you think you are trying to organise my life? I'm not a charity case, you know, it's so typical—' Terry was slightly out of breath, his words tumbling over themselves in his haste to get them out.

'Whoa, keep your hair on, what are you talking about?'

'The milk round. You said he needed a hand for a few days, not that he was packing it in and you were going to buy it for me, you've just—'

Phil interrupted. He raised his hands, palms open towards Terry in a vague apology. 'I didn't say I was going to buy it for you. It was going to be a loan. You could pay me back once you get it going?'

'I don't need your money. We're fine. What makes you think I want to be a milkman anyway?'

'I didn't think he'd mention it straight away. Typical Mike, subtle as a brick, I thought he might wait to the end of the week, see how it was going.'

Terry stabbed at his own chest with his finger. 'I'll decide what I want to do, not you. And I'll pay for it. We don't need you to sort our lives out for us.'

'Come on, Terry, I was just trying to help. I knew if I told you straight about it, you'd just dismiss it. It could be a great opportunity for you to get back on your feet. Back working again. What's wrong with being a milkman anyway? I reckon you'd be great at it.'

'I didn't say there was anything wrong with it, it's just you thinking you're better than me, thinking you can just click your fingers and—'

'That's not true, and you know it. It wasn't that at all. I was just trying to help.'

'Well, I don't need your help. Why don't you stick to sorting your own life out?'

Phil flinched as though prodded with something sharp. 'What's that supposed to mean?'

At that moment, the front door opened, and both men turned as Julie shouted up the path. 'Hi, Terry, you alright? What's going on?'

'Nothing,' Terry replied, stomping back around his car, 'I was just leaving.'

Terry slammed the car door and drove away, leaving Julie, who had walked up the path as far as the gate, and Phil, looking after him.

By the time he got back to the caravan site, Terry's breathing had calmed down, and his face didn't feel quite so hot, but he was still angry. He sat down and took off his boots, tossing them onto the mat in front of the door. Dennis immediately leaped off the floor and onto his lap but then jumped down again as Terry got up to make himself a tea. While the kettle boiled, Terry paced the caravan, still muttering to himself about Phil. He turned on the electric fire and flicked on the television in the living room, then picked up his coat from the kitchen table where he'd thrown it coming in, hung it up and straightened his boots on the mat.

When he woke in the armchair later, a presenter on *Pebble Mill at One* was outside the studio in a thick coat and gloves, trying hard to look interested as an expert explained how to protect your outdoor plants during the winter. Terry got up and relieved his aching bladder and then made himself a cheese sandwich and another mug of tea, throwing the almost full cold remains of his earlier one down the sink.

It was dark by the time Pat came home. Terry jumped up when he heard the door open and walked through into the kitchen.

'How did the milk round go?' Pat asked him, taking off her scarf and coat and dropping them over the back of a chair.

'Yeah fine, apart from the fact that Mike's emigrating to Australia and Phil's cooked up some crazy plan to buy it off him for me, the cheeky sod.'

Pat filled the kettle and sat down at the table. 'What? What do you mean?'

'Mike's moving to Australia and is trying to sell his round, and Phil apparently told him that I'd be interested. He told Mike that he'd give him the money and that I'd pay him back when I got it going, as if it was all decided, done and dusted.'

'So Phil would give Mike the money and you'd pay Phil back?'

'Yeah, crazy, huh?'

'How much? How much does he want for it?'

'I don't know – I didn't ask. I just went round Phil's and told him we didn't need his money. That's not the point – it's just him thinking he can organise our lives and then pay for it like we're some kind of charity case.' Terry was pacing back and forth across the floor. He stopped to take a couple of mugs from the mug tree, throwing a tea bag in each.

Pat watched him pour the water into the mugs and then resume his pacing. 'Did you enjoy it, the round?'

'I'm not taking Phil's money. We don't need his help to get back on our feet. I'd rather stay on the dole.'

'Oh don't be stupid, Terry.' Pat pulled a newspaper from her bag and threw it down onto the table. 'Look at that.' Terry stopped at the change of tone in Pat's voice and bent to read the headline.

3,000,000

Below this was a picture of a long queue of people outside a jobcentre.

'You're forty-five, Terry. Do you think you can just walk back into another job? Because it doesn't look that easy to me.' Pat got up from the table and took over making the tea. Terry sat down.

'Why don't you see how the rest of the week goes?' said Pat, placing the tea on the table in front of Terry and sitting down opposite him. 'Find out how much he wants for it. We've got that bit left over from the house remember.'

'That was meant to be our rainy day fund.'

'Yes, well in case you haven't noticed, it's raining.'

Pat pushed herself up from the table and took her mug through into the living room, leaving Terry with the newspaper.

FIVE

'I thought I might do us some beans on toast,' said Tom, 'or I could do you a boiled egg if you prefer?'

Fiona continued to gaze at the television and, without turning to him, muttered almost inaudibly, 'I'm not really that hungry.'

'OK,' said Tom, 'well I'll do us some beans then. We had eggs yesterday.'

In the kitchen, the surfaces shone. Tom pulled a tin of beans from among dozens lined up in a cupboard on the wall and heated them in one of the new pans. Once warmed, he transferred the beans onto two plates – white toast for him, brown for her – and put the pan in the sink to soak. When he placed Fiona's tray onto the coffee table in front of her, he saw her eyes flick down briefly from the television and then back up again without expression. He went back to the kitchen for his own tray, turning off the light with his elbow on the way out.

'We're playing at home tonight,' he said, cutting a corner off his toast, 'so I shouldn't be too late.'

Folded into the armchair, her cheek resting squished against her fist, Fiona showed no sign of having heard him. Her hair, parted crookedly in the centre, hung in limp curtains either side of her flushed and puffy face. The beans steamed on the plate in front of her. When the programme finished, she bent forwards to the coffee table but only to retrieve the remote control. She sat back and changed the channel.

'I thought I might get us a new one,' said Tom, 'telly – we've had that one years.'

Fiona turned her head to look at him, her small round eyes made smaller still by the pouches beneath them. A wedge of loose fat shook below her jawline.

'Why do you always think we need new things?'

Tom swallowed a piece of soft toast. 'I don't know,' he said. 'It seems like we've had that one for ages.' He put down his knife and fork and moved the tray from his lap. 'I thought it might cheer you up.'

Fiona made a snorting sound through her nose and turned back to the television. Tom gave it a couple of minutes and then said, 'I got a letter through. We've got that appointment the week after next at the adoption agency. Remember? I'll take the afternoon off and come pick you up, save you having to drive. It's at three.'

Fiona nodded almost imperceptibly.

'OK then,' he said, taking this as a good sign. 'I'll just get the dishes washed up, then I'll be off; I shouldn't be late back.'

SIX

The White Hart was a Marston's pub – a local – and Terry and Pat had been drinking there since their late teens. Moving to the caravan was not going to change that. There were plenty of other people they knew who had left the immediate area but remained regulars, and it had not crossed Terry's mind to do any different, in spite of having to now drive to get there.

The pub occupied the corner of a narrow residential street, lined with dark terraced houses, and a busier arterial road through the city. There was a small car park on the main road, between the pub and the yard of a local builder's merchant, but it was full. Terry found a space down a side street opposite.

For a Wednesday night it was busy, the air dense with nicotine and the hum of competing voices. Behind the bar, Linda, the landlady, was drying a glass with a red-checked tea towel, a gold crucifix leaping around her freckled cleavage. She hung the glass from its handle on a hook above the bar, picked up her cigarette from an ashtray and drew on it deeply, blowing out the smoke above Terry's head.

'Hiya, Pat, Terry, pint and a half?'

Tom and Dave were at the dartboard, and Terry scanned the room for the others. Phil appeared from the direction of the toilets.

'Where's Julie and Fiona?' said Terry. 'I thought you said they were coming.'

'They were supposed to be. Julie's got some meeting at school, and apparently Fiona has a headache. Sorry, Pat. Dave's latest, Karen, is in the lounge.'

'I think I'll be fine here thanks,' said Pat, pulling up a stool.

Phil stopped Terry on the way to the dartboard. 'Look, I'm sorry about the round, about that stuff with Mike. I should've known he'd blab it all out straight off the bat. I just thought… I was just trying to help you out; I thought you'd appreciate it.'

'I don't appreciate you thinking I need some kind of handout, especially not from you.'

Phil's face puckered into that slightly aggrieved look that Terry knew well. He seemed like he wanted to argue the point but instead just said, 'OK fair enough.' Terry, though, could see that he was a bit put out.

'Who are we playing anyway?' he said, changing the subject.

'Red Lion,' said Phil. 'I don't think they're much good.'

'Alright, Terry,' said Dave, as they reached the others, 'how's the round going?'

Terry felt Phil looking at him. 'Yeah, OK,' he said.

'They want to get started straight away,' said Tom, indicating with his head a huddle of four men at the bar. 'Let's stick to the same pairings as last time and then see how the singles go from there, yeah?'

Phil was right that their opponents weren't very good, but Tom and Dave still managed to lose their first match. Tom came back to the others grumbling that Dave, who had disappeared over to the other side of the room, didn't seem to be taking the game seriously enough. Terry checked the flights on his darts and stepped up to the oche. As he was about to throw, the jukebox started up and the flat, burred voice of Benny Hill spilled from a speaker on the wall.

Terry checked his throw. When "Ernie (The Fastest Milkman In The West)" got to the chorus, Phil and Tom joined in. Dave came back across the pub laughing. Terry shook his head but couldn't help but smile at Dave's idiotic grin. 'Prat,' he said.

He turned from Dave and steadied himself, trying to ignore the noise around him. But he pulled his first dart into the treble five and then overcompensated with the other two. Seventeen.

'He's got milk on the brain,' said Dave. 'What's that Terry, the price of a gold top?'

'Shut up, you pillock – you'll put him off,' said Tom, elbowing Dave and causing him to spill the top of his new pint.

'Serves you right,' said Terry, as Dave shook the beer from his hand. 'I can't concentrate with that stupid song on.'

In spite of the inauspicious start, Terry and Phil played well, and Phil closed out the leg with a double twelve. They stayed on to play their opponents' other pairing and won that too, Terry, this time, hitting the winning double.

'I reckon you were inspired by that song,' said Dave. 'Maybe I should get my own theme tune.'

'I could think of a few that would be suitable,' said Terry.

When Dave and Tom won their second game, the match score was 3-1, and Tom went on to seal the victory with a win in the first singles.

'Well played, fellas,' said Phil, raising his pint. 'Only another eleven months and God knows how many rounds and we'll be in the final.'

'I'll tell you what, Dave,' said Terry, 'if we get that far, I'll even let you play Benny Hill as my intro.'

They wandered over to join Pat at the bar, who was chatting to Linda.

'Well done, fellas,' said Linda. 'You done us proud.'

'Yes,' said Pat, bending forwards on her stool to kiss Terry, 'at least you're good for something, you lot.'

The others laughed, and Terry took a long pull on his pint. This was where he was happiest. Swaddled in warm, hoppy air rich with cigarette smoke and stale beer; the inside of a pub was as comfortable to him as an old woolly jumper. It was dark outside, and the damp streets would be empty. In here, the soft glow from the wall lights was reflected in the polished brass of the bar rail and pumps, and people laughed and told each other stories. Friends and familiar strangers sharing private moments in a public space.

Dave had disappeared off into the lounge to find Karen. Tom looked at his watch. 'I suppose I better get off,' he said. 'I told Fiona I wouldn't be too late.'

'It's a shame she couldn't make it,' said Pat. 'I haven't see her for ages. Give her my love.'

'Yeah, thanks, I will,' said Tom, finishing his pint. 'See ya.'

They watched Tom cross the room, his little legs barely visible beneath his long sheepskin coat.

'He doesn't seem himself,' said Pat. 'He's usually got some crazy scheme or other to tell us about. I hope Fiona's OK.'

'I'm not convinced about the headache,' said Phil, wiping his moustache. 'Apparently he told Dave she was at her sister's.'

Terry turned his head back towards the door. When he'd spoken to Tom earlier, Tom had admitted that he thought Fiona was depressed. But he'd also said that he had a plan that he was hoping might bring her out of it. Terry decided not to mention it.

'We should maybe get going as well,' he said. 'I've got to get up early.'

'Oh come on,' said Pat, digging in her purse and pulling out two pound notes, 'let's have another one. We hardly ever go out these days.'

'I thought I might go fishing on the weekend if you fancy it?' said Phil. 'Maybe down to the lakes at Shardlow, see if we can get a pike.'

'I dunno,' said Terry. 'I'll see how I feel. With the round and everything.' He sipped his pint and then took a deeper draw, draining it almost to the bottom.

'You should go,' said Pat, signalling to Linda for more drinks. 'It'll do you good. When was the last time you two fished together?'

Terry made no reply. He knew exactly when he and Phil had last fished together. The first week of September last year. But a lot had happened since then.

It was raining outside, and when they arrived back at the campsite, the track was pocked with deep puddles. Walking to the caravan from the car, Pat leaped onto Terry's back.

'Bloody hell, Pat,' he said, staggering for a step before catching her legs in the crook of his arms, 'how many drinks did you have?'

'I don't want to get my nice shoes wet.' She laughed, nibbling his ear.

As Terry turned outside the front door of the caravan, a bolt of pain seared through his groin, causing him to cry out and drop Pat onto the steps more abruptly than he had intended.

'Sorry, love,' said Pat, laughing, 'I'm heavier than I look.'

Terry straightened and edged gingerly around, but the pain had gone as quickly as it had come. Pat put a hand on each of his cheeks and kissed him loudly on the lips.

'The round'll be fun in the morning if this rain keeps on,' said Terry. 'I'll get soaked.'

'Look on the bright side,' said Pat with a giggle, 'if the river comes up any higher, you'll be able to fish straight out of the kitchen window.'

SEVEN

It was obvious that Phil and Mike had spoken at some point, because Mike had stopped hassling Terry about taking on the round. Not in so many words at least. It didn't, however, prevent him from talking non-stop while they worked, sharing with Terry what he called "the tricks of the trade": the best way to stack and unstack the float, what to do with breakages, the difference and relative merits of each of the types of milk sold with their distinctively coloured tops, how to take and manage orders and payments and a hundred other details that Terry had not even thought about. He also filled Terry in on many of the customers. Not simply what milk they favoured, or how punctual they were at paying their bills, but who they were, who they lived with and what they liked to talk about.

'That's the secret, Terry,' Mike said to him. 'You might not see them much in the winter, but once the mornings start getting lighter, you're the star of the show. Get to know them; take the time to have a chat and a joke. Believe it or not, for some of them, seeing you will be the highlight of their day.' Mike leaned closer and placed his hand on Terry's knee. 'Just be careful of the ones who invite you in for coffee in their nightdresses, if you get my drift.' He winked at Terry. 'Though I won't tell if you don't.'

When they got back to the dairy, he introduced Terry to Paul and Bob, "the two fly-by-nights who run this place", and to Maureen, who worked alone in the office upstairs amid a mountain of bills and scraps of paper piled unevenly on her desk and tacked to the walls around her. 'Watch out for that one,' Mike said to Terry loud enough for Maureen to hear, 'you wouldn't be the first to help her with her filing.'

By the end of the week, Terry was sick to death of Mike's voice. Australia was the best place for him. A couple of hours of fishing, he thought, was just what he needed. He hadn't fished since the end of autumn last year, and he was looking forward to it.

When he turned off the narrow lane onto the rough piece of ground that served as a car park for The Ponds, Terry saw Phil's red Saab tucked in against the hedge to the left of the gate and pulled in behind it. He removed his rod, basket and landing net from the boot, pulled on his wellies and climbed over the stile into the field on the other side. The earth on the path was hard. Old tractor tracks stood raised and frozen into place like varicose veins in the dry mud. He followed the path north along the hedge with the field to his right, brown and barren but for a solitary skeletal tree at its centre.

Phil was fishing the smaller of the two ponds, or East Lake, as it was confusingly known, which was roughly the length and width of a football pitch. The lake was fed at one end by a small overflow from the larger pond to the west. At its tip, the water trickled out to add its weight to the river Derwent.

As Terry approached, Phil raised his rod to cast his line overhand towards the centre of the lake, his lure landing with a small splash. He waited a moment then wound his reel to retrieve the artificial bait, before repeating the same action. Terry walked a slight curve so as not to impede his friend's cast, bringing him into Phil's eyeline.

'Hello, mate,' said Phil continuing to retrieve his lure. 'I left you the peg over by the reeds, thought I'd better give you a chance. How are you doing?'

'Yeah, OK. What are you using?'

Phil lifted his rod and swung the lure in, catching it in his other hand with an open palm. He showed it to Terry. 'Just a little spinner. I didn't have time to pick up any dead bait.'

Terry waited for Phil to recast his line and then walked up the lake fifty yards or so and placed his kit down on the bare ground close to the water. He took out the flask from his basket, sat down and poured himself a half cup of coffee. He was tired, but the cold and the caffeine cleared the fatigue from behind his eyes. Nothing moved. There was no wind, and wisps of mist floated a few feet over the surface of the lake. Other than the faint, intermittent splash of Phil's spinner breaking the water, there was no sound. Terry listened intently. Nothing.

He took out his rod and reel and began tackling up, choosing a slightly larger lure than the one Phil was using: a plug, lime green with red flashes along the flanks, articulated at the tail to mimic the movement through the water of a small fish. Albeit one with a large, triple-pronged hook trailing behind it.

For the next hour or so, Terry fell into a rhythm of cast and retrieve, cast and retrieve. Sometimes quickly, then more slowly. At times, he would wind the plug in smoothly, then at others he would stop and restart the winding motion in order to make the lure jerk through the water, a staccato dance that he hoped would prove irresistible to any waiting pike. He cast his line different distances and varied the angle. Although he thought the area closest to the reeds was the most likely spot for a pike to be idling, he tried in other directions also, sometimes hurling the lightweight plug as far out as he could send it, at others tossing it just a few feet from the bank.

Terry was just thinking about trying another spot when

Phil strolled along the bank, carrying his rod and net, his basket hanging across his back.

'I thought I might give it a go round the other side,' he said, stopping behind Terry. 'How are you getting on, any movement?'

'No,' said Terry, still focused on drawing the plug back through the water towards him. He lifted the rod high over his right shoulder and then brought it quickly forwards, finishing the movement with a sharp flick of the wrist to send the plug back out into the lake. He waited a few moments for it to sink to what he thought would be a good depth and then began once again to wind it in.

Phil had not yet moved, and though Terry was looking the other way, fixed on the lake, he sensed in the silence that Phil wanted to say something. The next time Terry raised his rod to cast, Phil spoke.

'Oh, did I tell you we got a bye in the next round of the cup?'

'Great.'

'And apparently the national final is going to be played on the same day as the world championship final, as like an opener, at Jollees in Stoke. Imagine that, playing on the same stage as Lowey and Bristow, in front of a crowd.'

'I wouldn't worry too much about that if I was you,' said Terry. 'You've got about as much chance of that as marrying Princess Di.'

'She's already married.'

'Exactly.'

'Still,' said Phil, 'it would be unbelievable, wouldn't it.'

'Very,' said Terry, recasting his line, 'you're twenty-five years older than her for a start.'

Terry heard Phil laugh, but he remained where he was, and Terry wondered whether it wasn't the darts that Phil wanted to talk about.

'Right, OK,' Phil said finally, 'I'll give it a try round the other side. I'll see you in a bit.'

Terry turned his head to watch Phil walk along the bank, before he disappeared behind some bushes and trees that grew right up to the water's edge. A few minutes later, Phil reappeared on the far side of the lake, the dull green and brown of his clothes and hat blending in well with the muted winter palette of his surroundings.

Terry moved along the bank in the direction that Phil had taken, but instead of skirting around the mess of undergrowth as his friend had done, he took two or three steps into the lake so that the water came two thirds of the way up his wellies. From here, he made a side arm cast parallel with the bank, landing his plug only a yard or two from the tangled shoreline underneath a tree that listed over the lake like the mast of a stricken ship.

Once again, Terry lost himself in the routine of casting his plug into the water and then winding it back in. Though the air temperature had risen marginally since he arrived, and with it the trails of mist over the lake, the water remained icy cold. Terry's wellies gave him little protection and, in spite of the thick socks he was wearing, he quickly lost the feeling in his feet. He came in and poured himself another half cup of coffee. While he drank it, he watched Phil fish on the other side of the lake. He thought of what Pat had said about the milk round and how hard it would be for him to find something else. Besides which, he was actually really starting to enjoy it. But there was no way he was going to accept the money from Phil.

He removed his wellies and socks, drawing each foot up in turn onto the opposite knee to rub some life back into his toes. He was reluctant to put his feet back into the water but felt sure that the spot under the overhanging tree offered him the best chance of catching a pike. 'Right,' he said to himself, suddenly coming to a decision and getting up, 'if I get one, I'll do it.'

He took off the green plug and replaced it with a smaller spinner. It had a simpler design, consisting of a scooped metal plate the length of Terry's thumb, silver in colour, which rotated quickly around on itself as it was pulled through the water.

With the slight difference in weight and flight through the air of the new lure, Terry misjudged his first couple of casts, sending the first further than he wanted, almost getting it tangled in the branches of the tree in the process and overcompensating on the second to leave it short. The third cast was just right. Terry waited, two, three seconds and began to retrieve the spinner. After a couple of rotations of the handle, he paused the winding action for a moment and then quickened it to increase the speed of the shiny metal fish through the water. Without warning, there was a sharp tug on the line and then heavy resistance, causing the tip of Terry's rod to bend sharply towards the spot where his line broke the water. Terry felt a surge of excitement. The rod bent further. The resistance increased, and Terry lowered the rod to allow the fish its initial flight. But it was heading for the dark water beneath the tree. Terry was scared his line would get caught in the confusion of weeds and tangled roots and snap. He took a step further out into the lake and immediately felt his left boot start to fill with freezing water. 'Shit.'

He stumbled back half a pace, the water sloshing around his ankle. For a moment, there was no movement from the fish. Terry raised the rod, thinking he might be able to begin winding the fish in, but it turned and took off for the centre of the lake. Terry had no option but to let it run again. He took the opportunity to reverse carefully out of the water.

Eventually, the resistance weakened, and Terry sensed that the fish was tiring. Each of its attempts to shake free carried less conviction than the last. Terry caught his first glimpse of the pike as he reeled it close to the shore, and the surface of the water exploded as the fish flailed and thrashed in a final attempt to escape capture. Terry lifted his rod high and, with his left hand, pushed the landing net under the pike and lifted it onto the bank. He put the rod and net down, placed a hand on top of the fish just behind the head and took out his long, curved nose forceps from his breast pocket. Carefully, he advanced the forceps into the fish's gaping mouth, gripped the hook, and, with a slight twist and push, managed to remove the spinner.

'Nice fish,' said Phil as he approached from behind the trees.

Terry wet his hands in the water and then lifted the pike from the net. It was slick and heavy, the taut dark-green line of the fish's back and olive, speckled flanks contrasting with its pale, fleshy belly.

'Yeah, not bad,' said Terry. 'Must be five or six pound.'

He stepped into the lake and lowered the fish into the water. For a moment, it didn't move, and then with a powerful flick of its tail, it struck out of Terry's hands and was gone from sight.

Terry stepped back from the shoreline, sat down on his basket and pulled off his boot, emptying the water onto the ground. He peeled off his sodden sock and wrung it out. 'My feet are bloody freezing though. I reckon I'm done for the day.'

Phil looked at his watch. 'Pub'll be open – fancy a pint on your way home?'

Terry replaced the boot without bothering with the sock, which he threw into his fishing basket. 'Yeah OK, I'll have a quick one. Just for medicinal purposes obviously.'

'Obviously,' said Phil with a smile.

The pub was empty but for a man with a scratchy ginger beard sat at the bar with a pint, reading a battered copy of *Oliver Twist*. A fire was lit in an open hearth on one wall of the low-ceilinged room, and the men took their drinks to a table close by it. The fire spat and popped as if the wood was sappy, but they were both glad of its faint warmth. Each man took a mouthful of beer and looked into the fire, which hissed and smoked with the wet wood.

'That was a lovely fish,' said Phil after another sip of his pint. 'When was the last time you caught a pike?'

Terry put his glass down and rubbed his hands together. 'Must be a couple of years ago at least, maybe more.'

Phil turned back to the fire. 'How's it going with Mike?'

'He talks a lot, mainly about himself. I've got another week with him, then I start on my own.'

Phil put his glass down. 'You're going to do it? When did you decide that?'

'When I caught that pike,' said Terry with a grin.

Phil hesitated. 'But what about the money?'

'Mike said he could sort something out with Bob. Some kind of loan that I pay back as I go along – with a bit of interest.'

'Oh, OK,' said Phil, 'but you be careful of those two; I'm not sure you can trust them. You know my offer still stands.'

'I know, cheers. But it's fine.'

Phil nodded, and both men turned to the door as an old man shuffled through it, carrying a stick in one hand and a copy of the *Daily Star* in the other.

'Well,' said Phil, 'I'm happy for you. Sorry about not being straight with you from the start, I just – well, you know – I wasn't thinking.'

Terry picked up his pint. 'It's OK, you're probably right – I probably wouldn't have done it if I'd known.'

There was a silence, and Terry remembered the feeling he'd had at the lake, that Phil had been wanting to ask him something.

Phil cleared his throat. 'What did you mean when you said that I should stick to sorting my own life out?'

Terry took a swallow of his beer. 'Oh, nothing. I was just angry. I didn't mean anything.'

Phil looked unconvinced. He paused for a few moments and then said, 'I think Julie's having an affair.'

'What? No, don't be daft. Julie? What makes you think that?'

Phil's shoulders sagged, and he sighed. 'I don't know. She's been late home from work a lot recently, said she's had meetings. Then I phoned her at school last week about something, and the secretary said that she'd gone out for a bit.' He shook his head, fiddling with his glass. 'She's been distant with me, not herself.'

Terry tried to think of something to say to his friend. Phil, though, spoke again before Terry had the chance.

'You do know something, don't you? I can see it in your face.'

Terry shifted his gaze to the old man, who was circling something in his newspaper with a broken pencil, and then looked back at Phil, whose eyes had remained fixed on him.

'It's probably nothing. But she's not having an affair. Pat told me not to say anything cos of patient confidentiality and all that, but she saw Julie at the hospital last week.' He paused, but Phil said nothing and continued to stare at him so that he was forced to continue. 'She said she didn't think anything of it at first, but then she reckoned that Julie saw her and pretended not to, went the other way.'

'Where? Where did she see her at the hospital?'

'It's probably nothing, my guess is she was probably visiting someone.'

'Where?' repeated Phil. 'Which ward?'

Terry hesitated. 'Oncology.'

'Cancer?'

Phil, who had been leaning forwards against the table, spat out the word like a cough, as though it tasted bad in his mouth, and flopped back in his seat. The man with the beard at the bar glanced up from his book at the sudden change in tone and volume of the conversation.

'She was probably just visiting. I'm sure she's fine.'

Phil looked crestfallen. All the air appeared to have gone out of him. 'Why didn't she tell me then? If she was just visiting someone, she would have told me.'

'Maybe she forgot. You said she'd been busy at work.'

'Yeah, but has she? Or is that just a lie as well?'

Terry couldn't think what to say. He felt suddenly exhausted and wished he hadn't said anything. Wished he hadn't come to the pub.

'Oh well, you never know, she might just be having an affair with a doctor.'

Terry regretted his weak joke immediately, but fortunately Phil was staring blankly at the glass in front of him, lost in his own thoughts.

'What?' he said, looking up.

'Nothing. I'm sure she'll be fine. If it was anything serious, she'd have told you.' Terry tried to inject a note of optimism into his voice, but Phil looked completely deflated. He snatched a look at his watch and finished the remains of his pint. 'I'm going to have to go,' he said, getting up. 'Don't worry, she'll be OK, I'm sure of it. Give me a call when you've spoken to her.'

'You haven't got a phone.'

'Oh yeah. There's one in the farmhouse we can use – I'll call you tomorrow teatime when you've finished work.'

Phil just nodded.

Outside, the cold air after the warmth of the pub seemed to grip Terry by the throat. He felt momentarily dizzy, and the crunch of his boots on the gravel in the car park filled his ears. On the drive home, he struggled to keep his eyes open.

EIGHT

Phil hosed the mud off his boots, stepped out of them and let himself in the back door. The smell of a roast dinner filled the kitchen, and Phil lifted the lid on a pan of potatoes frothing under a high heat. Julie was in the hallway with her back to him, on the phone.

'I'll try,' she said. 'I can't promise anything.'

Phil walked around her and mouthed hello with a little wave. Julie leaped backwards, almost dropping the phone.

'Jesus,' she said, recovering the handset from the crook of her arm. 'OK, no, no I'm fine; I'll do what I can, bye.' She put the phone down. 'For Christ's sake, what are you doing creeping around like that? You almost scared me to death.'

'Sorry,' said Phil. 'Who was that?'

Julie hesitated and then moved past him towards the kitchen. 'Oh no one,' she said, 'just someone from school.'

Phil followed her into the kitchen and watched her bend to take the beef out of the oven. 'Shall I carve?' he said.

Julie threw a tea towel over the joint and then drained a pan of carrots in the sink, the steam clouding the window. 'No, let it rest for a minute – you sort the wine out.'

Phil dawdled for a second, but Julie was busy with the

vegetables and gravy, so he went through into the living room. He picked out a bottle of Merlot from the rack on the floor, opened it, sniffed the cork and then emptied the contents into the crystal decanter his parents had bought them for their fifteenth wedding anniversary.

'No roast potatoes?' he asked, as he carved the beef and laid out strips on the warm plates.

'No, sorry,' said Julie, 'I completely forgot.'

'What do you think of the wine?' he said. 'It's perfect with the beef.'

'Hmm,' Julie acknowledged, 'very nice.'

'Terry came fishing with me,' said Phil.

'Yes,' said Julie, putting a battoned carrot into her mouth, 'you said.' She chewed her carrot slowly and speared another but reached for her glass instead. 'Did you catch anything?'

'He did. A pike, a really nice fish.'

'Oh,' said Julie, nodding, 'good.'

'He's going to take the milk round on. Your brother's done him some sort of deal with Bob. I told him to be careful.'

Julie looked at him but made no reply. Phil reached for the wine bottle and topped up Julie's glass. He took a sip from his own and placed it back down on its coaster, then cleared his throat. 'He mentioned that Pat had seen you at the hospital. Coming out of the oncology ward he said she thought it was.'

Julie cut a slice of beef and slid it into her mouth.

'And last week, I called the school, and they said you'd gone out.'

Julie swallowed the beef and took a mouthful of wine. 'It's nothing,' she said, looking directly across the table at him. 'I didn't want to worry you. I found a lump in my breast and thought I'd better get it checked out. But it's fine. It's nothing.' She stretched her mouth at him in a thin smile.

Phil let out an enormous sigh. 'Oh thank goodness,' he said. 'I was so worried. I know things haven't been that great lately,

49

but you should have said something, shared it with me.' He laughed and poured them both more wine. 'Terry was right,' he said, 'he told me it'd be nothing. Either that or you were having an affair with a doctor.'

NINE

Terry woke to the sound of rain drumming on the caravan roof. The luminous green hands and numerals of his bedside alarm told him it was not yet 2am, and he lay for a few moments listening to the incessant beat of the downpour, which, if anything, appeared to be increasing in intensity.

He needed a pee, and he knew that he would have to get to the dairy early, since it would take him longer to load the crates on his own. But the bed was warm, and the rain didn't sound like it was stopping anytime soon. The round, though, would also take much longer without Mike. He reluctantly reached for the alarm clock to turn it off.

Sandwiches and an empty flask lay on the kitchen table, and Terry boiled the kettle for coffee.

The loading bay at the dairy was under the cover of a high roof, but as soon as Terry began his deliveries, walking back and forth between the doorsteps and the float, he got wet. By the third street, he was completely soaked. The hood of his jacket stuck to the side of his face each time he turned his head one way or the other, transferring water onto Terry's hair and cheeks, which then inevitably made its way down his neck and inside his shirt. His trousers clung to his legs. His feet squelched in his boots. The seat in the cab of the milk float was slick with rain that blew in the open sides to drench Terry even when he was driving.

By the time he was halfway into his round, Terry realised that he was miles behind schedule. It was already beginning to get light, though with the thick cloud, it was difficult to tell, and soon the early morning rush of cars and buses would clog the streets to slow him up further.

It was almost 11am by the time he got back to the dairy. All of the other floats were parked up empty, hundreds of crates stacked one on top of the other in row after row of blue and white, like scarves on a football terrace.

It rained again on Tuesday – and Wednesday. By the end of the round on Thursday, Terry had developed a hacking cough that tore at his throat with each convulsion. And his lower back ached. For now though at least, the physical discomfort was not his biggest concern. Working alone and having to accustom himself with the round and the float, in addition to the unrelenting rain, meant that he was slow. Far too slow.

Scuttling down a garden path on Bedford Street with his head hunched against the rain, Terry didn't notice that the front door was open until a pair of pale pink slippers with stockinged legs attached appeared on the doorstep.

'What time do you call this?'

Terry looked up. A drop of rain detached itself from his hood and ran between his eyebrows and off the end of his nose.

'You've been late every day this week. The kids have already gone to school – what use is that?' The woman inclined her head to one side in anticipation of an answer to her rhetorical question, her arms pressed tightly beneath her bust, her thin lips barely visible.

'Yeah sorry, I'm new.' Terry held out a bottle of milk to the woman, forcing her to unfold her arms to take it. She looked deflated at the lack of confrontation.

'Yes, well,' she said, apparently unsure of what to say next but determined nonetheless to have the last word, 'it's no use to me, I can tell you.'

Four houses further along the street, Terry had just placed the bottles down and turned to leave with the empties when he heard the front door open behind him.

'Oi.'

Terry stopped. A man in loose jeans and a grubby vest stood in the doorway, a cigarette smouldering in the nicotine-stained fingers of his right hand. The man was bald on top of his head, but a curtain of lank, greasy hair hung from the sides and back to his shoulders.

'You're useless. If you're gonna turn up at this time, you could at least get it right.' He bent to pick up one of the bottles from the step, giving Terry a view of a hallway and staircase stuffed with bags and boxes and towers of old newspapers and magazines. The front wheel and handlebars of a bike poked through the clutter like a conceptual sculpture.

'This is semi-skimmed; do I look like I drink that shit?'

Terry resisted the urge to give the man an honest answer. He returned to the float and came back with the correct bottles.

Two streets further on, the rain miraculously stopped. Unfortunately, this appeared only to encourage more people to come out to complain so that by the time he got back to the dairy, Terry had added a thumping headache to his list of afflictions.

It was late morning when Terry got back to the campsite; it was no longer raining, but the sky was black with threat, the dense clouds seemingly within touching distance. A dark, wide puddle filled the patch of rough ground in front of the gate. Negotiating the flooded potholes on the track, Terry glanced across at the lower section of the campsite, shimmering under several inches of water. Pat was at the kitchen table cradling a mug of tea when Terry walked in.

'I thought you'd be in bed,' he said.

'Thought I'd wait up for you. How was it? Must have been awful in that rain again.'

Terry sat down and pulled off his boots. He told Pat about the complaints, his account of the day broken by fits of frenzied coughing.

'You need someone to give you a hand,' she said, putting a tea down in front of him as he bent over the table spluttering and wheezing, 'and a doctor.'

Terry took a breath and then a cautious sip of his tea. 'I can't afford to pay anyone. I'll be fine if it ever stops raining.'

Pat sat down. 'What about Martin?'

'What about him?'

'He could give you a hand. He told me him and Pete have been quiet with the removals, with the weather and everything, I'm sure—'

'You've spoken to him?'

'I'm sure he'd help you out.'

Terry looked across the table at Pat, at the dark pouches of skin beneath her eyes. Her hair was dragged into a tight bun, hollowing her cheeks and accentuating the line of her jaw and cheekbones. She looked thin.

'I don't know. I can't see that lazy toerag getting up in the middle of the night. Especially to give me a hand.'

'I'll ask him,' said Pat, as Terry began coughing again. 'Come on, let's go to bed. I'll do us a hot water bottle.'

In spite of Terry's coughing, Pat fell asleep almost immediately. She was probably right, he thought, he probably could do with a hand just until he got used to things. But he couldn't imagine Martin being too keen to help him out. They had been close once, but not for a couple of years. Not since Martin had suddenly announced he wasn't going to university. Terry regretted now some of the things he'd said, but at the time he'd been angry, and disappointed. He couldn't just let

Martin throw away his life like that. He had brains; he could make something of himself. Dropping out of the youth training scheme without even bothering to tell Terry had been the last straw, and the rift between them had deepened further. For the last eighteen months or so, they had been strangers in the same house, avoiding each other if possible and saying the bare minimum to one another if not. Since Martin left home prior to the move to the caravan, they had not spoken. Terry missed him.

TEN

'I hope the car will be alright here,' said Tom, looking around.

A sign stuck in a patch of unkempt grass alongside the disabled access ramp advised visitors "not to leave valuables unattended". Dog dirt littered the strips of soil either side of the paving slab path, providing much-needed nourishment to the scratchy shrubs attempting to grow there. The discarded sweet wrappers and crisp packets less so.

The low, flat building itself looked relatively new, the bricks still pinkish red as though recently fired. As Tom and Fiona got out of the car, a dog appeared ahead of its aged owner and cocked a leg over a corner of the wall, leaving a dark stain.

Sandy, as she had asked them to call her, sat reclined behind her desk in a loose-fitting lilac kaftan, with peacock motifs running across the chest and sleeves. Her lower arms, pale and flabby, were bare, her thick wrists hidden beneath a collection of silver and gold and copper bracelets. A poster tacked to the wall behind her showed a child hugging her knees on the floor of an empty room. "Make a difference", it said, in bold type, "Adopt".

'So,' said Sandy, pressing out a roll-up in an ashtray on her desk, 'how have we been since I last saw you, have you had a chance to chat?'

'Yeah, great,' said Tom, 'we're still really keen.'

'Fiona?'

Tom swivelled his head.

'Yes, fine,' she muttered.

Sandy held her gaze on Fiona for a second, before turning to Tom. She smiled. 'Did you bring those bank details I asked you about, Tom? Your business sounds like it's doing really well, but as I said, I'm obliged to check everything out.' She smiled again. 'I'm sure it won't be an issue.'

Tom handed over the papers, and Sandy studied the top one for a moment. 'Marvellous,' she said. 'And Fiona, you mentioned that you're not working currently, but,' she looked down, 'I see from your questionnaire that you used to help out part-time at a nursery. That must have been rewarding. Why did you stop?'

'It got a bit complicated, didn't it?' said Tom. 'I was really busy with work and—'

'I just couldn't do it anymore,' said Fiona, 'being with all those kids every day. The parents. I just couldn't do it.'

'I see,' said Sandy, writing something in her notebook with a sympathetic smile.

'She loved it though. Didn't you?' said Tom. 'It was just difficult. It made her realise how much she wanted a kid, what she was missing.' Tom's voice trailed off, then he said, 'But it's me that can't have them; it's not her.'

'Yes,' said Sandy, 'you said. But you both have to be committed. Adopting a child is a big decision. You both have to want to do it.'

'We do,' said Tom. 'We've thought about it a lot. We think we have a lot to offer.'

'Fiona?'

'Yes,' said Fiona.

Sandy dragged a file across the desk towards her. 'OK. Well, I have a couple of possible candidates. We usually start with an afternoon, say, at the park, with a social worker present, and then work up to a weekend with you when everyone's ready. How does that sound?'

'Yeah, great,' said Tom, leaning forwards over the desk. 'Can I have a look?'

'This is not a supermarket,' said Sandy, shutting the file. 'You can't just pick the one you like off the shelf. At this stage we prefer you not to have too much background information on the child. Let's just see how the first meeting goes and take it from there.'

'Oh, yeah sure,' said Tom, shifting back in his seat. 'We don't mind anyway, do we, Fiona? Boy, girl, black, white – whatever.'

Sandy smiled. 'OK, well I'll be in touch about the dates.'

Outside, a boy of around ten or eleven was peering, his nose against the glass, into the BMW.

'Oi,' shouted Tom.

The boy's head shot up, and he raced off between some houses and a pebble-dashed community centre across the road.

Tom circled the car for any damage. 'Why isn't he at school anyway?' he said. 'Bloody kids.'

ELEVEN

Finally, on Monday morning, the blanket of dirty white cloud lifted and tore apart so that, as the day broke, the low winter sun streaked through the holes to offer, if not discernible physical heat, at least a level of psychological warmth.

'You not got a radio in this thing?' said Martin, leaning over to peer at the milk float's almost featureless central console.

'No. We can hardly drive around at this time in the morning with music blaring, can we?'

Martin straightened up, dropping his chin to his chest and plunging his hands into his jacket pockets. 'It's bloody freezing.'

'You're lucky, at least it's not raining. It pissed it down all last week.'

Terry stopped the float. 'OK, it's like I explained,' he said, picking up the clipboard with the delivery schedule on it. 'You're this side, I'm the other – odds and evens, see? Fill your bottle carrier so that you can deliver two or three houses on each trip.'

Martin turned just his head to glance at the top sheet of paper. 'You should divide it into two columns, that's just confusing. And you're writing's terrible.' He slid out of the float before Terry could think of a reply.

As the round progressed, and the gaping mouths of the empties outnumbered the shiny foil tops of the full bottles on the float, Terry had to admit to himself that Martin had picked the job up pretty quickly. In spite of appearing to spend barely any time at all studying the schedule, he seemed able to memorise what half the street had ordered without making a mistake so that it was often he who was waiting for Terry to catch up.

As a result, when a front door opened as he approached, Terry assumed despondently that he was in for another earbashing from a moaning customer.

'Mornin'.'

Terry was thrown for a moment by the lack of hostility in the greeting. 'Morning,' he replied, stopping in front of the woman.

'You the new boy?' she said, in a slow West Indian drawl.

Terry laughed. 'Yeah, I suppose I am. Terry.'

The woman held out her hand. It was cool, the skin slack but soft. 'Rose Johnson, delighted to make your acquaintance.'

The woman was tiny, no more than five feet, and wore a pair of large, thick-rimmed glasses that looked too big for her delicate face. She wore a mustard-coloured jumper and an orange skirt to mid-calf with a pair of dark wool stockings and neat black shoes.

'Would you mind taking a look at my washing machine? It just pack up and died again.'

Terry took a second to understand what the woman had said. 'Er, I don't know. What's wrong with it? I'm not very good with mechanical stuff.'

The woman didn't answer. Her small, dark eyes, magnified slightly by the huge oval lenses of her glasses, were fixed on Terry. He had the sense that if he didn't say something, she would remain there, looking at him, indefinitely. He looked at his watch, then half-turned towards the milk float.

'Martin, come here a second. This is Mrs Johnson. She's got a problem with her washing machine. Why don't you take a look? I'll do the last couple of streets and then swing back round to pick you up. He's quite good, Mrs Johnson, he used to have a scooter that he was always fiddling around with.' Terry turned back to Martin. 'Take the toolbox out of the float – there's a couple of spanners and screwdrivers in there that might be useful.'

Terry watched while Martin fetched the toolbox from the milk float and then turned to find the woman had already disappeared back inside. Martin shrugged and followed her into the house.

When Terry returned after completing the round, he expected to see Martin waiting for him, but the pavement in front of the house was empty. He parked up and leaned back against the plastic sheeting that separated the bed of the float with the crates from the cab. His back ached and, although he was coughing less, his chest felt tight. And he was desperate for the toilet.

The street was awake now. Most of the curtains were open, and the road was busy with cars. Children in burgundy blazers trudged sleepily under heavy bags towards school. Terry looked again at the front door of the house, but it remained closed, and he really did need the toilet.

When he rang the doorbell, it was not Mrs Johnson who answered the door but a much younger woman, a girl perhaps in her late teens. She was dressed in men's checked pyjamas bottoms with thick red socks and an oversized grey sweatshirt with YALE written across the chest. The girl raised a hand to shield her eyes from the low sunlight that appeared suddenly over Terry's left shoulder and which picked out wisps of the girl's hair come loose from the parallel rows plaited tight to her head.

'You must be Terry,' she said.

Martin appeared in the hallway behind the girl. 'Hi, Dad, this is Alma. She's a photography student, Mrs Johnson's granddaughter.'

'Great to be exact,' said the girl.

'Oh yeah, great-granddaughter. She's done some brilliant photos – she's really good.'

'I'm really sorry,' said Terry, 'but can I use your toilet please?'

'Sure,' said the girl, stepping to the side, 'top of the stairs, first door on your right.'

When Terry came back down the stairs, Martin and Alma were still stood just inside the door. She was telling him about the college course she was on.

'Right, thanks,' said Terry. 'You ready? Shall we go?' He stopped to allow Martin to pass through the doorway first and then followed.

Halfway up the path, Martin turned so that Terry almost bumped into him. 'Bye, Alma,' he called out, raising his hand in a sort of half-wave. 'Sorry, Dad.'

'How did you get on with the washing machine?' asked Terry as they drove back to the dairy.

'Yeah good. It wasn't the machine – it was the socket – a wire had come loose. Only took a minute or two.'

Terry glanced across at him. 'Oh, OK good.' The traffic lights turned red and Terry stopped at the pedestrian crossing. An old man shuffled across, pulling a shopping bag on wheels.

'Alma showed me some of her photos,' said Martin. 'She's got them on the wall in the kitchen – and the living room. Black and whites mainly. She's really good.'

'Right,' said Terry. 'How old is she?'

'Dunno. She's at college, nineteen, twenty maybe.'

Terry pressed on the accelerator, and the milk float moved away. 'She looked younger.'

By Wednesday, they were getting back to the dairy almost an hour earlier than Terry had done working alone. And, to Terry's surprise, Martin had been on time all three days.

Each morning, Terry turned into the street where Martin

shared a house to find him already on the pavement, stood, like some kind of crime novel detective, beneath a streetlight with his head in his chest, his body clenched taut against the cold.

They spoke little on the round, but, though he wouldn't have told Martin as much, Terry was enjoying having him there. It was the most time they'd spent together for years. Terry had taken Martin fishing when he was little, and back then Martin had talked incessantly. Terry remembered him constantly asking questions that he scarcely gave Terry time to answer before launching into the next. He'd been a voracious reader too, gobbling up books about dinosaurs and space and soldiers. But by the time he was thirteen or fourteen, Martin had begun to withdraw into himself. He was still reading, though by now he was churning through crappy horror novels where rattlesnakes or giant rats terrorised horny teenagers, but the questions stopped. In fact, he hardly spoke at all, other than the occasional grunt in reply to a request to help clear the table or tidy his room. Terry had been so happy when Martin had got a place at university. When he changed his mind and said he wasn't going, they'd had a massive bust-up. Martin had shut himself in his room, emerging only to use the bathroom or raid the fridge when Pat and Terry were out.

Towards the end of the round on Thursday, Terry stopped the float at a zebra crossing outside the front of the primary school where both he and Martin had been pupils. A lollipop lady, shorter than her stick and as round as the disk on top, marched into the centre of the road to halt the traffic. A girl, in navy socks to her knees, skipped forwards ahead of a small boy. Midway across, the boy turned to the milk float and gave them a cheery thumbs up. Martin returned the gesture, and the boy ran to the pavement and in through the school gate.

'I remember when you were that age,' said Terry, as the lollipop lady ambled back to her post. 'Always asking questions, wanting to know what everything was for, how it worked. Used to drive us mad sometimes.' In the playground, the children shrieked and chased one another around in circles. 'Seems like five minutes ago.'

Martin made no reply, and they went on with the round in silence once more. It was still cold. The ragged holes in the cloud had patched themselves together so that the sun shone through only as a flat disk devoid of heat. They were on a wide street lined each side with boxy council houses: semi-detached, with the front doors alongside one another in the middle. A single garden path served both houses. Halfway along, Terry returned to the float to refill his bottle carrier as Martin did the same from the other side.

'I've decided to go to college,' he said.

Terry stopped what he was doing and looked across the float at Martin, who continued to take out his empties and replace them with full bottles of milk. 'When?'

Martin looked up. 'September,' he said, 'when the new term starts,' and he turned to set off delivering his milk. Terry quickly finished filling his carrier and scurried down the path to the next doorstep. When he got back to the float, Martin was almost ready to set off again.

'That's great,' Terry managed to say before Martin headed off again, his bottles clinking in the carrier. Terry once more rushed off, and when he got back, Martin was already in the cab of the float. Terry jumped in alongside him but paused for a moment before pulling away. 'That's great, Martin,' he said. 'When did you decide that?'

Martin gave a slight shrug of his shoulders and continued to look ahead down the street. 'Dunno, the other day.' He stopped as though he thought this enough of an answer but then went on. 'I bumped into Alma in town the other day. She was telling me how good it is. Different from school.'

'Right,' said Terry, 'fantastic. What do you want to study?'

Martin shrugged again. 'Dunno, engineering maybe, or electronics. Something useful.'

Terry nodded. 'OK, brilliant.' He was tempted to interrogate Martin further but thought better of it. Instead, he said simply, 'Good idea, your mum'll be pleased.'

Back at the dairy, Martin was quick to jump out of the cab and begin unloading. It was obvious he wasn't keen to talk any more about it for now, so Terry let him be. He was looking forward to telling Pat though.

Once the crates of empties were stacked and the bed of the float cleared, Terry set off across the yard to the car.

'Actually, I'm alright for a lift, Dad.'

Terry stopped and turned.

'I'm going into town again. I'll get the bus back from there later.'

'Oh, OK, no problem.'

'I've got to work with Pete tomorrow and Saturday, moving some bloke to Long Eaton.'

'Yeah, course,' said Terry, 'OK.'

Martin made no move to go. The automatic lights of the dairy went off, and Martin glanced up at them and then looked back at Terry. He had Pat's eyes.

'I might try and find some temping work, save some money,' he said. He flicked at his fringe with his fingers. 'But I can still give you a hand until I get something – if you like. I quite enjoy it,' he added.

Terry smiled. 'Course. I'll see you Monday same time.' He looked across at the old clock on the dairy wall. 'No, let's put it back twenty minutes; we've done well the last few days.'

TWELVE

By the middle of the next week, though the weather had improved, Terry's cough had returned. This time, however, the dry, scratchy hack had been replaced by something looser, more greasy. It began with a rattle in his chest as he inhaled and often finished with him spitting a clod of waxy mucus into the gutter. Concerned that the damp mornings would transform a chest infection into pneumonia, and knowing full well that he would never do it himself, Pat booked Terry an appointment with the doctor for Friday morning, after the round.

The surgery was on the ground floor of a three-storey sandstone townhouse, in the centre of a row of rather grand-looking Georgian terraces. The city jail, now a greyhound track, had once looked down the street, and Terry imagined the inmates peering through the bars at the ladies and gentlemen pushing through the doors of these neat little houses. He unlatched the gate and mounted the steps to the front door, painted black with a shiny brass knocker and handle. Inside, a tiled corridor led Terry past a door that would once have been the house's drawing room into a small waiting room. Plastic chairs lined three of the walls around a low table covered with magazines. Behind a glass hatch in the fourth wall, a receptionist in a white office sat painting her nails. She looked up and slid back the glass.

'Mr Fletcher?'

'Yes.'

'Take a seat please.'

The only other people in the room were a woman in perhaps her early thirties and what was presumably her young son. The woman was flicking through a *Woman's Own* magazine without appearing to read any of it. The boy, whose feet failed to reach the floor, swung his legs back and forth and stared at Terry. Terry poked his tongue out at the boy but then convulsed into a fit of coughing. The boy was unmoved. The glass partition slid open.

'Mr Fletcher, Doctor Barnes will see you now.'

Terry fished a handkerchief from his pocket and stood up, still spluttering and attempting to clear his throat.

Doctor Barnes looked as though he should have retired years ago. His broad, square face was heavily lined, and his white hair stood out from his head as though blown by a strong breeze. He was sat reclined in his chair behind a massive desk, the surface of which was almost entirely invisible under piles of folders and files and loose sheets of paper. Picture frames stood in the gaps in the chaos.

'Come in, Terry,' he said.

Terry sat down. A large window behind the doctor, though half concealed by a blind, gave the room lots of light. Shafts of it picked out dust in the air above the thick carpet.

'Nasty cough you've got there.'

Obviously nothing wrong with his hearing, thought Terry. 'It's not too bad. Pat was worried.'

The doctor nodded. 'OK. Take your shirt off and sit on the bed. Let's have a listen to your chest.'

The doctor got to his feet and moved slowly around his desk. He pressed the stethoscope to Terry's back, breathing loudly through his nose. Terry could hear him moving a mint around his mouth as he listened, but it failed to disguise the smell of tobacco on his clothes.

The doctor said nothing while Terry put his shirt back on and sat down again. He pulled a prescription pad from the top drawer of his desk and scribbled one out. He reread it before he passed it across to Terry. 'Anything else bothering you?' he said.

Terry looked at the prescription but could decipher nothing from it. 'No, not really.' Outside, a church bell chimed somewhere nearby. 'My back aches a bit, but that's just the carrying at work and the cold. I seem to need to pee a lot, I suppose.'

'When?'

'Er, well whenever really.'

'Do you have to get up in the night?'

Terry shrugged. 'Yeah, I guess so, sometimes. But I just put that down to my age – or the beer.' He laughed.

'Does it hurt?'

'Not really.'

The doctor nodded again and then took a big breath in and exhaled heavily.

'I'll make you an appointment at the hospital for a blood test. Sheila will have your number – she'll call you with the date.'

'Oh, we've moved,' said Terry. 'We don't have a phone at the moment.'

'Alright, give her your new address and she'll send it through the post.'

In the waiting room, the woman was skimming a new magazine, but the boy was still swinging his legs. He was sending them further now so that on each back stroke he kicked the underside of the chair with his heels. When he saw Terry, he stuck out his tongue.

Outside, the sun shone brilliantly. Tiny buds of blossom

studded the branches of the trees that lined the street, and sparrows pecked at them.

Terry hated hospitals. They made him uneasy, uncomfortable. Actually, it was more than that; there was something flat and heavy and black that crawled up from his stomach to sit in the centre of his chest, constricting his breathing. Anxiety, fear – dread.

He shifted in his chair. The hard plastic squeaked under him. A droplet of sweat slid down the crease in the centre of his back, and he rubbed himself against the chair to interrupt its passage. The smell of – what? Disinfectant? Chemicals? Illness? – filled his nostrils. He hated that smell, the smell of hospitals. And he hated the white spaces: the shiny floor, the bare walls, the overhead lighting. And these plastic chairs, he hated them too, shackled to one another in rows as though they themselves might try to escape.

He was not alone in the room. All but one of the seats around him were occupied by other bodies sitting silently, waiting to be poked at, prodded and pricked. From time to time, the woman behind the desk would call out a name, or a nurse or doctor would come, and someone would get up from their chair and shuffle off in one direction or another, watched by those left behind. Before long, the seat would be filled. A new victim would push open the swing doors, announce themselves at the desk and drop into the still warm chair.

When Terry arrived forty-five minutes ago, the woman at the desk had ticked off his name and handed him an empty test tube with a plastic cap. 'Toilets are over there,' she said, pointing. 'Bring it back here when you're done.'

For a moment, Terry was confused. He was here for a blood test – what was he supposed to do, jab himself?

Inside the toilet cubicle, he stood with his trousers around his ankles, his penis in one hand and the test tube in the other, but nothing came. He'd been pushed for time this morning and hadn't done himself a flask. He'd had nothing to drink since last night. Now, for once, he didn't feel the urge to go. He waited and then sat down. Maybe it would be easier like this. But he couldn't push himself far enough back on the seat, and anyway, he didn't like the idea of lowering his hand that far into the toilet bowl. Suddenly, he felt something, and a trickle of urine ran down the porcelain, rippling the water at the bottom. Terry clenched the muscle below his balls to stem the flow, pushed himself up with his free hand and shifted awkwardly around in the tight space. He put the test tube close to the end of his penis and released the muscle. But nothing came again.

'Oh, come on,' he said aloud.

Then a squirt shot out, hitting the top of the tube and spilling down the sides over his hand. Unable to let go of the tube, he tried to stop again but succeeded only in raising the jet a centimetre or two, splashing the toilet lid and seat.

'Fuck,' he said.

He relaxed the muscle and allowed his bladder to empty. In an instant, the tube was full and overflowing the rim, pee running between his fingers. He pulled the tube out of the torrent until he was finished, and then, with his trousers still around his ankles, poured some of the excess liquid into the toilet. Taking care to keep the tube upright, he dug in the pocket of his crumpled trousers for the cap and then inched his pants and trousers up his legs with one hand. He managed the zip but was unable to fasten the button at the waist.

At the sink, he laid the tube down carefully behind the taps while he washed his hands. When he turned to leave, he remembered the mess he'd made in the cubicle and went back inside to clean it up. He tore off sheets of toilet paper and attempted to wipe his spray from the seat, but the paper was waxy and unabsorbant, and the pee just smeared. He gave up, rewashed his hands and walked back into the waiting room.

He handed the warm tube to the woman behind the desk and made his way back to his seat, watched all the way by the silent spectators.

Terry leaned forwards in his chair, causing it to creak again, and rested his forearms on his thighs. The grout between the floor tiles was black from years of waiting feet. High heels, flats, work boots, school shoes scuffed and scratched. His, back then, he remembered, had been black, low on the inside of each heel, the leather worn white at the toe.

When his dad had first been admitted, the visits had seemed almost like fun. A special time between the three of them. His mum would pick him up from school and they'd walk together to the hospital, chatting about his friends and teachers and what he had done that day. His mum would ask lots of questions and laugh at his stories, encouraging him to embellish them for her benefit. They would stop off at the shop on the corner of Woods Lane to buy grapes, or a bar of dark chocolate, and his mum would let Terry pick out a few sweets with the change.

At the hospital, it was pretty much the same routine each time. His dad would be sat up in bed, propped on pillows, waiting for them to arrive. He would give them both a tight hug and then look surprised when Terry handed him the grapes or chocolate from behind his back. He'd ask the same questions Terry's mum had done earlier, and Terry, sitting in the chair closest to the head of the bed, would recount the same stories, making her laugh again. After a while, he got to know the other men in the beds around his dad, and sometimes they would laugh at his stories too.

Things changed when his dad was moved to the other place. Terry was only allowed to visit twice a week, and the men in the other beds were always asleep or looked miserable. They came and went more often too so that Terry didn't know who would be there from one week to the next. Him and his mum still brought grapes or chocolate, but his dad didn't always fancy

71

them straight away, so Terry would put them on the bedside table next to the photo of him in his school uniform. Sometimes he was too tired for one of Terry's stories.

'Mr Fletcher.'

Terry started at the sound of his name being called and looked up. A nurse, her dark hair pulled into a neat ponytail, was stood to the left of the reception desk with a clipboard in her hand. She smiled as Terry approached and then turned to head down the corridor. Terry followed. A porter passed them in the other direction, pushing an old man in a wheelchair with his head slumped to one side, his tongue visible between large, dry lips. The nurse opened a door and held it for Terry to enter the room.

'Take a seat,' she said, indicating a chair next to a metal trolley laid with swabs and gloves and various other medical supplies and instruments. The nurse put her clipboard down on a desk and took a pen from her top pocket. She scribbled something down on the top sheet of paper. 'Take off your jacket please.'

Terry did as he was told and draped the jacket over his knee, but the nurse held out her hand.

'Oh, thanks,' he said, handing it to her, and she hung it on a stand behind the door. She came back to the trolley, put on a pair of thin gloves and unwrapped a syringe. Then she took Terry's wrist, straightened out his arm and swabbed a cold, clear liquid on an area just below the crease of his elbow. Terry watched her place the swab in a metal tray shaped like a cashew nut and then pick up the syringe. He looked away. Through the window in the wall opposite, the branches of a short tree bent with the weight of a full blossom, white as an old man's beard. Terry felt a prick and then a dull ache in his forearm. A blackbird, or possibly a small crow, landed in the tree, upsetting the blossom which fell to the ground like snow.

'OK,' said the nurse, 'all done.' She asked Terry to hold a swab to his arm while she peeled open a plaster, which she flattened over the wound. She retrieved his jacket from the stand and handed it to him.

'Is that it?'

The nurse pulled open the door. 'For now, yes. Just make sure the desk has your contact details right, and we'll be in touch.'

Outside, Terry stopped with his back to the door and sucked in a great lungful of air. Thank God that was over. In fact, it had been easier than he had expected. But it was still nice to get out. Even this car park was better than that suffocating neatness inside, that smell.

He wondered whether he should find Pat and tell her. She was here somewhere, in another wing, working away, oblivious to him just around the corner. But he couldn't face going back inside. And he had nothing to tell her anyway. He felt fine. It would be better to wait until he got the results back, he thought.

THIRTEEN

Tom watched through the windscreen as Adam chased pigeons off the path through the park, while his social worker strolled behind him, sucking on a Pall Mall.

'I don't think he'd actually stamp on one if he managed to catch up with them,' said Tom. 'He seemed like a nice enough kid.'

Fiona made no reply. The social worker pulled up the collar of his donkey jacket as the first drop of rain struck the roof of the car.

'We timed that well,' Tom said, looking up at the leaden sky. 'Looks like it's going to chuck it down.'

In the park, close to the far gate, Adam collided with a pushchair and fell to the ground under a barrage of abuse from the fierce-looking mother. He picked himself up and shot past her into the street beyond. The social worker, far enough behind to disclaim any responsibility for Adam, appeared to offer no apology as he passed the woman fretting over her little angel in the pram. Instead, he took a long, last drag on his cigarette and flicked it in the general direction of an overflowing bin just inside the park gate.

'He was a bit of an odd fish, didn't you think?' said Tom.

'Adam had him round his little finger. It was easier when he went off to get his paper and left us to it.'

'He didn't even buy a paper,' said Julie, 'just a packet of fags.'

Tom turned his head to look at her. In profile, her face appeared almost flat, her little nose barely a bump. She had made an effort to put some make-up on but had overdone it, the rouge on her cheeks only highlighting the pallor of the skin around her jaw and throat. The rain, heavier now, streaked down the side window in uneven lines.

'I think that was just an excuse to leave us on our own with Adam for a bit,' said Tom. He listened for a moment to the rain pounding against the car roof and then said, 'What do you think of him? Adam, I mean.'

Fiona continued to stare at the windscreen, though it was impossible now to see much through it. Her fingers scratched at the strap of her handbag in her lap. 'To be honest,' she said, turning to look at him, 'it wouldn't have been my first choice, a nine-year-old with a foul mouth. But I suppose beggars can't be choosers.'

'Hmnn,' said Tom, 'maybe I'll have a word with Sandy. See if she's got one a bit younger.'

He turned the key in the ignition and jabbed on the windscreen wipers. Above the trees on the far side of the park, the sun cut through the tattered, grey cloud, and a rainbow arced over the shining rooftops.

FOURTEEN

Phil and Julie lived two miles out from the city centre, on a street of neat front gardens and wide pavements with clipped maple trees evenly spaced along the kerb. The house itself was a solid, 1920's semi, with large bay windows one above the other, in the living room and front bedroom. The gable over the upper window, alongside that of its neighbour, was mock Tudor: painted black beams on white render.

Phil's Saab was on the drive, its nose against the garage door, with Dave's sky-blue Capri pressed up behind it. The spaces on the road in front of the house were also occupied so that Terry was forced to find a spot further up the street between a camper van and an Austin Princess.

'Do you think we should have brought a bottle of something or a few beers?' said Pat, as the two of them approached the house.

'No, Phil said he still had loads left over from Christmas.'

Terry pushed open the gate and then closed it behind Pat. The front door was set back in an open brick porch with a flat roof. Pat stepped inside and rang the doorbell. It was Julie who answered in a long, green dress, cinched at the waist and flared at the hem across her calves. Her hair, with a bounce that suggested it had been recently cut, was parted in the centre and then rolled in waves to rest neatly on her bare shoulders. Terry thought she looked remarkably well for a woman that had recently had a health scare.

'You two didn't need to ring the bell – come in.'

Pat handed Julie a card and a present wrapped in shiny silver paper. 'I'm sorry it's not much. I didn't know what to get you. Happy birthday.'

'Oh you didn't have to,' said Julie, putting her free arm around Pat in a sort of hug. 'Thank you – you're a sweetheart. And you, Terry.'

Julie took Pat's coat and tried to find a hook on which to hang it. Eventually, she removed a man's jacket and tossed it over the banister to make space. Terry, concerned that Pat would see the letter from the hospital that he'd stuffed into his pocket earlier, folded his on top, and they followed Julie into the house.

The living room was a riot of different shades of pastel. Dusky pink curtains hid most of the front wall, and an enormous floral three-piece suite, in flesh tones, filled the room with its swollen arms and overstuffed cushions. Tom was buried in one of the armchairs, chatting to a couple Terry didn't recognise on the sofa. A mousey woman sat primly in the other armchair, staring into space.

'Of course, we should have seen it coming,' said the man to Tom, raising his voice further as he saw the others approach, 'South Americans are notoriously hot-headed. And the Argies are the worst of the lot.'

'Terry, Pat,' Julie checked that they had followed, 'this is Sandra, a colleague from work, and her husband Roger. He works for the council.'

'Planning,' said Roger, before resuming his analysis of the Falklands invasion.

'And that's Barbara,' said Julie, indicating the woman in the armchair, who gave them a weak smile.

Dave and his girlfriend Karen were stood in the centre of the room in conversation with Phil and another couple Terry didn't recognise. A low, smoked glass table between them displayed nibbles, carefully arranged on napkins: bowls of nuts and crisps, a plate of vol-au-vents and a hedgehog of cheese and pineapple cubes on sticks. Karen had kicked off her shoes and was pawing the thick pile of the cream carpet with her painted toes. She was wearing a sleeveless silk blouse, unbuttoned just far enough to show glimpses of a pink bra.

'Until yesterday,' she said, 'I'd never heard of the place, never mind knew where it was.'

'It looked like Dartmoor to me,' said Dave.

'This is Bob and Anne,' said Julie, putting her hand on the latter's shoulder to interrupt the conversation. 'And that's Keith, Barbara's husband.' Keith had his back to them, stood at the hi-fi rifling through Phil's record collection. He wore beige trousers, flared at the bottom but too tight around his backside and thighs. He turned at his name, revealing thick sideburns to his jawline and a tuft of dark chest hair.

'Hi,' he said.

'Fiona not here?' asked Pat, glancing around.

'Er, no,' said Julie. 'She couldn't make it. Migraine apparently, so we're thirteen.'

'Unlucky for some,' said Dave.

'What can I get you to drink?' said Julie. 'Phil'll tell you what beers we have, Terry; I'm on the Babycham, Pat, but there's Malibu, Cinzano – and Karen's making snowballs, aren't you, Karen? You name it.'

Pat glanced around the room. 'A beer'll be fine for me too thanks,' she said.

'Two beers coming up,' said Phil. He left the room and returned with a bottle of Bass in each hand. Terry followed him to the drinks cabinet where Phil took out two half-pint glasses and filled them from the bottles.

'Cheers.'

'Cheers,' said Terry, raising his glass before taking a long swallow. He wiped his mouth with the back of his hand and scanned the room. 'Looks good,' he said. The dining table, extended with another borrowed from the kitchen, protruded through the arch that divided the two living spaces. Each place was already laid with cutlery and glasses, and a tall ramekin of prawn cocktail. On the wall behind, a "Happy Birthday" garland hung between a couple of framed prints of white lilies, and pairs of balloons had been tacked in the corners.

'Shall we sit up?' said Julie. She took a setting from the far end of the table and relaid it at the head that pushed through into the living room. 'I had done boy-girl-boy-girl, but now we're odd, so I'll sit here as it's closest to the kitchen.'

'Definitely odd,' said Dave.

Julie lifted a chair around and put her hands on the back of it. 'Six down each side, and you're not allowed to sit next to your partner. Tom, you go where you like.'

Terry wandered over to the table and then everybody shuffled about behind the chairs discussing where to sit. It was Dave who plonked himself down first, right in the centre of one side of the table.

'OK, someone's got to make a decision around here,' he said, 'the rest of you can fight to sit next to me.'

'I'll sit here,' said Pat, pulling out a chair next to Julie. 'I can give you a hand serving.'

Terry sat down across from Dave and two seats along, with Anne to his left and Bob, at the end of the table, on his right. When Karen made a move to sit opposite Bob, Keith, evidently an accomplished player of musical chairs, practically barged Sandra out of the way to sit next to her. 'A thorn between two roses,' he said.

Phil began moving along the table, with a bottle of red wine in one hand and white in the other, filling people's glasses.

Opposite Terry, Keith had beaten Phil to it and was serving Karen from a bottle he'd taken from the centre of the table.

When everyone had a drink, Phil picked up his own glass and tapped it with the side of his dessert spoon.

'Ladies and gentlemen – and those who don't qualify as either – just a quick toast before we begin…'

'Make sure it is quick,' said Dave. 'I'm starving.'

'And those who don't qualify as either,' repeated Phil, clipping Dave with his free hand. 'Firstly, thanks everyone for coming. As you all know, it's been a worrying time for us over the last few weeks – and months.' He paused to look down at Julie, who pressed her lips together in a tight smile. Terry saw her eyes flash down the table towards Karen, or Keith, before she turned back to Phil. 'But fingers crossed that's all behind us now, and it's at times like these that you realise just how important your friends are.'

'Hear hear,' said Anne.

Pat placed her hand over Julie's.

'Anyway,' Phil continued, 'I'm sure you're all dying to eat.' He looked down at Dave.

'Yes,' said Dave.

'So I won't go on, but if you'd all like to raise your glasses, I'd like to wish my beautiful wife a very happy birthday – Julie.'

Everyone repeated the toast and applauded as Phil sat down. Keith leaned towards Karen and whispered something in her ear, and she laughed politely. Terry removed the lettuce leaf from his prawn cocktail and took a mouthful. After the glug of red wine, the Marie Rose sauce was sharp and sweet on his tongue, so he rinsed his tastebuds with a swig of beer.

'How's the round going?' said Tom. 'Martin still giving you a hand?'

'No, he says he's found himself a temping job, but I'm not sure doing what exactly. He's very secretive about it. He's supposed to be trying to save some money to go to college in

September. But the round's going OK – I'm enjoying it – getting to know the customers.'

'I reckon it suits you,' said Tom, 'working for yourself, all that fresh air.'

'It's definitely fresh,' said Terry. 'Most of the time it's bloody freezing.'

Julie and Pat got up and began clearing people's starters.

'I'll give you girls a hand,' said Sandra, pushing back her chair.

'Hey, Terry,' said Phil, 'next round's in three weeks; don't know who against yet but—'

'Well you've got no chance without me anyway,' said Dave. 'I got that promotion I was after; they're sending me to Head Office in Brum for a few months.' He looked at Karen. 'But I should be back by August, September sometime.'

'Oh, well you won't get any of the winnings then,' said Phil. 'Embassy are putting up twenty grand for the team that wins the final.'

'Twenty grand,' said Terry. 'Bloody hell, that's 5k each. I could pay off the round with that, maybe put a deposit down on a house – get us out of that caravan.'

'I thought you liked it,' said Phil.

'I didn't say I wanted to spend the rest of my life there; besides, it'd be nice for Pat.'

'Five grand would definitely come in handy,' said Tom.

'What are we going to do though?' said Terry. 'We need to find someone if Dave's not here.'

'There's a Dutch guy at work who's really keen,' said Phil. 'Hans, says he used to play a lot in Holland.'

'As long as he's not an Argie,' said Roger, butting in.

'Maybe we won't miss you at all, Dave,' said Terry. 'You might not get your place back in the team. Still, I'll try and remember to give you a mention in my victory speech, and I'll get Bristow's autograph for you as a little memento.' He raised his glass and took a slurp of beer.

'Yeah,' said Tom, 'and I'll send you a postcard from Barbados.'

'Mind your backs,' said Julie. She leaned through and placed a plate in front of Bob and then another as Bob passed the first down the table. 'Beef Wellington, Phil's favourite.'

'Hey, Keith,' said Phil, leaning forwards in his chair to look along the table. Keith had his back to him, in conversation with Karen. 'Keith,' Phil said again, 'do you want to put another record on, maybe Steely Dan or that Fleetwood Mac one? Or I've got some tapes in the stand.'

'No, it's OK, you choose,' said Keith, without turning around.

By the time Roger and Terry had split the last portion of sherry trifle, the number of empty wine bottles that Phil had cleared from the table had passed double figures, and the noise level of the various overlapping conversations had risen considerably. The next time Phil stood up, he nodded his head in the direction of the door in a signal to Terry to follow him.

As Terry came into the kitchen, Phil was inserting candles into a birthday cake.

'You go in first and turn off the lights,' he said, putting a match to the candles, 'and I'll come in behind.'

'Try not to set fire to the kitchen,' said Terry, as Phil sent a newly struck match arching across the kitchen.

'God yes, Julie would kill me,' said Phil, lighting another.

When Terry got back to the living room, the music had been turned up and Julie, Pat and Karen were dancing in a loose circle around the coffee table. Keith was on the perimeter, the cuffs of his shirt folded back to his forearms, attempting to slide his way in. Terry stopped Phil with one hand and indicated to Pat to turn the music down with the other. The others turned as he flicked off the lights and moved aside to let Phil pass him with the cake. The women moved back to the dining table while everyone sung "Happy Birthday". Julie waited for them to finish and then took two attempts to blow out the candles. Everyone cheered. As Terry turned the lights back on, there was a rumble and then a thump of something heavy hitting the ground behind him. Dave lay in a heap at the bottom of the stairs, clutching Terry's coat in his hand.

'I'm fine,' he said, as Terry pulled the coat from him and then hooked him under the armpits to his feet, 'just missed a step.'

'You need to take it steady,' said Terry, pushing the letter back into his coat pocket and replacing it carefully over the banister rail. 'Come and get some cake. Karen's wondering where you are.'

'I doubt it,' slurred Dave. 'She's pissed off with me cos I'm going away. I asked her to come with me, but she won't.'

Dave stumbled back into the living room, colliding with the door frame on his way through. Pat and Phil were moving the coffee table to make space in the centre of the room. Keith was back at the record player. He took off an album and replaced it with a forty-five.

'Oh I love this one,' said Karen, putting down her untouched piece of cake and getting up to dance. Dave lurched forwards and began swirling her back and forth across the carpet, crooning the song's chorus in her ear: "Yes Sir I Can Boogie".

Behind them, Keith put his hand on Julie's forearm, as if inviting her to dance, but she shrugged it off and turned quickly to make conversation with Sandra.

Terry reversed back into the hallway, dug out the letter from his jacket pocket and nipped up the stairs to the toilet. He sat on the edge of the bath and turned the letter over in his hands. He'd been lucky earlier when Mr Langley had handed it to him that Pat had gone back into the caravan to get Julie's present. But it meant he'd still not read it. And he hated hiding things from her. If it was nothing, then he could throw it away and forget all about it. He pushed his index finger beneath the corner of the flap and tore open the envelope. The letter was brief:

Dear Sir,

The results of your blood and urine tests of 17 March show abnormalities. You are therefore kindly asked to return to the hospital at 9am on Monday, 12 April in order to undergo further examination.

Terry reread the letter. "Abnormalities", what the hell was that supposed to mean? He looked again at the date for the next appointment. *Surely if they were worried, they'd have made it sooner than that*, he thought. He heard a noise on the landing and stood up, waiting for a hand on the doorknob. But it went quiet again, so he shoved the letter into his trouser pocket and had a pee. When he came out, Julie appeared from the bedroom, straightening her hair. Keith was halfway down the stairs, so Terry waited until he was out of earshot and then said, 'Look, Julie, I'm really sorry about letting it slip with Phil – I was angry and...'

Julie looked confused. She glanced down the stairs.

'About the hospital, he just sort of asked me direct and, anyway, I'm really glad you're OK.'

'Oh,' said Julie, 'oh that, don't worry about it – it's fine, I—'

'What's fine?' said Phil, coming up the stairs.

'Oh nothing, darling,' said Julie, 'well, everything actually, everything's fine.' She put her hand on Phil's arm as he reached them and then shot off down the stairs.

Terry and Phil watched her go.

'Hey, guess what,' said Phil. 'I backed the winner of the National.'

'You're joking,' said Terry, 'the jockey was older than me.'

'I take it you didn't then,' laughed Phil.

'Did I heck. I've not had a winner since Red Rum. I backed Martinstown, didn't I. I think it's still running.'

Downstairs, Terry poked his head inside the living room door. Karen was still dancing, but Dave was slumped in an armchair asleep. Keith was reading the inside of a Pink Floyd album. Terry found Pat in the kitchen with Tom.

'It's a shame Fiona couldn't come,' she said.

'Yeah,' said Tom, 'she seems to get these migraines a lot lately.'

'Oh,' said Pat, 'has she seen a doctor?'

Tom shook his head. 'She won't.' He took a long drag on his cigarette and then put it out in the remains of a vol-au-vent. 'Actually,' he said, 'I think she might be depressed.' He looked up at Pat, who was leaning with her back against the sink. 'We're trying to adopt; it's me but, anyway, it's difficult.'

In the living room, someone turned up the volume on a David Bowie song. Terry took a beer from the fridge and offered it to Tom.

'I'm fine thanks,' said Tom, getting up. 'I've got a scotch in the other room.'

Terry watched him go and then cracked open the can.

'You go steady,' said Pat, coming over to put her arms around him. 'You don't want to get ill again.'

'I've only had a couple,' said Terry, lifting three fingers to his forehead, 'Scout's honour.'

Pat laughed and gave him a squeeze. 'You were never in the Scouts. Too busy chasing Gail Mathews around the park from what I heard.'

Terry could feel the letter in his trouser pocket. 'Just biding my time while I was waiting for you to notice me, darling,' he said, releasing himself from her. He raised his chin and drew in his belly. 'And with these looks, I don't know what took you so long.'

At the caravan later, Pat was already in bed when Terry came through from the bathroom. He sat down with his back to her and tugged off his socks.

'Did you think Phil and Julie were a bit odd tonight, with each other, I mean?'

Terry stood up, unbuckling his belt. He let his trousers drop to the floor and stepped out of them. 'No more than usual,' he said. 'In what way?' He lifted the covers and got into bed.

'Oh, I don't know,' said Pat, shuffling across, 'they hardly said a word to each other.'

'Hey,' said Terry, 'you're naked.'

'Well, it is Saturday night – seems ages since we've had a cuddle.'

Terry grinned and snuggled up to her, reaching over to put his hand on her bare backside. She flinched.

'God,' she said with a giggle, 'your hands are freezing.'

FIFTEEN

The Cricketers was a low, squat building of Derbyshire stone, with a slate roof and hanging baskets. It occupied a prime spot in the centre of the village, between a prize-winning butchers and a local branch of a national bank. Opposite, across the road, was the cricket ground; A black hole now in the centre of surrounding clusters of lights from living rooms and kitchens. On summer afternoons, the male occupants of these houses – solicitors, accountants, dentists – lumbered around in heavy white pullovers and flapping flannel trousers, while their wives prepared teas of egg sandwiches, sausage rolls and sponge cakes. Trees sketched the perimeter of the pitch, with one particularly impressive oak, bearing a canopy almost as wide as it was tall, actually standing inside the boundary. At long on, bowling from the church end, Terry remembered. He had played here just once, as a slogging number eight for a mate's work team in a pre-season friendly. Unfortunately, he'd swung the bat and missed and hadn't been asked to play again.

The pub sign, hanging from an iron post, showed a match in progress with the players in top hats and the church clock forever stuck at ten to three.

Terry pulled open the thick wooden door and was hit by

warm air and the buzz of conversation. Brass plaques, horseshoes and copper plates studded the dark beams that supported the low, plastered ceiling. The pub was busy. Groups of people sat around tables and stood at the bar smoking. A woman in tight jeans and knee-high boots, clutching a tall glass of something clear and fizzy, stepped to one side with a smile to allow Terry access to the bar.

The dartboard was in a smaller room at the back of the pub. At one end of the bar, the landlord had made space for a tray of sandwiches and a bowl of pickled onions. As the four of them came in clutching their pints, a man in a mustard waistcoat walked over.

'Ah, you gents must be The White Hart. Peter. Welcome, welcome.' He put his hand on Terry's shoulder. 'Come on over – I'll introduce you to the troops. Got rather a strong team out tonight, so I'm twelfth man, drinks and so forth.' He laughed. 'Donald's rustled up a few sarnies here in case we finish early.'

Three men were practising at the dartboard, alongside a woman with masses of gold jewellery and shoulders like a second-row forward. Terry glanced at Tom, who smiled and shrugged.

'That's Kate,' said Peter rather proudly, as the woman at the oche, her rings flashing in the overhead lights, sent a dart smack into the treble twenty, 'and this is her lucky little bulldog, Bill.' He threw his arm around the shoulder of a short, round man puffing on a fat cigar. The man's upper lip was hidden beneath a thick black moustache. Two equally dense patches of dark hair sprouted over his ears, on an otherwise glistening bald head. 'Lawyer, divorces mainly. Seems it's a growing market. John here's in garden centres, and James does something with wine; none of us is entirely sure what. Or it might be the other way around. I have trouble telling them apart.'

Terry had never seen a pair of adult twins so alike. If they hadn't been wearing different coloured shirts, he'd have sworn he shook hands with the same one twice.

Phil was looking around the room. 'I can't see Hans,' he said. 'I knew I should have picked him up.'

Half an hour later, he came back to the table where Terry and Tom were sitting. 'They said they'd give us another twenty minutes or so, then we'll have to forfeit. They're alright, but the twins don't want to hang about anymore.'

'Probably late for the Mad Hatter's tea party,' said Terry glumly. 'I can't believe it. I finally talked Pat into letting me put a board up on the outside of the caravan, and we're gonna get knocked out on a forfeit. I've been practising like there's no tomorrow.'

'What about rescheduling?' said Tom. Phil shook his head and picked up his pint. He sucked an inch off the top. 'No, they're not having it, said it's got to be tonight.'

The door to the room opened, and all three men swivelled to look. A short man in a tired suit and a pale green shirt came in, flattening his hair with his palms. Phil shook his head. 'I'll go outside,' he said, 'see if I can see him.'

On the back of Phil's shirt was an image of a badger in a yellow jersey, riding a bicycle. Above it, the printed lettering was cracked, with bits missing completely, so that it looked like it could have originally read "The Barber".

'I was going to get new shirts done if we won this,' said Tom. 'I had a great idea for yours.'

'Better than this one, I hope,' said Terry.

When Phil got back, Tom was telling Terry about a new machine he'd bought at work that printed on fabrics and clothing, but Terry wasn't really listening. Tom always had some project on the go. For a while, last year, he'd got into restoring old furniture, buying up clapped-out armchairs and settees – and in one case a chaise longue – to strip down and reupholster. He'd sold a few of the revived pieces through ads in the local paper but lost money on them by all accounts. Before that, he'd tried unsuccessfully to get Fiona into Latin-American dancing. Terry had trouble imagining the pair of them locked in an Argentine tango in sequins and tight trousers.

'No sign,' said Phil, sitting down. 'I can't believe it; he seemed so keen.'

'Hang about, what if just the three of us play?' said Terry. 'We can forfeit the two doubles that Hans would've played, but that still leaves five games, and we only need four to get through.'

'Worth a try,' said Tom. 'We've got nothing to lose.'

'OK, I'll go and tell them,' said Phil. 'You two can play the doubles, and then we'll take it from there.'

Phil got up and pushed his way through the tight mass of people towards the dartboard at the far end of the room. Terry took out his darts case from his jacket pocket and began putting them together. He was still smoothing out his flights when Phil came back.

'Right, we're on. Two practice throws each and then nearest the bull for the darts. They want to get on with it.'

Though Terry was closer than Tom with his attempt at the bull, he looked on helplessly as Kate, with the nonchalance of a child throwing a paper airplane, stuck hers in the outer ring to get the advantage of throwing first. When she followed up with a score of ninety-five, grouping her three darts in a cluster around the treble twenty, Terry knew that they were not going to win four games out of five.

Which was a shame, because he felt good, and the hours of practice at home were clearly paying off. He threw well. He shook the tension from his shoulders before each visit and concentrated on keeping his action fluid. Strangely, this looseness actually appeared to increase the power in his throw so that each dart flew straighter and landed with more authority. Nevertheless, he and Tom lost the first leg. Kate, her bright pink nails matching the flights on her darts, set up her partner perfectly, and he hit the double with his second dart.

'Nice one, Princess,' he said and craned his head up to meet hers as she bent to kiss him on the lips.

The second leg went much the same way as the first. Though Tom and Terry had the darts and scored respectably, the odd couple, as Terry had christened them, were always ahead. This time, the lawyer returned the favour, leaving "Princess" with a double for the game. She missed with her first two darts but hit it with her third to earn another kiss as a reward.

'You played well, Terry, not much we could do.'

Tom fiddled with his flights and then decided to change them for another set, which he pulled from his darts case on the bar. Terry looked across the room to where Phil was stood clutching his pint against a wall, with a vantage point to the door. Phil shook his head and then shrugged.

Terry threw first in the next match against the twins. The likeness really was uncanny, and it wasn't until each had thrown a few times that he noticed that one of them was left-handed. Even so, he was still convinced that, at one stage, blue shirt had thrown twice in succession.

He and Tom won the first leg, but when they lost the second, their chances of winning the match overall looked slim at best. Without Hans to play the other doubles, Terry and Tom would need to win the next leg just to keep the match alive. Then they'd all have to win their singles for a pretty unlikely victory.

When Tom threw a hundred with his first darts, however, it looked on. But the twins wouldn't go away, racking up good scores themselves to stay in it.

'Are you sure there's two of them,' said Tom in Terry's ear while one of the twins was throwing, 'and it's not the same bloke?'

Eventually, the twins drew ahead so that when Terry stepped up to the oche still needing ninety-three, their opponents were already on a double. Terry thought for a moment and decided to go for treble nineteen, which, if he hit it, would leave him double eighteen for the game.

He lowered his eyes to the bottom of the board and settled himself, trying to block out the noise of the busy pub. As the dart left his hand, it looked good. But at the last instant, it failed to drop enough, landing in the thin part of the wedge for a single nineteen. Terry did a quick calculation. Seventy-four left. No choice. He moved his gaze to the treble eight, his head and body remaining perfectly still. The dart landed with a satisfying thud in the heart of the bed. Fifty left. One dart – bull. Again, he swivelled only his eyes to the new target. He breathed in deeply and then exhaled. The pub was silent. He drew back his arm, but at the precise instant that he moved it forwards to release the dart, Phil yelled out, 'Hans,' shattering the apparent silence. Terry felt the tiniest jerk in his action; the extra pressure on the tip of his finger that told him he had held onto the dart a fraction of a second too long. He watched it drop low into the outer ring – twenty-five.

'Fucking hell, Phil,' he said, turning, 'I had that.'

Phil was not looking. He was making his way to the door where a man with a round face and unruly blond hair was scanning the room over the heads of the crowd of people.

Terry retrieved his darts and then watched dejectedly as the left-handed twin hit the double with his first dart to take the game. And the match.

'Good game,' said the right-handed twin, coming over to shake Terry's hand.

'Yeah, well played,' said his brother.

'Our other player's here now,' said Terry, as Phil led Hans towards them. 'We can carry on the match.'

Hans raised his hand, a broad smile across his soft, fleshy face. 'Hello, sorry I'm late,' he said, pronouncing sorry as if he had a boiled sweet tucked into the corner of his mouth.

Though tall, six three or four at least, Terry thought, Hans had narrow shoulders and a relatively small frame, so that, from the back, he might almost have appeared slim. Front on, however, Hans's T-shirt was stretched tight over a swollen, bowling ball belly that Terry knew could only be beer.

'But you've already forfeited the other games. It's too late – we've won,' said the lawyer, looking up at them.

'Oh come on, that's ridiculous,' said Phil. 'He's here now. I said we'd forfeit if he didn't turn up.'

The twins, standing next to one another, each lifted an arm to look at their watch in perfect symmetry.

'It's OK,' said the woman, putting her hand on her partner's shoulder. 'It's fair enough; let him play. It's a long way from Holland.'

'Great,' said Tom and Terry together.

'No practice though,' said one of the twins, 'just carry straight on.'

'I agree,' said the other.

Hans fumbled in his pocket. 'I'll just get a drink,' he said.

'You two get yourselves ready,' said Tom, putting out a hand, 'I'll get these.'

'You hold this please.' Hans handed Terry a solid wood darts case with a reddish tinge in the tight grain and fastened with a small brass clasp. Carved into the top was Hans's name above a profile of a dart in flight. Hans flicked it open and took out a skinny tungsten barrel not much wider than the point.

'My wife bought it for me. For my birthday. We have a friend who is a wood worker. It is nice, no?'

'Beautiful,' said Terry.

Hans picked out a shaft and screwed it into the barrel. Then he chose an orange flight with the number fourteen on it and inserted it carefully into the shaft. When the dart was complete, Hans ran the point through the pinched thumb and index finger of his left hand as though removing an invisible sheath, before placing the dart back into the case. He repeated the exact same procedure for the other two darts.

When he was finished, he lifted the three darts from the case and laid them in the palm of his hand as though gauging their collective weight. He shut the lid of the case and snapped shut the clasp. 'You look after it,' he said to Terry.

From where they were standing, it was no more than four or five feet to the oche, but it was enough for Terry to see that Hans moved awkwardly. There was a stiffness in his hips, and he was flat-footed – his feet splayed at ten to two so that he shuffled forwards like a mechanical toy. Each leg appeared to work independently of the other. He reminded Terry of a robot that Martin had once owned, and he pictured Hans with an enormous metal key in his back.

Once at the oche, however, in his stance and ready to throw, a transformation occurred. All of a sudden, poised, sideways on, his body seemed to soften and relax. His shoulders were loose, and his elbow moved with an oiled smoothness his legs could only dream about. Terry knew before the first dart was released that Hans could play.

His attempt at the bull, however, though perfect in height, pulled left into the thinnest part of the eleven. "Princess" again hit the twenty-five to take the darts.

'I need a beer,' said Hans.

'Sorry,' said Tom, appearing between a group of men with a pint in each hand, 'took ages to get served.'

Hans accepted one of the pints and took a long pull. 'Ah, that's better,' he said, wiping his mouth with the back of his hand. Terry took the other beer, and Tom disappeared back to the bar.

'OK,' said Phil, 'you go first, Hans, and I'll finish them off.'

As it was, Phil was little more than a spectator. Hans completely dominated the leg and finished it off with a double fourteen at the first attempt.

'My favourite double,' he said to Terry.

The second leg was even more emphatic. Hans scored 140 with his first throw and increased the advantage with each subsequent visit to the board. Phil missed the double, but their opponents were miles back, and Hans finished off the leg, and the game, with ease. The divorce lawyer looked irate. Like he'd just been informed that it was *his* client that was having the affair. And by the way her jewellery was rattling, Terry sensed that his partner was also regretting her decision to carry on the match.

The twins stood no chance. Hans continued to throw with astonishing accuracy, each beautifully flighted dart landing with the same soft thump, like a cushion being plumped. By the end of the two legs, and with the score back at all square, Terry could hear the opposition grumbling to one another about a "ringer".

'Wow,' said Tom, 'well played, Hans, mustard!'

'Unbelievable,' said Terry. 'Anyone missing Dave?'

'Dave who?' laughed Tom.

'More beer?' said Hans, heading off to the bar.

'Bloody hell,' said Tom, watching Hans go and then turning to Phil, 'where did you find him?'

'He's over from some engineering firm in Holland – on a placement. He said he could play a bit.'

'That's what Mozart said about the piano,' said Terry, laughing.

'Yeah, I didn't realise he was that good.'

Hans came back with the beer, with a smile like a bear who'd found four jars of honey.

'Er, you go first in the singles, Hans?'

'OK,' he said, taking a deep drink from his new pint.

The home team had obviously decided that none of them were going to beat Hans, so as he stepped forwards, it was one of the twins that was pushed towards the oche to face him. *A sacrifice*, Terry thought. They were gambling on "Princess" and the lawyer winning their games to seal the match.

Perhaps word had got around, but by now, a few of the locals were taking an interest in the game, and Terry was keen to play again. He was enjoying himself. It was inspiring watching Hans, and he wanted to show him that he was a decent player too.

'I'll go second,' he said to the others, as they watched Hans thrash the twin in the first leg of their game, 'save you 'til last Tom – if that's alright with you, Phil?'

'Er yeah, that's what I was going to suggest.'

The twin threw first in the second leg, but it made no difference. Hans peppered the treble twenty and then rubbed salt into the wound with a neat 102 checkout, finishing with his favourite double fourteen.

'Bloody hell,' said Tom.

Terry took a quick gulp of his pint and checked his darts, making sure that the shafts were screwed in properly and the flights were secure.

'Good luck,' said Phil.

Terry was surprised to see that he was up against the lawyer. They obviously thought Tom was stronger and were saving "Princess" to play him. *Right*, he thought, *show them what you're made of.*

In the end, it was easier than he thought. Although he played well, it wasn't really necessary, as his opponent beat himself. From his first weak attempt at the bull for the darts, he was agitated, muttering away to himself and becoming increasingly frustrated at his inability to land the dart where he wanted to. And the better Terry played, the worse it got. His body stiffened up; his moustache twitched; and he lost any kind of rhythm. First slowing down his action and then, when that didn't work, throwing much too fast, his darts slamming into the board like missiles. Terry tried not to let it bother him. He knew that by staying calm and continuing to throw good scores, he was making it harder and harder for his opponent, pouring coal on the anger that was visibly burning within him. He also wanted to impress Hans.

Having taken the first leg, he knew when he came to the board at the end of the second with a big lead, that he should throw the obvious dart to give him two at the double. Sixty left. Twenty, double top – simple – with a dart to spare if needed. But he wanted to make a statement. Put on a show that wouldn't matter if it didn't come off but that would feel fantastic if it did. He'd had three goes at the bull tonight and missed them all, but he was sure that one would have gone in if Phil had kept his mouth shut. He stepped up and focused on the single ten. He'd look a right prat if he missed this. The dart sunk snug into the black sisal, dead centre of the fat part of the wedge. Fifty left. He took a breath and set his gaze on the small red circle in the centre of the board. He blocked out the pub and the people around him. Just the thin metal of the barrel between his thumb and fingers and that red dot. It took less than a second for the dart to travel the seven feet nine and a quarter inches from Terry to the board, but it was long enough for him to know before it landed that it was in.

As the dart hit, Terry didn't move. There was a cheer from somewhere behind him, and a ripple of surprise from the locals, before the babble of conversation resumed. But Terry wanted to savour the moment. He wanted to leave those two darts there as long as he could. His opponent had turned away, and it was Peter who stepped forwards to shake his hand.

'Jolly well played, chaps,' he said. 'Thought we had you for a moment there. That big fellow of yours certainly had a good knock.'

'Brilliant, Terry,' said Tom with a huge grin. 'Where did that come from? I'm going to have to get those shirts done now.'

'I don't know,' he said. 'I think that's the best I've ever played. That bull felt huge, big as a cricket ball. It felt like I couldn't miss.' He looked again at the board, at his final dart planted in the bullseye like a climber's flag in the summit of a conquered peak. He glanced around the room and then finally walked forwards. He removed the first dart from the ten and then, after a moment, the one from the bull.

When he got back to the others, they were all looking at him with broad smiles. Phil handed him his pint.

'That was fantastic, Terry – I've never seen you play like that. That bull to finish.'

'I'd have got that one earlier if you hadn't put me off.'

'Yeah, well you normally miss; I thought the distraction might make you hit it.'

'Very good darts, Terry,' said Hans. 'You are a better player than Phil I think.'

The others laughed.

'He just got lucky,' said Phil. 'We don't want his head getting too big.' He moved towards the bar. 'One for the road, chaps?'

'I'm just going to the loo,' said Terry.

The toilet was at the other end of the pub, through the lounge. With fewer people standing, it appeared marginally less busy than the bar but was jammed with tables. Terry navigated through them, still thinking about the darts, replaying the checkout in his head.

There were two other men in the toilets. Terry contemplated using the cubicle, but one of the men zipped up and moved to the sink, so Terry took his place. He unzipped and waited. After a few seconds, the lack of activity made him self-conscious, and he shuffled slightly to face further into the corner. Judging by the noise, the man two urinals along had a hosepipe going. Eventually, a dribble dripped from the end of Terry's penis, and then a stronger stream. Relief.

He looked down into the bowl of the urinal. A sodden crumple of toilet tissue lay in the bottom and, at first, he thought that the blood was seeping from this. That perhaps someone had had a nosebleed and had used the paper to stem it, chucking it in the urinal afterwards. But then he saw that the pee was red before it hit the paper. The blood was coming from him. He inched further towards the corner. And then it was gone. His urine turned pale again, and he wondered if he'd imagined it.

He'd been thinking of the bullseye; maybe that was the red he'd seen.

When Terry pulled open the toilet door, the lounge appeared to have cleared a little. Terry rechecked his fly and set off across the room. Four men at the bar were discussing the war. One of them was taking issue with another who was adamant that it was just a plot to keep Thatcher in power and that, as far he was concerned, "a poxy little island in the middle of nowhere was not worth fighting for".

'Nonsense,' said the first, 'a firm hand's what's required. Give them a good thrashing; we can't have dagos setting up shop where they like. It'd be Gibraltar next if your reds were in charge.'

Terry stopped. Martin was sat with his back to him, at a low table in the far corner of the room. Or at least, it looked like Martin. But what would he be doing out here? With a step closer, it was definitely Martin. He went over and placed a hand on his shoulder.

'Hello, matey. What are you doing all the way out here on your lonesome?'

Martin looked up and then his eyes shifted for a second to the table, to a tall, thin glass of what looked like Coke sat across from his pint.

'Oh – hi, Dad. What are you doing here?'

'Darts,' replied Terry. He indicated with his thumb. 'In the other room. You should've seen me, kidda, like Bristow. But shorter and fatter.' He patted his stomach, smiling, but Martin was not really listening. He had half turned on his stool and kept flicking his gaze towards the toilets. Terry spun his head and saw the girl from the milk round walking towards them. The one whose washing machine had broken down. Mrs Johnson's granddaughter, or great-granddaughter. Terry glanced down at Martin, but he had turned back to the table and was taking a drink from his pint. *So that's what you've been up to*, thought Terry.

'Hi, Mr Fletcher,' said the girl with a big smile, walking around the table to sit down opposite Martin.

'Hiya,' said Terry, looking at the girl and then down at Martin, 'er, Terry, call me Terry.'

There was a silence. The girl smiled again and took a gulp from her glass.

'Er, this is Alma, Dad,' said Martin without looking up. 'You remember her, from the round? She's the one I was telling you about – who goes to college.'

'Yeah,' said Terry, 'photography, wasn't it?'

The girl nodded. 'Yeah.'

There was another silence. Terry shifted closer to the table to allow someone to pass. The girl was staring at Martin. and Terry noticed her eyes widen slightly as though she were trying to pass some silent message over the table.

'Right,' said Terry, 'I'll leave you two to it. Get back to the others.'

Martin lifted his head quickly. 'OK, see you, Dad.'

'Bye, Terry,' said Alma with another broad smile.

SIXTEEN

Phil's legs were suddenly wobbly. He flopped backwards onto the sofa, his feet lifting for a moment off the floor.

'Keith!?' he blurted out. 'The David Bowie fan? The one from your party with the chest hair and the too-tight trousers?'

'He's the deputy head,' said Julie. 'He started in September.'

'Oh, the deputy head,' said Phil, with a sneer, 'well, pity the poor headmaster. So has this thing, as you euphemistically call it, been going on since then?'

'It's a headmistress,' said Julie, 'she's a woman. No…' she hesitated, 'just the last couple of months or so.'

Phil hitched up the knee of his suit trousers and shook his head. 'And I suppose he's been comforting you during your little scare? Been very sympathetic, has he?'

Julie released a large sigh and sat down, perched on the edge of the armchair. 'There was no scare. I was visiting him. I didn't know what to say. I'm sorry about that.'

Phil stared at Julie. He opened his mouth as though to say something but shut it again. Eventually, he managed to mutter, 'You weren't even ill? You lied to me about that?' He shook his head again. 'So, does *he* have cancer?'

'No,' said Julie, in a low voice, 'he was having his tonsils out.'

'His tonsils!' exclaimed Phil. 'His fucking tonsils! How old is he, twelve?' He got to his feet and paced towards the mantelpiece. 'But Pat saw you,' he said, turning, 'in oncology.'

'I took a wrong turn coming out,' said Julie.

Phil swivelled his head and gazed out of the window. Neither of them spoke for several minutes.

'Why?' said Phil finally, looking down at the top of Julie's head.

Julie lifted her face to him and then to the ceiling. She looked around the room before her eyes came back to Phil. 'I was bored, I suppose,' she said. 'Bored of this room, bored of the pastel walls and the pastel curtains, bored of *your* armchair and *my* corner of the sofa, bored of the news at six and pork chops and roast on Sundays, Hugh flamin' Johnson and that sidekick of his with the big glasses.'

'Jancis Robinson?' said Phil.

'Yes,' said Julie, 'bored of her too.'

'But everybody has roast on Sundays,' said Phil.

'Yes,' said Julie again, exasperated, 'that's the problem – we're all bored of roast on Sundays.'

Phil was silent for a moment and then asked firmly, 'Do you love him?'

Julie sighed, the noise of the air escaping her nostrils audible over the tick of the clock on the mantelpiece.

'I don't know, Phil,' she said. 'It's not as simple as that.'

'Well, it seems fairly simple to me.'

Julie made no reply. Phil straightened his shoulders. 'I think you should go to your mother's,' he said.

Julie looked up at him.

'Just for a few days. Until you can make up your mind.' Phil's voice cracked ever so slightly with this last statement, and he turned and marched out of the room. Julie dropped her head into her hands.

SEVENTEEN

When Terry pushed open the heavy swing door at the hospital, he found himself in the same reception area, with the same plastic chairs, and the same bored-looking woman behind the desk, as the last time he was there. The anxiety had not changed either. He felt the familiar churn in the pit of his stomach and that dark weight on his chest constricting his breathing.

Coming home from the darts the other night, he had decided to tell Pat. Tell her about the tests, and the letter, and maybe even the blood in his pee. But he'd bottled it. He just couldn't seem to find the right moment. Now, here, he wished he had. Though he wasn't technically lying, it felt wrong keeping things from her, and the fact that she was here somewhere, in the same building, made it worse. Also, right now, he'd be glad of the company. Her calm hand in his, clammy as it was, would have been a comfort.

But the way their shifts had worked out over the last few days, they had hardly been in the caravan at the same time. And when they had, one or other of them had been sleeping. On the one occasion when they'd been actually sitting down in the same room together, Terry was just about to say something, when Pat asked about the darts, and he ended up telling her about seeing

Martin with Alma instead. She hadn't been as bothered as him that Alma was only seventeen, and they'd ended up disagreeing as to how much they could trust Martin to take precautions. If things had gone that far.

Terry handed the letter to the receptionist, expecting the same instruction to take a seat with the others as on his previous visit. Instead, the woman read the letter, looked down at a list of names and handed it back to him.

'Second floor,' she said, pointing past him to a staircase to the right of the entrance, 'top of the stairs, through the doors. There's a desk on the left. Or there's a lift if you prefer.' She indicated the same direction with a flick of her head. Terry took the stairs. He wasn't a fan of lifts at the best of times.

There was nobody behind the desk on the second floor. Beyond it, behind a wall of windows, two nurses were slumped at a table cradling white mugs. Terry stood at the desk for a moment, but neither of the women looked his way. They looked exhausted.

Four chairs were pushed against the wall to his left, one of which, Terry only now realised, was occupied by an old woman in a faded pink dressing gown. She wore slippers and looked as frail as a small bird. Terry glanced again in the direction of the nurses, who were still seemingly fully engaged in their conversation, and then sat down in the seat furthest from the old woman. He leaned forwards and picked a magazine from a loose pile on a low, glass table. It was a *Woman's Weekly* with a cover story about a minor soap star whose husband was a sailor preparing to leave for the Falklands. Beneath the headline, the bow of an enormous battleship loomed towards the reader, six wide guns trained forwards. Below this image, in bold type, were written details of the size of the ship, how many men and what type of armoury were on board and how long it would take to sail to the Falklands. *So much for the element of surprise*, thought Terry.

Before he had a chance to open the magazine, a third nurse appeared in the room behind the glass and said something to the two sitting down. They both nodded and the new nurse came out to where Terry and the old lady were sitting. She wore an upside-down watch pinned to her uniform, with a badge above it that read "Joanne".

'Mr Fletcher? Hi, I'm Jo. Would you like to come with me please?'

Terry tossed the magazine onto the table and stood up.

'You should be getting back to the ward now, Mrs Finch.'

The nurse bent and took the old lady by the arm, gently lifting her upright. Without a word, the old lady shuffled her feet around and inched off down the corridor. The nurse smiled at Terry, and he followed her in the other direction, their shoes tapping out an uneven beat on the polished floor. Though she looked not much older than Martin, and her uniform newly starched, there was something in the way the nurse held herself, something in the softness of her expression, that calmed Terry, that gave strength to the weakness in his legs.

Not far along the corridor, the nurse pushed open a door, and Terry walked into a room with no window. At first, he was puzzled where the light was coming from, light that flooded the room entirely, but a large, plastic dome in the ceiling revealed a patch of clear, blue sky. Otherwise, the room was like any other he had been in, or seen on television, in a hospital. Sparsely furnished, but somehow busy with metal cabinets and cables and trays of medical equipment. There was one plastic chair against a wall and a bed on wheels, half cocked, with a shiny mattress. Terry hesitated, unsure whether to go for the chair or the bed.

'Take a seat,' said the nurse, indicating the chair.

She went through a door on one side of the room, leaving Terry alone for a few seconds. When she returned, she was taking something from a clear wrapper that she screwed up and tossed into a bin at the end of the bed. She took Terry's hand and turned it palm up. 'This shouldn't hurt, just a quick prick.' She pressed the instrument she had taken from the wrapper against the pad of Terry's ring finger and pushed down sharply. He felt the needle pierce his skin and then the nurse squeeze his finger. A ball of blood bubbled to the surface quivering, round and viscous, in the centre of the fleshy tip. The nurse sucked the spot of blood into a pipette, let go of Terry's wrist and released the red liquid into a thin glass tube which she plugged with a plastic cap and placed upright in a rack on a metal trolley. She peeled off her latex gloves and dropped them into a tall pedal bin, whose lid sprung open with a loud rattle.

'OK?' asked the nurse, before returning to the back room without waiting for an answer.

Terry relaxed. *That was easy*, he thought.

The nurse returned with some kind of light blue material in her hand, which she passed to Terry.

'Just pop that on,' she said, pulling a paper cover over the bed from a roll attached to the frame at its head. 'I'll be back in a minute.'

The gown was patterned with crescents a centimetre apart like the scales of a fish. He placed it on the bed and undressed. He stuffed his socks into his shoes and pushed them under the chair and folded his clothes into a neat pile on the seat, his underpants on the bottom. The gown was long, reaching almost to his ankles. He pulled it around himself and tied the string in a bow at the front.

When the nurse came back, Terry was standing in the middle of the room.

'Just jump up here for me,' she said, straightening the paper sheet.

Travelling along the corridor, Terry felt a draught on his legs and groin that made him conscious that he was naked beneath the thin gown. He pushed his feet together and dropped his hands into his lap.

The second room was bigger than the first. There was a window in the wall opposite the door, but a blind pulled down to within an inch of the bottom meant that Terry could see little through it. The nurse parked the bed on one side of the room and applied a brake with her foot. A set of stirrups hung from a pole close to Terry's feet. A doctor appeared from an adjacent room in a pair of white latex gloves.

'Hello, Terry,' she said. 'I'm Doctor Harvey.'

Terry sat up while she leaned across him to lower the bed, and he caught a trace of perfume. She had a small brown mole on her upper lip and flat silver earrings in the shape of a bird's footprint.

'I'm going to do a quick digital examination of your rectum,' she said, smiling. 'It might be a little uncomfortable, but it won't take long. If you just turn over for me onto your side, Jo will pop one of your legs into the stirrups.'

Terry turned his back to the doctor. Her use of the nurse's christian name seemed somehow wrong in the circumstances. His gown was parted and balanced on his hip. But it slipped over and landed in a rucked pile on the bed in front of him. The doctor pulled his cheeks apart with one hand and used the other for the digital examination. It felt a lot less technical than it sounded. It also went on much longer than Terry had thought. He stared at a mark on the wall, shaped vaguely like Australia, and tried to think about something else. But he was unable to shift his mind from the doctor's finger. He felt like a fish, foul hooked, writhing while the angler tried to unsnag him. It came as a relief when the doctor finally finished probing and Terry heard her snap off her gloves. The nurse unhooked his foot from the stirrups and threw the gown back over him.

'OK,' said the doctor, 'you can turn back over now, Terry.' She was no longer smiling. 'We're almost certainly going to need to do a cystoscopy,' she said, 'but I think for today it might be best if we take a small sample from your bowel, just in case. We'll let you rest up here for a while, and I'll be back later, OK?' She placed her hand on his knee, and Terry nodded. He had no idea what a cystoscopy was, but it didn't sound pleasant.

The nurse had moved to the window and was pulling on a cord that shifted the slats of the blind from vertical to horizontal. The view was of another part of the hospital, a block three storeys high with a flat roof. Sunlight blanched the render and glinted off the glass of the top-floor windows. On the middle floor, almost directly opposite Terry, four nurses stood in a huddle chatting. One of them, side on to the window, was Pat. Terry shrunk into the bed in an instinctive attempt at making himself less visible, and at the same time, Pat turned from the other nurses and moved out of sight. Terry had the sudden irrational thought that she was coming to see him. When the door opened, he jumped, but it was Doctor Harvey leaving the room, not Pat coming in.

'Is that OK for you?' said the nurse. 'Not much to look at, I know, but it's better than nothing.'

There was no clock in the room, and for some reason – force of habit, he supposed, since he always removed it at night when he undressed – Terry had taken his watch off with his clothes earlier, so he had no idea how long he was alone. The sunlight had moved down the facade of the block opposite to reach the ground-floor windows, but then the cloud must have obscured it, and Terry was no longer able to use this to mark the time. His eye was naturally drawn back to the room in which he'd seen Pat, but she never reappeared. He wondered whether she had ever been in this room, without possibly imagining that he would one day be in it. Had he always been destined to be here at this time? Were there other rooms, other spaces, he was fated to occupy, irrespective of his actions? He had a weird sensation that this room had been waiting for him, that the path of his life, everything he had ever done, had been leading him inevitably here. And that there were other places, other rooms like this one, doing the same – waiting.

He must have dropped off at some stage, because the sun was now visible through a thin cloud and the building opposite in shadow. He was hungry. His stomach gurgled, and he felt slightly nauseous. *I wonder if Pat is having her lunch*, he thought. Perhaps she'll come back to the room opposite to eat her sandwiches. Ham were her favourite, on brown bread with a thick layer of marg and a dab of mustard.

Later, when the nurse came back into the room, followed closely by Doctor Harvey, Terry was thinking back to the pub the other night, about bumping into Martin, with Alma. He was thinking of the contrast between Alma's wide brown eyes and those of Martin, washy blue, almost colourless. Hers a deep pool of calm water, his flitting, furtive; shallow water rushing over stones. She might be only seventeen, but the girl had held Terry's gaze easily, while Martin had found it difficult to look at him.

'OK, Terry,' said the doctor, putting her hand on Terry's knee, 'we're going to put you on your side again – same position as before – and then I'm going to take a small sample with this little machine.' She pulled a trolley towards her and showed Terry a long, tubular contraption that looked like something Pat would use to curl her hair. The nurse closed the blinds.

Lying on his side with his face to the wall again, he tried to think about the darts to take his mind off things but realised immediately that this was a mistake. He had an awful image of his vast, flat backside as a dartboard with his anus as the bullseye. He didn't want to picture the probe as the dart.

In the end, the biopsy was no worse than the digital exploration earlier. *It might even have been better*, he thought. Though that didn't seem quite the right way to put it.

'OK, all done,' said the doctor. 'I'll have a look at these and see you later. Jo will take you back to the other room.'

The breeze beneath the gown as the nurse pushed Terry back along the corridor felt more invasive than the first time. As though a door had been left open for the air to blow directly in. When they got back to the first room, Terry's clothes were no longer on the chair. His shoes had gone also.

'I'll go and get you a cup of tea,' said the nurse. 'You can get dressed now, just leave the gown on the bed. Sugar?'

Terry scanned the room.

'They're under the bed.'

Terry looked at her.

'Your clothes.'

He was still confused. When had she put them there?

'Sugar, in your tea?'

'Oh, yes please, two, thanks.'

Terry swung his legs to the floor and stood up. His clothes were stacked in a neat pile on a shelf beneath the bed. His shoes on the bottom, his white underpants folded on top. He put these on first and then took off his gown and placed it on the bed. When the nurse came back into the room with his tea, Terry was still fumbling with his trousers. He tried to pull them up quickly but one foot snagged in the loose material so that he had to hop on the other leg in order to free it. The nurse placed the cup and saucer down and left the room.

Sliding his watch onto his wrist, Terry was surprised to see that it was already gone 2pm. *No wonder I'm hungry*, he thought. An aeroplane crossed the skylight, leaving a vapour trail of four distinct parallel lines before one broke up and drifted to merge with another.

It wasn't long before the nurse returned to take Terry back to the waiting area where the old woman had been sitting earlier. She had been replaced, or had somehow morphed into, a man in his sixties in various shades of brown who was studying the blank wall opposite. A woman in a red skirt to below the knee was reading a gardening magazine. Terry's old spot was free, and he sat down next to the woman.

'I'll give you a shout when we're ready,' said the nurse, before heading into the room behind the glass windows.

Terry looked at his watch and wondered whether he had time to go and find something to eat. Pat finished at four. *At this rate she'll be home before I am*, he thought.

Eventually, it was Doctor Harvey who came to get him. Terry followed her along the corridor to a room alongside the one in which he had had the biopsy. It was much smaller than the one next door, with a desk along a side wall and two chairs, one at a microscope, the other pushed under the table. The doctor turned them to face one another.

'Sit down.' She smiled.

A window in the back wall gave Terry the same view as earlier, but the room where he'd seen Pat was empty. The doctor was looking at him, one hand resting on top of the other in her lap.

'There are some abnormal cells,' she said. She paused, and Terry heard a trolley go along the corridor past the door. 'It's what I suspected we might find from the blood and urine tests, but my examination confirms it.'

The mole on the doctor's lip was perfectly round and, against her pale skin, looked like a tiny knot in a freshly cut piece of wood. Terry tried to make sense of what the doctor had said to him. In her lap, the middle finger of her right hand was gently stroking the spot on her left where a wedding ring would have been.

'What does that mean, abnormal? Abnormal cells?' said Terry, the words hanging in the air as though spoken by someone else.

The doctor glanced down and stopped rubbing her ring finger. For a moment, Terry had the sensation that she was going to put her hand on his knee again, but she only interlocked her fingers.

'A tumour. The cells are cancerous,' she said. 'You have cancer. We'll monitor things over the next few weeks and then decide on what treatment is best. I'm sorry.'

In the short silence that followed, the word cancer came like a rushing in Terry's ears, like air escaping from a balloon. He was suddenly aware of having been awake since 2am and not having eaten. The doctor appeared to be waiting for him to say something, or maybe for him to leave the room. But he was light-headed. *If I get up now*, he thought, *I'm going to fall over.*

EIGHTEEN

Tom leaned over his desk and snatched up the phone. 'Peat Street Printing,' he said.

'Mr Richards, Tom? It's Sandy – from social services.'

Tom lifted the flex over the stacks of catalogues, and files and paper samples, and moved around to the other side of his desk. He shooed Trevor away with a couple of sharp flicks of his hand and sat down.

'Oh, hi, Sandy, I… er, I was going to call you.'

'Yes, well, I wanted to have a quick chat with you about the paperwork you left with me last time – the bank statements and accounts.'

Tom scrabbled on the desk for a pen, then pulled open the top drawer and took one from there.

'OK,' he said, sliding a scrap of paper in front of him, 'is there a problem?' He scribbled "Adam" on the paper and underlined it.

'Your printing company,' said Sandy, with a rising inflection, 'is it a big business?'

'Not really,' said Tom, 'just me and a couple of lads on the machines.' He looked up and saw Trevor through the open doorway thumping the side panel of the old Palmerston with the side of his fist in an apparent attempt to unjam it.

'Oh,' said Sandra, 'because you do appear to have rather a large overdraft.'

'Yes,' said Tom, 'er, I've had to get a couple of new machines recently, and cash flow's been a bit of an issue.' He wrote down "cash" on the paper.

'I see,' said Sandy.

'But I have applied for a business loan – well, it's more of a grant actually. You know how much Mrs T loves an entrepreneur.' "Thatcher", he wrote.

'Hmm,' said Sandy sceptically, 'I'm not sure you should be relying on her to help you out.'

'No,' said Tom, crossing out the word "Thatcher", 'it's not going to affect the adoption though, is it? Scupper our chances I mean.'

'Well, not necessarily,' said Sandra, 'it depends. But it is important that an adopted child enters into a stable environment,' she paused, 'that there are no unpleasant surprises.'

'Yes,' said Tom, picturing Sandy behind her large desk in her large dress, her bracelets jangling. "Kaftan", he wrote.

'There are also a number of quite substantial outgoings from your personal bank account each month – in addition to your mortgage, I mean – which appears,' she paused again, 'a stretch: car, television, video recorder.'

'Er, yes,' said Tom, 'we don't use that much – I was thinking of sending it back.'

'OK,' said Sandy, 'well I'm going to have to let the finance department have a look at these, see what they think.'

Tom glanced down at the sheet of paper and scribbled out the word "Kaftan" and replaced it with "Kafka".

'Anyway,' said Sandy, 'how did you think it went with Adam? The social worker said that Fiona was very quiet.'

'Er, yes a bit,' said Tom. 'He's a nice kid, but I think Fiona was hoping for one a bit younger.'

'Hmm,' said Sandy, 'well, as I said before, you're not picking them off a supermarket shelf, Tom.'

'No,' said Tom.

'But I might have one that is perhaps a better fit, more suitable.'

'Great,' said Tom.

'But we'll have to see what the finance guys come back with. I'll let you know.'

'Oh, OK,' said Tom, 'thanks.'

He put the phone down. Through the door, Trevor had the side panel off the old Palmerston and his head inside it. Screws and bolts and bits of metal lay strewn on the floor around him. Tom looked down at the piece of paper on his desk and wrote on it, "bollocks".

NINETEEN

There were no other vehicles in the church car park. Terry pulled to a stop close to the worn grey stone. The back door, dark within the arched alcove, and solid, was closed. The slim window above it was also in shadow.

Terry didn't know why he was here. When he'd left the hospital, something had prevented him driving straight home and drawn him to this place. He got out of the car, shivered suddenly in the shade of the church steeple and turned down the track that ran behind the line of trees beyond the cemetery. He passed through the kissing gate into the field on the other side. From here, he took the usual route, following the narrow path in the grass, around the perimeter of the field, until he came to the river. Two minutes further upstream, where the water deepened and slowed, Terry stopped on the bank and sat down.

It was one of those glorious spring days. Birds dipped and danced against a blue sky puffed with fluffy white clouds, and chirruped and chattered in the trees. The leaves swayed on the gentle breeze. The river moved without a sound. He tried to think back to the first time he came here. He would have been six or seven, and it had been much colder. He'd cried, and he remembered his dad pulling off his wellies and socks to breathe on his toes to warm them. Or maybe that had been another time. This had been a favourite spot of theirs. Terry watched a small bird hop down to the edge of the water and dip its head to drink. A plastic bag was snagged in the lower branches of an overhanging tree, flapping in the light wind. Another image came to him, of his mother, dragging herself through the front door of their house on Milton Street carrying a plastic shopping bag. She had been to the hospital to collect his dad's things and had not allowed him to go with her. Later, he saw the bag in the corner of his parents' room and sneaked in to see what was inside it. It was his dad's best shoes, creased and worn but still polished to a military shine.

A cloud passed in front of the sun. The church bell rang five. *Am I going to die too?* he thought.

Terry sat in the car outside the caravan listening to the cracks and shudders of the chassis as the engine settled and cooled. Billy, the neighbour's boy, was peddling his bike up and down the track, tugging on the handlebars to lift the front wheel a few inches off the ground. Dennis was crouched in the weeds beneath next door's lounge, stalking a supplementary supper.

It was warm inside the caravan when Terry entered. The window above the sink was pushed open, but the kitchen was filled with a rich, earthy smell that reminded Terry of coming home from school. The television was on in the lounge, and he could see Pat's slippered feet through the archway. He slid off his shoes for the second time that day and padded through to the lounge in his socks. Pat looked up.

'Hi, love, you OK? Where've you been?' She kicked off her slippers and brought her feet up onto the armchair. Her toenails were painted the same red as the foil top on a bottle of skimmed milk.

Terry flopped onto the sofa. 'I've been at the river.' He turned from the television. Pat was looking at him.

'Did you catch anything?'

Terry shook his head. 'No.'

Pat glanced back at the screen, pushing a loose strand of hair behind her ear. Curled in the chair with her feet tucked beneath her, her head angled against her palm, she could have been seventeen, Terry thought. The age she'd been when they'd first met. Yes there were more lines around her eyes, around her mouth, but it was the same girl. He had to tell her.

'I was at the hospital.'

She looked at him. There was a scratching noise at the front door, and she unfolded herself from the armchair. 'That'll be Dennis. I'll just let him in and check on the oven – shepherd's pie.'

Terry turned back to the television. On screen, someone slammed a door and the *Crossroads* set shook ominously. He heard the front door open and then Pat speaking to the cat.

'Ugh, Dennis, you can leave that outside.'

'He's got another mouse,' she said when she came back, 'poor thing's not even dead yet.' She settled back into the crook of the chair.

'What do you mean? What were you doing at the hospital?'

She looked at him with curiosity rather than concern. There was no fear in her eyes yet. Terry was ashamed. Ashamed that he hadn't told her earlier about his visits to the hospital. Ashamed that he was ill. Pat was waiting for him to answer, her gentle blue eyes fixed on his, the crease in her forehead deepening in the silence.

He cut out some bits. The urge to pee when nothing came. The dribble when it did. The blood. Especially the blood. By the time he got to the biopsy, she held her fist in front of her mouth and was shaking her head slowly from side to side. She no longer looked seventeen. When he'd finished, she was close to tears, her eyes beginning to pink at the edges.

'What do you mean – abnormal?'

118

The room appeared to expand and then retract again in an instant. Terry had the sensation that Pat was suddenly huge and he tiny, like Alice after drinking the shrinking potion. He wasn't sure if his feet were touching the ground or just dangling from the sofa. His voice, when it came, was distorted. Like a record played at the wrong speed.

'Cancerous,' he said. 'Cancer. She said they'd look at it for a bit and then see what treatment I needed.'

Pat was crying now. Tears filled the corners of her eyes, before one fell and ran slowly down the side of her nose. She sniffed.

'How?'

'I don't know.'

Pat took her hand away from her mouth and used the back of it to wipe her cheeks and eyes. 'Why didn't you tell me?'

Terry looked down, and then at the television, before facing her again. 'I don't know. I didn't think it would be anything. Then I didn't want to worry you. I just kind of ignored it.'

Terry closed his eyes and felt something wet on his cheek, then Pat's arms around his neck. She kissed him in the soft flesh above the collar of his shirt. His head spun, and his stomach churned. He didn't know whether he was hungry or was going to be sick.

TWENTY

Terry heard them before he saw them, though he didn't recognise the booming laugh and would have been unable to judge the sex of its owner if he hadn't have already known to whom it belonged. He tossed his third dart at the board without waiting to see where it landed and moved a few yards to peer around the end of the caravan.

Alma was still laughing, trying to push Martin into a puddle in the centre of the track, as they came towards him. It was no longer raining, but a low mass of grubby white cloud lay snug against the caravan roofs, reflected in the shallow pools of water dotting the track like spots on a set of dominoes. With a leap, Martin was able to avoid muddying his trainers in the stagnant water. He noticed Terry and waved. His hair was longer than he usually had it, giving him a slightly feminine look that Terry remembered from when Martin was little. Alma was an inch or two taller than Martin and more athletic. Her shoulders were narrow, but she stood tall, her spine long and straight, so that she appeared to glide over the ground as if on wheels. She wore a dark coat with a broad collar buttoned to mid-thigh and a tight skirt in the same tone to just above the knee. Her legs were covered by black woollen stockings, her feet in black shoes with a low, square heel. Terry thought she looked dressed for church.

'Hi, Dad,' said Martin.

Alma was smiling at him, the creases at the corners of her mouth the only lines in her otherwise flawless skin, which appeared buffed to a soft shine. Her nose was a contradiction, strong and sharp down the ridge, the nostrils flared and plump. Below it, a deep, wide groove, like the impression made by a child's finger in moist clay, appeared to tug gently on her upper lip. But it was her eyes that made her truly beautiful. Around the deep black of her pupils, the irises were a chestnut brown that was almost orange at the edges. Terry wondered what she saw in Martin.

'Hi, Terry,' she said, without breaking her smile.

When they reached the steps to the caravan, the door and most of the windows were propped open. Pat was crouched at the oven with her back to them, checking on the roast, which spat and sizzled in the tin. Columns of steam spouted from each of the pans on the four hobs. She didn't hear the three of them arrive so that when she shut the oven door and turned, they were lined up looking at her from behind the kitchen table.

'Oh hiya, Martin,' she said, tucking a tea towel under the string of her apron and pushing back loose strands of hair behind her ears, 'and you must be Alma – it's so nice to meet you, sweetheart. Martin's told me lots about you.'

This was news to Terry. As far as he was aware, she only knew what he had told her from meeting Alma on the milk round and in the pub.

'Let me take your coat, love,' she said, edging around the table and chairs. 'I'll put it on the bed; don't worry about your shoes.'

Alma unfastened the last of the buttons on her coat and handed it to Pat. Beneath it, she wore a gold, sleeveless blouse. The skin on her arms shone like her face.

'You take them through, Terry.'

When Pat turned towards the bedroom, Alma slipped off her shoes and lined them up on the mat behind the front door. Terry led the way into the lounge and sat down in the armchair. Martin and Alma took the sofa. When Pat came in, she pulled the footstool to the side of Terry and sat down on it.

'I can't believe you kept this old thing,' said Martin, patting the arm of the sofa, which sagged in the middle so that Alma's thighs and his fell together in the crease between the cushions. 'How did you get it in here anyway?'

'With difficulty, mate. Do you want a beer? I've got a couple of cans in the fridge.' He pushed himself up out of the armchair.

'What about you, love?' said Pat. 'Do you want anything?'

Alma shook her head and smiled. 'No thanks, I'm fine, honest.'

'I'll have a mouthful please, love,' said Pat, 'just a drop of yours in a glass.' She glanced at her watch. 'Actually, I'll come and check on the chicken.'

Terry was bent at the fridge when Pat put her hand on his shoulder and whispered to him, 'She's very pretty. Are you sure she's only seventeen?'

Terry took out two cans of beer and stood up, shutting the fridge door. 'Didn't Martin tell you?' he said. 'I thought you knew all about her.'

Pat hit him in the chest with the back of her hand and silently shushed him with her lips.

As Terry came back through the arch with the cans, Martin and Alma stopped whispering to one another, and Alma removed her hand from Martin's thigh. Terry handed the unopened beer to Martin.

'Are you sure I can't get you something, Alma?' he said, dropping back into the armchair without waiting for an answer.

'No honestly, I'm fine thanks,' she said, raising a hand. The skin on her palm was pale, pinky in comparison with that of her arms and face.

'How's your nan, no more trouble with her washing machine?'

Alma glanced at Martin. 'Oh no, Martin was great with that.' She paused. 'He's been a great help.' She put her hand back on Martin's thigh, who smiled awkwardly at Terry and then shifted his eyes as Pat came back into the room.

'Couple of minutes,' she said, using the arm of Terry's chair to lower herself back down onto the footstool. As she leaned against his knees, Terry noticed for the first time a grey hair behind Pat's ear. It was thicker than the dark hair around it and more wiry, like a long white bristle of a painter's brush.

'How's Pete?' she asked.

Alma swivelled her head to look at Martin, who shifted in his seat in an apparent attempt to pull himself from the middle of the sofa. He looked briefly at Pat and then lifted his eyes to meet Terry's. Terry recognised his son's discomfort. He looked like he'd been caught nicking sweets from the treat drawer.

'Yeah, he's OK. I think he's OK, I er…' Martin scratched the side of his nose, and Terry thought for a moment that he was going to pick it like he'd done as a kid when he was hiding something. 'I, I couldn't afford the rent anymore, so I moved out.'

'Oh,' said Pat, hooking an arm over Terry's knee.

Martin glanced at Alma, who gave him a quick smile before turning back to look at Terry. Martin addressed Pat.

'Yeah, so Mrs Johnson, er, Alma's nan, well great-grandma, said I could move in with them – just for the time being. They've got a spare room.'

'Since when?' said Terry.

'He's been great,' said Alma, 'a real help with my nan. She's getting old, and she's diabetic, so it's been nice for her to have Martin around the house while I'm at college.'

'Oh that's nice,' said Pat.

'What about work, the temping?' said Terry, sensing that this was not quite the whole story.

'Yeah, it's been a bit quiet. I'm sort of looking for something more full-time now.'

'What about college? I thought that was the plan in September.'

'Er… yeah it was…'

Martin dropped his eyes to Pat. She patted Terry on the thigh and pushed herself to her feet. 'Right,' she said, 'shall we go through? The chicken'll be ready. Can you carve, Terry?'

There was not enough space on the table for the chicken, so Terry tore off the legs and sliced the breast with it still in the baking tray on the kitchen worktop. He transferred the dripping meat onto plates that had replaced the pans on the now unlit hob, and Pat added a Yorkshire pudding and four or five roast potatoes to each. The gravy and two bowls of steaming vegetables crowded the centre of the table.

'Help yourselves to veg,' said Pat, putting a plate down in front of Alma and then passing one to Martin. 'Mind, it's hot, I would've done cauli cheese, I know you like it Martin, but I was struggling for space in the oven. There's a crumble for pudding, your favourite.'

'Thanks, Mrs Fletcher, this looks great – I love Yorkshire pudding.'

'Call me Pat, love.'

Terry put the other two plates on the table and sat down. Alma plunged a serving spoon into a glass bowl filled to the brim with peas. The same glass bowl, Terry remembered, that had once been used to cut Martin's hair when he was four or five. Two fat peas dropped to the table like escapees over a prison wall. Terry filled his plate, then poured the remainder of the jug of gravy over the mound of food and speared a piece of chicken into his mouth. Martin was sat opposite him but had his head down, evidently enjoying his meal. When he took a sip of his beer, Terry caught his eye, but Pat spoke before Terry had the chance.

'So, Alma,' she said, slicing a gash into each of her roast potatoes, releasing puffs of steam, 'it's your nan you live with, is it?'

'She's actually my great-grandmother, but I call her nan. I've lived with her since I was little. My mum died when I was three, and my real nan, her mum, went back to Jamaica. I've got a half-brother in London somewhere, but I don't see him.'

'What about your dad?' asked Pat.

Alma forked a carrot into her mouth and shook her head. 'Never met him.'

They went on eating. Martin with his head down, the knives and forks clinking from time to time against the plates.

'There's more of everything,' said Pat, directing the statement at Martin whose plate was almost empty. He looked up.

'I'm fine thanks, Mum. I better leave some space for the crumble.'

Pat smiled and pushed back her chair. She picked up a tray of Yorkshire puddings and tipped the remaining potatoes into it.

'Alma?' she said.

'Oh yes please, thanks Mrs F.'

Pat spooned another Yorkshire onto Alma's plate and added a couple of roast potatoes. She did the same with Terry's before heaping on more chicken. She refilled the gravy jug and put it in front of Alma and then sat back down.

'Nan worked for the NHS like you, Mrs F, as a nurse. She did all sorts, old people, kids, cancer wards, everything.'

Pat and Terry looked at one another. Pat arranged her knife and fork together on her plate and pushed it an inch or so towards the centre of the table. Terry's mum had given them the cutlery set when they'd got married. A gift she'd received herself on her wedding day. The dark wooden box was on top of the wardrobe in the bedroom. Terry looked at the knife in his hand. Pat picked up her glass and finished off the shallow puddle of beer in the bottom. When she put the glass down, she pushed her fork a millimetre straighter on her plate and tidied an imaginary loose hair behind her ear.

'Actually,' she said, her voice coming out deeper than usual, 'we've got some bad news.'

Martin reached for his drink, knocking over the salt cellar, which he quickly rescued and stood back up. Pat began absently collecting the spilled grains into a small pile with her finger. Something brushed against Terry's leg, and he leaned back to see Dennis angling his head against his calf.

'Your dad's been for some tests. At the hospital.' Pat swallowed. 'And he's got cancer.'

The word hung in the silence like a gunshot. Alma stopped chewing and looked at Terry, and then at Martin. Behind Pat, a bird flashed past the window, black and shapeless. Martin continued to stare at Pat, apparently unable, or unwilling, to look across the table at Terry.

'It's probably not that serious,' said Terry, 'but we wanted you to know. I start my chemotherapy a week next Wednesday. Obviously, I'm a bit worried about losing my hair.' He lifted his hand to his bare scalp which was damp with sweat. Nobody laughed.

'Shit,' said Martin. 'What kind? What did they say?'

Terry felt Pat's hand on his knee. 'Bladder. Hopefully it's not gone further than that. I've got to go in for treatment every couple of weeks for a few months. Then we'll see how it goes.'

Terry was surprised how matter of fact he sounded. It was as though by saying it out loud, he was talking about someone else. Telling them about a bloke down the pub.

'I'm really sorry, Terry,' said Alma. 'Nan had cancer a few years ago, but she's completely recovered. I'm sure you'll be fine.' She pressed her lips together in a sympathetic smile that Terry couldn't help but return.

'I might need you to do the round for me on the odd day,' he said, 'when I'm at the hospital. If that's OK?'

Martin nodded. 'Yeah, yeah of course.'

The short silence that followed was punctured by the dull thump of a raindrop smacking against the caravan's metal roof. The next seemed to hit directly over the table. It was followed quickly by a volley of others that transformed rapidly from a staccato percussion into a continuous drumbeat. Everyone lifted their heads to the ceiling.

'Hope you've brought a brolly,' said Pat, getting up. 'Everyone finished?'

The sink and surrounding worktop were already piled high with oven trays, pans and empty dishes so that Pat was forced to slide the dirty plates and cutlery into whatever space she could find, or create. Alma moved around the table to hand Pat the vegetable bowls and the gravy boat, which Pat added to the crooked stacks.

'Thanks, love,' she said.

Terry was watching Martin watch his mother take the crumble out of the oven. She set it down on the mats in the middle of the table, followed by a bowl for each of them, which she took from a cupboard on the wall. The bowls were white, with a ring of interlocking roses, faded from repeated washing, around the rim. Terry couldn't remember eating a pudding out of anything else since Martin was born – probably longer. The hot fruit in the crumble bubbled through the edges of the topping and oozed down the side of the dish like lava. It looked like it might be cool enough to eat sometime around Christmas. Pat placed a glass measuring jug down alongside it, filled with steaming custard, thick and buttercup yellow. She served each of them a helping of molten crumble, and they took turns pouring on the custard.

'It might be a bit hot,' she said, as they each sunk their spoons into the pudding to let out some heat. No one dared yet put a portion anywhere near their mouths. Eventually, Martin brought a half spoonful to his mouth, blew on it and touched it to his lips. He pulled away sharply and put the spoon back in his bowl. He looked at Pat and exhaled air through his nostrils in a small shrug of a laugh.

'Actually,' he said after a moment, 'we've got some news as well.' He glanced at Alma, who was blowing on her spoon. 'We're having a baby.'

The rain, which had been pounding the roof, stopped abruptly the moment Martin looked at Alma, as though someone had turned off a tap, so that this last declaration was announced with a confidence that Martin did not look like he felt. A loud silence followed.

'Alma's pregnant,' he added helpfully but with no apparent conviction.

Terry felt Pat turn to look at him.

'When?' she said. 'When's it due?'

Martin looked at Alma, but she had a mouthful of hot crumble and was unable to immediately answer.

'January,' said Martin.

'Eighth,' said Alma, still struggling with the crumble.

'What about college?' said Terry.

Martin pushed at his nostril as though scratching an itch inside. 'I'm going to get a job. We'll need the money.'

Terry dropped his spoon onto the side of his bowl, causing the handle to clatter against the rim. It fell the wrong way, splattering custard in a yellow arc across the table. 'For fuck's sake, Martin. That was your chance. Finally, I thought you'd screwed your head on properly. That you were going to make something of your life. I should've known you'd find some way to fuck it up.'

The room was suddenly stifling. Terry could feel his neck reddening. Across the table, less than three feet from him, he saw the change in Martin's eyes. From hope – uncertain, hesitant – but definitely hope, to defiance, anger even. Martin's shoulders stiffened. He laid his hands flat against the table and appeared to lean harder against it.

'You never went to college; you did alright.'

'Oh yeah, look at this.' Terry threw his arm around the room, twisting in his seat. 'I did great, just great. I don't want you to do what I did; I want you to do better. Do you think this is what you want? You're just kids.'

'You and mum weren't much older when you had me.'

'Your mum was twenty-one – there's a big difference – and we were married. College was your way out.'

Terry's voice cracked. He pushed himself back from the table and stood up, and the other three looked at him as he turned and marched into the bedroom. He came back with his jacket.

'Where are you going?' said Pat, as he fought to cram his foot into a shoe and push his arms into his jacket at the same time.

'Pub.'

He pushed open the caravan door, still trying to squeeze his foot into the second shoe, aware that the others were watching him. In the end, he flicked the shoe through the open doorway and followed it down the steps with an enforced limp.

He was almost at the gate to the site before he felt the wave rise in his chest. He reached out a hand to grasp a flaking rail as his knees folded under him. The metal was rough against his palm, and cold. He flattened his other hand against the wet grass to stop himself from falling. The sobs came in bursts, in splutters and gasps, his tears heavy like raindrops.

TWENTY-ONE

Phil straightened a picture on the mantlepiece and brushed off a layer of imaginary dust with his palm. He cocked his head to read the titles of the paperbacks on the bookshelf and pulled one out by Penelope Lively but put it back after a cursory glance at the blurb on the rear cover.

At the window, he watched the woman across the street watering her garden, the evening sun firing her long, blonde hair and catching the colours in the mist from the hosepipe. He had always found her attractive and felt guilty for doing so. He looked at his watch. 6.15pm. He had eaten already: a bowl of oxtail soup with a slice of buttered toast. And the dishes were washed up, the kitchen tidied. At her mother's, Julie would be still having her tea, something home-cooked no doubt. He would give it another half an hour or so and then call her.

The phone was picked up on the second ring. It was Julie's mother.

'Oh, hello, Pru, it's, er, Phil, I wondered if—'

'I'll get her,' said the clipped voice on the other end. And the phone went silent. Phil picked up a pencil from the hallway table and wrote "Pru" on the notepad. Then he added "nella" after it.

'Hello.'

Phil looked up. 'Oh, hi, Julie, it's Phil, er... I wasn't sure if you'd have finished eating. How are you?'

'I'm fine, Phil. I'm fine.'

'Oh, OK, good,' said Phil. He scribbled "Pru" again on the pad and then added "ne" to make "Prune". 'Er, I just wondered if you'd had a chance to think things over. About what you're doing, I mean.' Beneath "Prune", he wrote "Prudent".

He heard Julie sigh on the other end of the phone. 'You were the one who wanted me to come here.'

'Yes,' said Phil, 'but just for a few days, I thought. That was three weeks ago.' He heard Julie's mother in the background and imagined her pretending to be occupied with jobs that caused her to be close enough to the phone to overhear the conversation. "Prussian", he wrote. Then he said quietly, 'You are coming back, aren't you?'

Julie, perhaps waiting for her mother to move away, was silent for a few seconds and then eventually said, 'I don't know, Phil. Not yet anyway.'

Phil jabbed dots in the pad. 'Are you still seeing him?'

'Well, I see him every day at school.'

'You know what I mean.'

There was another pause. 'No, I'm not seeing him. I just need a bit longer, Phil.'

Phil gave a little clench of his fist. He looked at the pad and noticed that he had written "Keith", and now he crossed it out heavily, scoring the paper.

'OK, er, great,' he said, 'well, you know where I am; just give me a call, or just come round, whichever.'

'OK, I've got to go. I'll speak to you soon.'

'Great,' said Phil, 'bye.'

He put the phone down and dropped the pencil onto the pad. He opened the front door. The woman opposite was at the window in her bedroom looking out. She drew the curtains. *Prurient*, Phil thought to himself.

131

TWENTY-TWO

Ten days later, Terry was sat in a chair on the second floor of the hospital with a drip in his arm, reflecting on how he seemed to be moving up a floor with each visit. As if each successive storey represented an increase in seriousness of the diagnosis. Surgery perhaps another floor up. Just the flat, black roof beyond that.

He looked down at the rubber tube going into his arm, through which the blood-red liquid was being fed into his body. Or was it being sucked out? It was hard to tell. The only sound in the room was the continual hum of the machine and the *tick tick tick* as it measured out each dose. Like an overwound clock or a bomb in an old war film. Already, Terry felt a tingling in his fingers and toes but not yet the numbness the nurses had warned him about. They had also said, in what he suspected was classic British understatement, that the treatment might make him feel a bit poorly. Then they'd put a bowl on the table across the bed in case he was sick. So far, though, he felt no nausea – other than that from his own dread at being here.

Gazing at the blotched and flabby flesh of his forearm, he thought of the pike he had caught three months earlier. He had a clear image of himself, on the bank of the lake, with the sleek, wet fish in his arms, showing it to Phil. The machine hummed and ticked; the red liquid flowed. Terry had the weird sensation that he was outside of his own body, looking down at himself in the bed with the drip in his arm. He had experienced this strange sensation once before. He was seven and had broken his leg falling out of a tree down by the canal. When she brought him home from the hospital, his mum had propped him on the sofa with a pillow and moved it so that he could see through the living-room window. She went to fetch him a glass of milk, and it was then that he had felt it, watching the clouds scuttle across the sky, his leg throbbing. When his mum came back with the milk, he tried to explain it to her, how he had floated and seen himself on the sofa, but she just laughed and told him it was the medicine. When his dad came home from work, he washed his hands and face at the kitchen sink and leaned over Terry, dripping water onto his bony chest. That was the year before he'd died.

Terry felt the first wave of nausea. Could it be working that fast? He closed his eyes, but that made it worse, so he opened them again. He tried to focus on the machine, but it was better if he kept his head straight, his chin on his chest. If he kept perfectly still, he might not need to use the bowl.

When Pat got home at 6.30pm, Terry was on his knees, throwing up into the toilet. At 9pm, she told Terry that she was going over to the farmhouse to call Martin, to see if he could do the milk round in the morning. Terry had protested but with little conviction. The truth was, he felt weak as a newborn. His stomach rolled wildly, and his head thrummed, as though it had been filled with quick-setting concrete, ready to crack along a jagged line across his forehead and down behind his ears. Right now, forget tomorrow, he was never going to work again. Pat forced him to drink a half cup of water, into which she dropped a broken-up paracetamol, and then helped him into bed. She placed the washing-up bowl on the floor alongside him.

For a long time, he lay awake, unmoving, his knees drawn up to his chest, unable to sleep but incapable of thought. His body had taken over from his mind as the seat of consciousness. No reflection, just wretched sensation. When he did finally drift off, his sleep was frantic. Dreams, like spliced newsreel, ran continuously behind his eyes, cutting rapidly from one scene to the next. In one, Martin was driving the milk float, but instead of stopping and walking to each doorstep to deliver the milk, he was hurling the bottles as he drove so that they landed on lawns and in hedges and smashed against people's front doors. When Terry woke, the sheets were damp and tangled amongst the blankets and bedcover, draped half on, half off the bed. The curtains were drawn, but the room was no longer in darkness. Dust particles floated in a shaft of light that broke through a gap between the thin curtains and the wall, illuminating a patch on Pat's pillow. Terry lay still for a moment, watching the dust, trying to assess how he felt. Thankfully, the nausea had gone, and while his head still pounded, it no longer felt like it would explode if he dared to move it. He rolled slowly over, keeping his head in contact with the pillow just in case, and lifted his eyes to his bedside alarm. It was almost 11am. He had slept for over twelve hours – well, apart from the dozens of sweaty awakenings after each weird dream.

Pat wanted to call Martin to see if he could do the round again the following day, but Terry was having none of it. By mid-afternoon, after two more paracetamol, he finally accepted Pat's offer of a bowl of tomato soup and a couple of rounds of dry toast. The soup went back to the kitchen untouched.

'If you can't eat anything for tea, I'm calling him,' said Pat, dropping another slice of toast onto the plate. She pulled the footstool an inch or two closer to the sofa. 'What about a cuppa?'

Terry agreed to the tea. A couple of hours later, he managed to get down a bowl of the reheated soup without feeling as though he was going to bring it back up.

The following morning, Pat fussed around him, making his flask and packing his bag, while Terry stumbled about still half asleep. But he actually felt much better – almost normal.

'I'll be at work when you get in, but ring me if you need to,' said Pat, putting her hands on his shoulders and puckering a kiss on his lips. 'I've told the girls at work, so they'd understand.'

'I'll be fine,' Terry replied, surprised that Pat had told her workmates about his illness. 'I'm feeling much better. I'll see you later.'

At the dairy, Bob, one of the managers, was trotting down the metal staircase from the office as Terry made his way across the yard. 'Your kid was back early yesterday, Terry, hope he didn't forget anybody.' Bob laughed and turned away into the warehouse. Terry scanned the float, but the flatbed behind the cab was empty. A slip of paper hung from the clip alongside the steering wheel, and Terry pulled it free, thinking that it was from Martin. But it was just a note from a customer changing her order for the following week, with no extra word from Martin on how the round had gone or how he was doing.

The weather over the next ten days or so was glorious, and Terry, in spite of his worries about Martin and his own health, was feeling strangely content, jubilant even at times. He wondered whether it was the chemo or the tablets he was on. Or perhaps his body's reaction to surviving the first attack of the drug, like a soldier's relief at dodging a bullet or bomb in a battle. Maybe he was de-mob happy.

Morning came quickly now, and the birds were triumphant in announcing its arrival. Terry loved to see the gardens change as the days grew longer, buds peeling open to reveal their brilliance, colour painting over the monochrome of winter mornings. Daffodils, like lanky schoolgirls, had slipped away, leaving the borders to the peonies and geraniums. The bushes had thickened; the lawns and leaves were a deeper green. For a week or more,

Terry whistled along with the birds at work and spent his afternoons happily practising his darts outside the caravan. Then the day of his next treatment drew close, and, like a soldier called back to the front, the bubble burst, and the fear returned.

Phil and Tom came round one evening after work before this change in Terry's mood. It was a warm evening with just the gentlest of breezes describing a delicate arc in the long grass down to the river. The leaves on the oak in the centre of the field barely wavered, their glossy faces flat to the six o'clock sun. Terry was outside practising, as he had been almost constantly since the last round of chemo. He was working on his doubles, and when he'd hit each one in turn, he gave himself a dart at the bull for the world championship.

'Alright, lads,' he said, as the other two approached, 'you brought your arrows? I'm on fire tonight.'

'No,' said Tom, 'but I did bring you this.' He raised both hands in front of him and allowed the shirt he was holding to unfurl like a dark sail. 'We've gone navy – a bit more classy – what do you think? I've made the stag's head a bit bigger, and the writing.'

'Brilliant,' said Terry, 'as long as you bastards wear 'em from now on.'

'OK, you ready for it?' said Tom. 'Ta-da.'

He spun the shirt around. Terry laughed. 'Fantastic,' he said, 'I love it. The bald eagle has flown the nest, long live the milkman.' He stepped forwards and took hold of the bottom of the shirt, pulling it up to get a better look. Across the shoulders, in white capitals, was printed "THE MILKMAN" and beneath it, in smaller letters, "cos he always delivers". Below that, taking up almost all of the rest of the back of the shirt, and in the same brilliant white as the lettering, was a side-on image of a milk float, complete with crates of milk, and "WestPark Dairies" stencilled across the base of the bed. There was even the profile of a driver in the cab clutching the steering wheel.

'I hope you've had some dough off the dairy for the advertising,' said Terry, 'must have cost you a packet. What've you two got on yours?'

'I haven't done them yet,' said Tom. 'Any ideas?'

'How about "THE MIDGET" and "THE MOUSTACHE",' said Terry, drawing an imaginary banner in the air, 'and something crazy like – "THE DUTCHMAN" for Hans.' The others laughed. Terry moved towards the open door of the caravan.

'Wait there – I'll get some beers.'

Tom looked at Phil, who shrugged. Terry came back with three cans and handed one each to Tom and Phil. He put his own down on the steps and went back inside, returning with two chairs. He cracked open his can and sat down in the doorway. 'Cheers.'

'Are you supposed to be drinking?' said Tom. 'I thought you didn't like lager anyway.'

'I don't mind it in the summer, when it's hot.'

'It's only May,' said Phil, 'could be five degrees again next week.'

'Ever the optimist,' said Terry.

'That's what Julie says,' said Phil, taking a drink from his can.

Terry and Tom glanced at one another.

'You heard from her?' asked Terry.

'Yeah,' said Phil, fiddling with the ring pull on his beer, 'I've spoken to her a couple of times. She's still at her mother's. Says she's not ready to come back yet.'

Terry looked across at Tom, but he had his head down, his mind apparently elsewhere.

'But she is coming back, right?' said Terry.

'I think so,' said Phil. He looked at Terry. 'It's weird, I keep tying it to the darts somehow, like if we can win this thing, everything'll be OK. I know it makes no sense.'

Tom looked up. 'I know what you mean,' he said, 'I'm the same. And it's not just the money.'

'Well, the money would come in bloody handy for me,' said Terry, 'especially if I have to start giving Martin something for covering for me during my treatment. Bob says Mike's been hassling him to up the repayments on my loan, but I'm sure they're in it together. I'm barely managing to cover it as it is.'

'I told you to be careful of those two,' said Phil.

A magpie flapped down from a branch above their heads, and they watched it for a moment pushing at a twig with its beak, before it took off again.

'Morning, Captain,' said Tom and Terry together.

'Anyway, I've had the info through from the darts association,' said Phil. 'The next round's a week on Saturday, the 29th. But the format's changed, multiple teams in a sort of mini-league. Winner goes through.'

Tom walked over and pulled Terry's darts from the board. 'Bit heavy for me,' he said, lining himself up behind the brick on the floor that was Terry's makeshift oche.

'That's cos you've got no strength,' said Terry. 'You seen Hans, Phil? He still up for it?'

Phil was taking a swig from his can and nodded. 'Yeah, yeah he loved it. He said he was a bit rusty in the last round but—'

'Flippin 'eck,' said Tom, stopping his throw, 'if that was him rusty, we're definitely in with a chance of winning this thing. We should start practising more, together I mean, make it more realistic. If you can manage it, Terry,' he added.

'Yeah, I'm fine,' said Terry, tipping back his head to drain the last of his can. 'Come on,' he stood up, 'let's have a quick game now; I'll get some more beers. Winner plays The Moustache.'

TWENTY-THREE

There was no question of Terry doing the milk round the day after his next treatment. And when Pat told him that she'd already called Martin for the following day as well, Terry barely had the strength to protest.

He was lying on the sofa at the time with a wet flannel on his head, not watching the FA Cup final replay on the television. When Glenn Hoddle slotted in the only goal from the penalty spot six minutes into the match, Terry was leaning off the edge of the cushion retching a thin, greasy bile into the washing-up bowl on the floor beside him. Pat retrieved the fallen flannel from the bowl and replaced it with a fresh one.

Friday morning, Terry no longer felt sick at the mere thought of food. He was even able to cope with the smell of Pat's bacon sandwich without it turning his stomach. By lunchtime, he managed to nibble at a few crackers with cheese and keep them down.

When he woke Saturday morning, although he still had a headache, the nausea had gone completely. But his fingers were numb. *How am I going to play if I can't feel the darts?* he thought.

He got out of bed and fumbled with his jeans but was unable to do up the button at the waist. He pulled on a shirt and went through into the kitchen, flicking on the kettle. His darts were on the worktop alongside the bread bin. The case felt unfamiliar in his hands, and he had difficulty snapping it open and extracting the darts. Though he managed after a while to screw the shafts and barrels together, he couldn't get the flights in. His fingers were clumsy, insensitive to the difference in weight and texture of what he was holding, as if they'd been dipped in icy water or scalded on a hot plate. He gave up on the flights, dropping a dart down hard onto the work surface and then leaping backwards as it rolled and fell to the floor inches from his bare feet.

An hour or so later, after a bowl of mushy Weetabix and two large mugs of tea, Terry tried again. This time, he was able to insert the wings of the flight into the narrow slits in the end of the shaft. The numbness in his fingers had gone, replaced by a tingling, like chilblains, just at the tips. He went outside to practise and was still there when Phil came to pick him up at 2pm.

'I thought I'd bring him with me this time,' said Phil, as Terry got into the back of the car, 'didn't want to take any chances.'

'Hello, Terry,' said Hans, half turning in the passenger seat, 'it is good to see you again.'

Terry spent most of the journey across town tapping the tips of his fingers against his thumb or pinching them with his other hand. If anything, the tingling was getting worse. His index finger in particular smarting as though he'd been stung by a nettle.

From the outside, The Trident looked like it might once have been a Victorian orphanage, or asylum, extended over the decades with whatever materials and in whatever style had been the cheapest at that particular time. It was not pretty. Also, it was located at the foot of one of six concrete bridges, known locally as "the spider", in spite of the missing legs, over a web of permanently gridlocked roads. Wasteland on three sides of the pub, with vicious weeds pushing through the cracked concrete between shopping trolleys and discarded mattresses, served as its car park. For a mile in every direction, the houses were the same. Grey, pebbledash boxes with the odd shabby parade of shops: newsagents, chippy, bookmakers.

Big as it was, the car park was rammed. Phil found a spot between an overflowing skip and a faded blue Escort up on bricks.

'My old man used to drink in here,' said Terry. 'I remember my mum telling me he got arrested once in the car park, can't remember what for.'

'It was probably him nicked the wheels off that Escort,' said Phil.

Inside the front door of the pub, a sign with the word "Darts" and an arrow had been handwritten on a sheet of A4 and pinned to the wall. Terry pulled open the internal door and stepped into an enormous room packed with people shrouded from the waist up in a yellow-tinged mist of cigarette smoke.

Pool tables occupied much of the space on one side of the room, their green baize surfaces patched with beer stains. To Terry's left, four dartboards had been set up, the parallel oches and surrounding tables crowded with clumps of pallid men pouring beer down their fleshy throats.

'Some athletes there,' said Terry.

'Tom could be lost for weeks in here,' said Phil, coming alongside Terry and scanning the room, 'like trying to find a grape in a barrel of plums.'

'Let's try the bar,' said Terry.

He made a path through the bodies, careful not to nudge any elbows or hands that might be attached to precious cargo. The others followed before the gaps reclosed, absorbing them into the mass. They took a new route out, towards the dartboards, and stumbled across Tom sat alone at a small table pushed against a wall.

'Blimey,' said Terry, 'how did you manage to get a seat in here?'

'I dunno,' said Tom. 'I think sitting down is seen as a bit soft by most of these fellas.' He stood up. 'How's it going? You OK, Terry?'

The opening bars of "Going Underground" were cut off, interrupted by the echoey *thwup thwup* static of someone tapping on a microphone.

'Gentlemen,' announced a gravelly voice with a cough, 'your attention for a moment please.'

Terry and the others turned towards the voice, but its owner was hidden behind the crowds. The drone of conversation in the room gradually reduced in volume, the clink of the pool balls and profanities at a missed shot rising in direct proportion. Terry sipped his pint as the disembodied voice outlined the rules and format of the competition. He held his glass in his right hand, his fingers prickling, the palm of his left supporting the base just in case.

'How are you feeling, Hans?' asked Tom, raising his voice over the sudden explosion of conversation as the announcer stopped speaking. 'Have you been practising? Not that you need it.'

'I'm going to see who we're playing,' said Phil. He handed Terry his pint and squeezed himself behind a man in a red T-shirt stretched taut across his back and bulging at the sides like a Christmas stocking.

'Yes,' said Hans, 'I have been training quite a lot.'

'Let's go and see if we can throw a few now,' said Terry.

High tables formed a sort of makeshift perimeter fence around the throwing area for the four boards, with men clustered around them smoking and assembling their darts amidst the pint glasses. Terry and the others slid in among them. They pushed aside empties and ashtrays to make space for their dart cases on the table's glossy surface. Phil squeezed in next to Terry as he struggled to slot his flights into the shafts.

'Nervous?' Phil laughed. 'Right, there's eight teams, split into two groups of four. You play the three other teams in your group and then the winners play each other to see who goes through. I think we've done alright, got the easier side of the draw.'

Terry finally managed to insert the last flight into his darts and looked up to see the other three all apparently watching him.

'I'm the weakest,' Phil went on. 'What about I partner Hans and you two play together, equal out the pairings?'

'I don't know,' said Tom. 'Why don't we put me or Terry with Hans? Try and guarantee two wins in the doubles. Then if Hans wins his singles, we'd only need one more to take the match.'

'Lot of ifs,' said Phil.

'You go with Hans, Tom,' said Terry, rolling his darts between his fingers. 'I'm not feeling that great anyway.' He jabbed a dart forwards as if throwing, then swapped it into his left hand and did the same with another, dropping the first dart onto the floor.

'I'll get more beer,' said Hans, sinking the final third of his pint and turning towards the bar with a belch.

From the first practice dart, Terry knew things were not good. The slim, aluminium barrels felt like broom handles between his fingers, and yet at times he couldn't tell if he was holding the darts too lightly or gripping them like a vice. When he dropped his third dart in two visits, he caught Phil looking at Tom, who returned Phil's puzzled glance with a raised eyebrow.

Fortunately, for the first two matches, Tom's plan worked perfectly. Terry wished now he had pushed to partner Hans, since they would have probably won in spite of his own difficulties. As it was, Hans and Tom cleaned up in the doubles and in their respective singles without dropping a leg. Terry and Phil losing both their doubles didn't matter; the matches were won 4-2, and neither of them were required to play their singles game.

'One more and we're in the final,' said Tom, as they watched the other matches going on. Terry sipped his beer and took in the room. The volume had gone up. He could still catch snatches of songs from the jukebox, but the buzz of lubricated voices, the shouts of support and, for the time being, friendly abuse had definitely increased. The afternoon had drifted unnoticed into early evening. With mid-summer's day less than a month away, it was still broad daylight outside, but inside the pub, it might just as well have been midnight. There were no clocks on the wall, and nobody was looking at their watches. A constant current of bodies cut a channel through the cigarette smoke to the bar and the toilets, and back again.

When Hans came back from the bar with another pint, Terry looked down at his own three quarters full glass.

'You guys are sure you don't want another one?' said Hans, taking a deep pull on his pint. 'You are not playing so well today I think, Terry.'

'I can't feel the darts properly. It's like I've got rubber gloves on. Must be the chemo drugs.'

'Don't worry,' said Tom. 'Bit of luck, we won't need you.'

In the final group match, Tom lost his singles. With Terry and Phil again failing to pick up a point in the doubles, the score was now 3-3, and one of them would have to win a singles for the team to get through.

'Sorry, fellas,' said Tom, after his defeat.

'The other bloke played well,' said Phil. 'What do you think, Terry, you want to be the hero or shall I?'

Terry spun a dart through his fingers. He wanted the responsibility, wanted to be the one to win the match, but...

'You should play, Terry,' said Hans. 'You are better than Phil – even today.'

Phil and Tom laughed. 'Thanks,' said Phil.

Terry looked at Hans, whose face showed no sign of humour. As far as he was concerned, his statement was a simple fact. 'OK,' said Terry, 'I'll give it a go.'

Midway through the first leg, Terry's opponent, a kid around Martin's age wearing an inch-thick gold chain around his neck and an enormous sovereign ring on his little finger, was put off his throw by an argument on the adjacent oche.

'For fuck's sake,' he said, as his third dart joined the previous two in the one bed.

'Bag o' nails,' someone shouted from the crowd.

Terry, already with the advantage of having thrown first, managed to block out the raised voices to his right to score a decidedly flukey seventy-five, thanks to a lucky last dart in the double twenty. With his opponent rattled by the ongoing confrontation next door, where play had been temporarily stopped to sort out the disagreement, Terry was able to maintain his lead. He was first to the double and chased it around the board before finally taking the leg with one in the basement: double three. He blew out a huge puff of relief as the dart landed the right side of the wire.

Tom gave him a double thumbs up as he came back to the others. 'Nice one, Terry, brilliant.'

'Relax,' said Hans, 'you are playing better now.'

Terry took a quick mouthful of beer. A group of skinny lads in jeans and buttoned polo shirts were singing along to "Oliver's Army" by the pool tables over the rolling thrum of conversation and the recurrent staccato thump of darts against the board. He cleared his throat and took another sip of his pint, hoping his luck would hold out for one more leg.

Unfortunately, the ruckus in the other match had, for the moment at least, settled down, allowing Terry's opponent to regain his concentration. When he slammed his dart into the double to take the leg, he pumped his fist at his mates in the crowd and then twisted it to kiss the sovereign on his little finger. Terry shut his eyes, but it did nothing to block out the cheers from his opponent's teammates three feet away. He was playing better though; Hans was right. And the feeling in his fingers was almost back to normal. *Maybe it's the beer*, he thought.

He was first to throw in the final leg but had a quick slurp of his pint before settling himself at the oche. Sixty with his first three darts was steady rather than spectacular, but at least the darts were flying straight. Terry threw first at the double but missed. He shook his head in frustration. The kid raised the fat gold chain to his lips, composed himself and missed also. Terry exhaled and stepped forwards. Fifteen left, seven, double four. He fixed his eyes on the middle of the blunt black wedge at the bottom of the board – seven o'clock. When the dart plunged into the next-door bed, into the white of the sixteen, Terry dropped his head to the floor. Bust. The kid kissed his ring with a loud smack, clearly thinking it luckier than the chain, and hit the double ten with his first dart. The celebratory cries from the opposition team were loud and guttural, but Terry thought he heard a groan from Phil before it was drowned out. There was noise from the other match too. One of the teams was obviously not happy with something and was questioning the ethics – and from what Terry could hear, the parentage – of the other. The announcer, who, it turned out, was not the tallest man in the room but looked like he had spent most of his adult life lifting very heavy weights, was trying to calm things down.

Terry trudged over to the others.

'Never mind,' said Tom, 'you gave it a good go.'

'Yeah,' said Phil, putting a hand on Terry's shoulder, 'better than I would have done.'

'We get more beer?' said Hans.

'Yes,' said the others together.

Terry followed his friends to the bar, replaying the missed seven in his head. 'My hands were actually feeling better,' he said, when the four of them were stood in a tight circle with their pints. 'I can't believe I missed that seven.'

A short squeal of static cut through the conversation, and the announcer's voice reverberated through the crowd. 'Sorry about that,' he said, moving his mouth further from the microphone. 'OK, so the winners of group A, with three wins out of three, are The Cross Keys.'

'Fucking cheats,' someone shouted.

'And in the other group, we had three teams with two wins and a loss each, and two of them were tied on games as well. So we've had a countback on legs and the winners, to play The Cross Keys for a place in the next round, are,' he paused for dramatic effect, 'The White Hart. Match to start on board two in fifteen minutes.'

'Hey we're through,' said Tom.

'Bloody hell,' said Terry, looking around at the others, 'I can't believe we're still in this thing.'

'Must be that leg you won, Terry, made all the difference,' said Phil with a laugh.

Terry led the others back over to the playing area where their opponents were already practising at one of the boards.

'You should give them your number, Tom,' said Terry. 'I reckon they could do with something a bit more quality.'

The four members of The Cross Keys team were wearing matching white T-shirts, with the pub name and crest printed on the front. On the back, each had a transfer of an animal's head, with its name written above it: "MONKEY", "DONKEY" and "TURKEY". When the fourth player turned, they all laughed at the picture of a mouse, with "MICKEY" printed over it.

Terry stood alongside Phil while Hans and Tom played the first game of doubles. Though the other six teams had been eliminated, nobody, it seemed, had gone home. When Hans won the first leg with a stylish eighty-three checkout, the crowd around the tables cheered and heckled abuse at the players from

147

The Cross Keys, getting ever more vocal as Tom and Hans ran away with the second as well.

Terry and Phil played their first game against the "Donkey", a tall, dark man with a long face and big ears, and "Mickey", inevitably the smallest member of the opposition team. Unfortunately, Mickey was also a very good darts player, scurrying busily between the board and the oche, his rapid-fire action relentlessly accurate. The two legs were over quickly, without Terry feeling like they were ever really in the game. When the winning dart landed, the Donkey threw back his head and brayed in celebration.

Phil and Terry stayed on for their second doubles game, and, while neither played badly, they just couldn't seem to get any momentum going and lost two legs to one. The disaster, though, came in the next game. Tom missed three darts at the double and the Mouse nipped in to steal the leg like a piece of cheese from a trap. Hans dragged Tom through the next leg, but in the decider, even his superb play was not enough. Both of their opponents threw brilliantly, and the Mouse finished the game off with a no-nonsense treble nineteen, double top, which, in different circumstances, might have brought acclaim, or at least a begrudging "lucky bastard" from the crowd. As it was, his playing partner again tipped his head to the ceiling to release an extended "hee-haw" at the top of his voice. This did little to endear him to the inebriated onlookers. The players and supporters of the team who considered themselves unfairly beaten in the previous game gave him dog's abuse, threatening things that no donkey should have to endure.

'It's like a bloody farmyard in here,' said Terry.

He looked over to where the announcer was again attempting to placate some of the most vocal members of the swaying mob. But they were enjoying themselves now and appeared to have gathered followers, who were joining in with the insults. Others had drifted over purely for the entertainment.

'This could get ugly,' said Tom. 'It doesn't look like The Keys have got too many friends in here.'

Hans beat the Mouse in the first singles contest, to massive cheers from the boisterous onlookers, who increased the volume further when they saw the Donkey trot forwards to take on Tom. A wide corner of the room now resembled a football terrace as much as it did a pub.

'I don't like the way this is going,' said Phil.

'No,' said Terry, misinterpreting his friend's comment, 'Tom loses here, we're out.'

Five minutes later, and it was all over. The Donkey, under a barrage of jeering, and much worse, came to the oche with three darts for double eleven. When the second landed in the middle of the bed, he again opened his throat to the ceiling in his now customary celebration. And that was when the mayhem broke loose. Tom had no time to shake his opponent's hand before the Donkey was drenched in beer. The glass followed. Fortunately, it missed its target to smash at the Turkey's feet. Taking exception to his soaking, the Donkey charged into the crowd, swinging and kicking out his legs. The last thing Terry saw before the whole thing fused into a twisted mass of bodies was the hairy hand of the Monkey reaching down to grab the thin end of a jettisoned pool cue.

'Come on,' said Phil, pulling at Terry's arm, 'let's get out of here.'

The drive home was subdued. Terry sat in the back of the car staring out of the window. Groups of lads, and parties of girls, tottering on high heels and tugging at their tiny skirts, filled the pavements and staggered into the road. Motorists who blared their horns were rewarded with a finger or a flash of an overstuffed bra.

TWENTY-FOUR

Tom turned off the car engine and sat for a moment. The curtains were drawn across the living-room window, but he could see the blue light flickering beyond them. Fiona was watching television. Another Saturday night gazing at the box. The two of them, three feet and several miles apart. In silence. At least the darts had saved him from that over the last few months, but now that was over too.

She was in the corner of the sofa with her legs up stretched out in front of her. The remote control lay within arm's reach on a low table alongside a bottle of coke, a glass and a family size pack of cheesy wotsits. Her toenails, dabbed messily with burgundy varnish sometime in the past, made an arch of broken squares over the pale flesh of her tiny feet.

'Hi, love,' said Tom, walking into the centre of the room. 'Can I get you anything?'

'There's a letter for you,' said Fiona, without turning from the television, 'in the kitchen.'

It was from the Enterprise and Opportunities Commission. The loan he had applied for. While they were still in the darts, he had told himself that he could sort everything out, that everything would be OK, the money, the adoption – now he was scared to open the letter. He just knew what it was going to say.

He read it through to the bottom without taking in the last few lines. It was all in the first paragraph. They were sorry, they said, but his application had not fulfilled all of the necessary requirements for the release of the loan. *So much for Thatcher helping small businesses*, he thought. He stuffed the letter back into its envelope and slid it into his pocket.

Fiona turned to him as he came back into the living room and flopped down into the armchair.

'Have you heard anything more from Sandy? I thought you'd said she might have another proposition for us.'

'Proposition?' snapped Tom. 'You mean a child. A boy or a girl. Yeah, well she probably thought you weren't interested after last time.'

Fiona looked right into him so that he had to turn his head to the television. 'Not interested?' she said quietly. 'I wouldn't be doing it if I wasn't interested. But to show interest, I would have to allow myself to hope, and you know what they say about that.'

Tom looked at her.

'Hope,' she said, her voice shaking a little, 'was what I had for years when we were trying. Look where that got me.'

She held his gaze, and for the first time in a long time, Tom had the urge to hold her. He thought of the letter in his pocket and Sandy running her pudgy finger down his accounts.

'I'll get back to her,' he said. 'I'll sort something out.'

TWENTY-FIVE

Terry didn't pick up his darts for the next few days. And he felt none of the euphoria that had followed his recovery from the first bout of chemotherapy; he was already dreading the next. And he was constantly tired. Most days, he went back to bed when he got home from the round and then spent the afternoons dozing on the sofa, half-watching old westerns on BBC2. When Pat got back from work on Thursday, Terry was awake and John Wayne was trapped under his own horse, staring death in the face.

'Hi, love,' she said, bending to kiss Terry on the top of the head before dropping into the armchair. 'How are you doing?'

'Yeah fine,' said Terry, without turning his head. On the television, John Wayne showed little emotion as his life was miraculously saved by a long-range shot from the singer Glen Campbell.

'I thought we could get away for a couple of days,' said Pat. 'A girl at work's got a chalet at Mablethorpe. She says we can have it for the weekend.'

Terry swung his legs to the floor and sat up, tossing the cushion that had been under his head to the other end of the sofa. 'This weekend?'

Pat nodded. 'Yeah. Before your next treatment. I thought we could ask Martin and Alma to come. It's got two bedrooms.'

She looked tired. Terry picked up the cushion he had thrown and placed it in his lap.

'What do you reckon?' said Pat. 'It'll do us good.'

'What about the round?'

'If we went straight after you finished on Saturday, you don't do Sundays anyway, we could come back Monday night and you'd only miss one day. Or I suppose we could drive back late Sunday and you wouldn't miss any. We'd still get almost two full days.' Pat ran her fingers around her ear as though tidying a loose lock of hair. But everything was neatly clipped into place.

'I could ask Bob. Or Paul, he did a shift for one of the other lads when he was off the week before last.'

Pat's face lifted. She got up from the chair and planted a kiss on Terry's mouth, her hands covering his ears. 'That would be brilliant,' she said, releasing him. 'That'd give us two nights and nearly three days. It'll be lovely. I'll make a cup of tea.'

He watched her head through the arch to the kitchen and heard her fill the kettle from the tap. *I've always liked her in that uniform*, he thought.

'We're only going for two nights,' said Terry, as Pat squeezed another bag into the already stuffed boot of the Allegro.

'We have to take our own bedding. And you never know what the weather's going to do.' She straightened up. 'Right, I think that's it; I'll just check inside.'

'Don't forget the buckets and spades,' shouted Terry.

'Bugger off,' she shouted back over her shoulder and disappeared into the caravan.

Terry was attempting to rearrange the boot when she returned. 'Who else you invited?' he said. 'We could feed the England football team with this lot – and most of the fans.'

'Well there are four of us,' said Pat, getting into the passenger seat, 'and I'm not sure what Alma likes. You sure you don't want me to drive?'

Terry dropped into the seat alongside Pat, which sagged and sighed under his weight. 'No, I'll be fine,' he said.

For the second time that day, Terry parked up in front of Alma's house and made his way down the garden path. It felt strange to be empty-handed. He knocked and then took a step back from the front door and turned to look at Pat, who gave him a brief smile.

'Hello, Terry, how are you?' said a rolling voice from behind him. He turned. 'It is so nice of you to invite Alma on your holidays with you, so nice.'

'Hi, Mrs Johnson. Well, it's only for a couple of days, but—'

'And this must be your lovely wife, Pat,' said Mrs Johnson, looking past Terry and brushing what appeared to be flour from the front of her apron with the back of her hand. Terry swivelled his head to see Pat coming down the path.

'Hello, Mrs Johnson, it's lovely to meet you,' she said, holding out her hand.

Mrs Johnson took it and held it in hers. 'And the same to you, darlin', Alma tell me so much about you and your quite exceptional Yorkshire puddings.'

Pat laughed and placed her other hand against the back of Mrs Johnson's. The skin at the corners of Pat's eyes as she smiled creased into thin parallel folds, as familiar to Terry as the lines across his own palm.

'Ha,' Pat said, 'I'm not sure they're that good, but I'm glad she liked them. She's a lovely girl.'

'Who is?' said Alma, bouncing to the bottom of the stairs and kissing her great-grandmother on the cheek.

'Never you mind, young lady,' said Mrs Johnson. 'You just take care of yourself.'

Martin came down behind Alma, carrying a battered brown

leather holdall in his hand and a rucksack slung over one shoulder. It was the first time Terry had seen him since the meal at the caravan.

'Hi, Mum,' he said, edging past them towards the car. Terry turned to follow behind him.

'He's a lovely boy,' he heard Mrs Johnson say to Pat.

Silver Sands holiday park was half a mile from Mablethorpe's main street and two roads back from the beach. A section of the site was allocated to caravans, but for the most part, it was dotted with small wooden chalets arranged in neat rows around clipped patches of grass. Terry rolled slowly between them, scanning for number thirty-seven.

'It should be your side,' he said to Pat. 'There.'

He pulled the car off the narrow tarmac road and parked up on a strip of gravel between their chalet and the one next door. They had arrived from the rear. The glass front of the chalet gave onto a square like a miniature village green with identical wooden boxes spaced evenly along all four sides. Two blond kids, who looked like brothers, were kicking a plastic football around in front of one of the chalets while their little sister sat on the front step, sucking a lollipop.

'Home, sweet home,' said Pat, getting out of the car. A song drifted across from a radio two or three chalets along: Blondie, "Heart of Glass".

The sun was on the roof of the chalet, and the air inside was heavy with the scent of warm wood. Terry put a box of food down on the narrow counter that separated the tiny kitchen area from the living and dining space and turned to go and get another. He changed his mind and followed Martin through a skinny passage to the back of the chalet. Three sliding doors were open to two bedrooms and a toilet.

'Well, I guess I'll take the top bunk then,' said Martin, taking half a step inside the room to toss his rucksack up onto the bare foam mattress. Terry poked his head into the other bedroom and then edged around the bed to open the window.

'Not bad, is it?' said Pat, throwing down a bag of bedding. 'I'll do this later; let's have a cup of tea – I'm gasping.'

When Terry walked back through to the living room, Alma was stretched out on the bottom bunk.

'Comfy,' she said as he looked in.

Pat was pulling food from a cardboard box, arranging it on the kitchen work surface and in a small cupboard on the wall above the two-ring electric hob. She unpacked four mugs wrapped individually in newspaper and lined them up in front of the kettle, tossing a tea bag in each that she took from a Tupperware box.

'Can you put the lecky on?' she said, bending to stock the fridge with packets of ham and cheese, boxes of eggs and a fat slab of bacon. 'Angie said there's a junction box in the loo.'

Terry found the box next to the hot water tank and flicked on the power. A light came on in the passageway.

'That's it,' Pat shouted.

When Terry returned to the living room, Martin was adding more luggage to the pile in the middle of the floor.

'Right, that's the lot,' he said. He picked up two canvas deckchairs that were leaning against the wall. 'I'll put these outside – it's boiling out there.'

Alma came through from the bedroom and followed Martin outside. Terry watched them wrestling with the deckchairs. Alma giggled and slapped Martin on the arm as he made fun of the difficulty she was having in getting hers the right way round. When Martin sat down triumphantly in his chair, Alma abandoned hers, throwing it to the floor in mock disgust, and plonked herself in Martin's lap.

They drank their tea outside. Terry took out a plastic dining chair, and Martin and Alma sat in the deckchairs, once Alma had instructed Martin to assemble hers. Pat was on the step in the open doorway. The blond brothers had been joined on the grass by a younger boy, though for the moment he just stood there, watching them kick the ball to one another. He wore a floppy-brimmed hat low over his eyes, his arms and the back of his neck white with suncream. The girl had gone inside, perhaps frightened away by a tall seagull that was now perched on her chalet roof directly over the door.

'We should make the most of this weather,' said Pat. 'Why don't I make some sarnies, and we'll take them to the beach.'

'I'll give you a hand,' said Alma, getting up.

Martin watched her go. Terry thought about taking Alma's spot in the deckchair but, in the end, stayed where he was. He leaned back in the chair and closed his eyes, the sun warm on his eyelids.

They chose a spot on the beach close to the base of the dunes, hoping that the clumps of thick, stiff grass that grew directly from the sand might provide some shelter. But the breeze was onshore, coming straight out of the east. The tide was out, the sea a distant brush stroke of Oxford blue beneath an azure sky. Terry flopped down. The vast expanse of beach was dotted with families: kids playing cricket, mums dozing and dads digging in the sand. Grandparents fighting with the newspaper hid behind windbreaks striped like summer dresses.

Terry spent most of the afternoon napping. At one stage, Pat told him, he'd fallen into a deep sleep and begun snoring steadily, so she'd nudged him with her foot to get him to stop. Now, she was lying on her side, facing away from him, propped on one elbow reading. She had sand stuck to her bikini bottom and the top of her thigh. Martin and Alma were not there, but Terry scanned the beach and spotted them paddling at the edge of the water. The sea had come in a way since earlier, and he saw Alma kick up some water at Martin and then skip away laughing. She wore a yellow one-piece bathing suit, a camera hanging around her neck. Martin looked down at his wet shorts and ran after her. His skin against hers when he caught her looked bloodless.

Coming back, Alma stopped and crouched to take a picture of a boy sat burying his own legs in the sand. When he saw her, the boy raised a small red spade above his head, as if in celebration, but then lowered it and used it to flick sand at Alma. Terry saw her laugh and run away in mock fear. She stopped again as she approached them and once more brought the camera up to her face. The shutter clicked twice and then she moved sideways across the sand to change the angle. Terry lowered his gaze from the camera but could make out no discernible swell in Alma's belly.

As the afternoon wore on, the wind dropped. The sun was still high in the clear blue sky, and Terry felt it hot on the back of his head and neck. A long, low ship was a bump on the horizon. Terry lay back on his towel and closed his eyes, his head nestled in the hollow in the sand it had made earlier.

Coming down off the dunes later, Terry waited while the others dropped their sandals and shoes onto the pavement and wriggled in their feet.

'Let's get chips,' he said, 'save you having to cook, love.'

They walked south for five minutes with the beach on their left until the main street cut across them. The pavements were busy with people eating ice cream or standing outside the front of pubs drinking pints of lager. There was a queue at the chip shop. Families moved in and out of the amusement arcades, the machines ringing and beeping and calling out in flat, electronic voices. Terry watched a row of pensioners on stools, purses in their laps, feeding coins into the one-arm bandits.

They took their chips up the slip road towards the beach and ate them out of the paper on a low wall facing the sea. Terry at one end, Martin at the other. The tide had come in, the sand barely visible between the pink and white bodies packed tightly together like maggots in Terry's bait box.

'These are fantastic,' said Alma. 'This is just the best way to eat chips.'

On the walk back, Martin and Alma pulled ahead. Martin's shoulders were sunburnt.

'You OK, love?' said Pat.

'Yeah, I'm fine,' said Terry.

'He'll come round, but it might be you who has to make the effort. You know how he is.'

'Yeah,' said Terry. 'We're as stubborn as each other. Or as stupid.'

Pat slipped her hand into his, and they walked on, watching Martin and Alma fooling around on the pavement ahead of them.

'Maybe we should go to the club tonight,' said Terry. 'I saw a sign by the gate, says they've got a band on.'

Pat looked up at him and smiled. 'That's a great idea, get dressed up, let our hair down a bit.'

'That might be difficult for me,' said Terry.

Pat laughed. She lifted his hand to her mouth and planted a kiss on it. 'You're lovely without,' she said.

The band was awful. Two guitarists and a keyboard player in cowboy hats and matching black shirts with wing collars, singing covers of old Johnny Cash and Merle Haggard songs. Fortunately, the acoustics were bad also, and most of the time the lead singer's voice was lost in the noise of conversation in the packed room.

'Thank God for that,' said Terry, as the band stepped off the makeshift stage for a break. 'I was beginning to think of buying them a drink myself to get them to stop.'

'Ah, they're not that bad,' laughed Pat.

'I don't mind them,' said Alma. 'I quite like a bit of country.'

'It's just a shame they're not in a different one,' said Terry.

Terry woke on Sunday morning to a half-light filtered through the thin curtains. For a moment, he experienced a flash of panic that he was late for the round but then remembered where he was. Pat lay curled with her back to him, still sleeping. He got out of bed, pulled on a pair of shorts and a T-shirt and crept to the toilet. There was no sound from Martin and Alma's room. He slid the doors slowly on their runners to reduce the noise and sat down on the toilet.

In the living room, the sun shone at an angle through a side window, casting a fan of light across the floor and into a corner of the two-seater settee. *Dennis would like that spot*, thought Terry, and he wondered how the cat was getting on at home without them. Pat's handbag hung from the back of a chair, and Terry dug into it to pull out her purse. He opened it, removed a one-pound note and slid it, folded, into the front pocket of his shorts. Shoes from last night lay where they'd been kicked off, singly, or in unmatched pairs, so Terry had to search to drag out his trainers from beneath his own black slip-ons and one of Alma's wedge high heels.

He pushed aside the curtain that covered the entire front wall of the chalet just enough to open the door and stepped outside. The kid from yesterday with the hat was sat in front of his own chalet, plucking daisies from the grass and dropping them into a small red bucket. Other than the odd broken line of blurred cloud over the sea, the sky was as blue as it had been the previous day. Terry strolled across the campsite to the shop by the front gate, sticking to the gravel paths that ran around and between the chalets, taking his time.

Most of what the shop was selling seemed to be outside on a low wooden deck under the projecting roof. Terry thought about buying a postcard for Phil and Julie but then remembered she'd moved out. Phil might be a prat sometimes, but they'd been mates for over twenty years; Terry knew he couldn't just let Phil's marriage fall apart without trying to do something.

He picked a *Sunday Mirror* from the rack of newspapers and cut between the displays of inflatable crocodiles and dinghies, footballs and cricket sets, sunhats and sailor's caps, into the shop. It was as rammed with stuff inside as out.

No one was up when he got back to the chalet. He left the door open, drew the curtains the rest of the way back and made two mugs of tea. Pat was awake when he took hers through.

'Oh you're a star, thanks, love,' she said, sitting up in bed and plumping a pillow behind her back. 'I could get used to this. You been out already?'

'Yeah, just to get a paper. It's a beautiful day again. How's your head?'

'Not too bad,' she said, running her fingers though her fringe and stretching out her shoulders. 'I think the band did more damage than the beer.'

'Tell me about it,' said Terry. 'I can't get "Ring of Fire" out of my head this morning.'

'It was a nice evening though, wasn't it?' said Pat, smiling.

Terry nodded. 'Yeah, it was nice.'

Pat switched on the bedside light and picked up her book. She glanced at her watch. 'I'll just have ten minutes with my tea. I didn't realise it was so late.'

'No rush, we're on holiday. I'll do breakfast in a bit, a nice big fry-up.'

Terry pulled the door across. He could hear Martin and Alma talking in low voices and giggling.

They spent the day on the beach again in the same spot as the day before. After a late breakfast and then coffee, Pat hadn't bothered making sandwiches. Instead, she'd thrown four apples and a packet of club biscuits into her bag to tide them over. Martin bought a plastic frisbee from the site shop, and he and Alma tossed it to one another while Pat read her book and Terry watched or dozed.

Towards the end of the afternoon, Alma took her camera from her bag and set off with Martin along the beach. Pat put down her book and sat up, hugging her knees.

'She's lovely, isn't she?'

Terry watched Martin put his arm around Alma's waist and nodded.

'And Martin looks happy.'

A cloud passed quickly in front of the sun, causing a shadow to glide along the beach, like a blanket dragged across a bed, and off the other side.

'Yeah,' said Terry, 'they're just young, that's all. I don't want Martin to throw away a chance of going to college.'

'I know. But he told me he really enjoys the milk round, getting to know the customers…'

Terry turned his head to face Pat. 'Really? When did he say that?'

'Last night, when you were at the bar. He said he doesn't even mind the early mornings. Can you believe that?'

Terry turned back around. Martin and Alma were a hundred yards or so along the beach on the firm sand below the high tide line. Alma was posing for a photograph, side on to Martin, with one hand behind her head, the other resting flat against her stomach, which she was pushing forwards to exaggerate the swell. Terry continued to watch them as they walked further along the beach, quieter now as the weekenders began packing up to go home.

Pat went back to her book but soon dropped off, her breathing slow and rhythmic. The breeze had died to nothing, and barely a ripple troubled the dark surface of the sea. Terry thought of his next chemotherapy session coming up when he got back. He wondered what was going on inside him. It was strange because he didn't feel ill. Other than that first day by the river, he'd given no thought to the fact that he might die. In his mind, the treatment was so awful it must be making him better. Now he thought about it. He tried to picture Pat and Martin and Alma without him. And the baby. But he found it impossible. Even if he removed himself from the scene, he was the onlooker. He could only see them through his own eyes, as if they needed him to exist themselves. But he knew this was not the case. He knew that however difficult it was to imagine, it was perfectly possible that he might die. And for the first time, he realised that he desperately wanted to be around to see Martin's child born and grow up.

Alma and Martin were gone for over an hour and came back through the dunes. Terry sat up. The beach was almost deserted save for the odd diehard family and a couple of dog walkers on the hard sand. A light, offshore wind had lifted, forming creases in the surface of the water that glistened in the evening sunlight.

'Shall we nip into town for a pint?' said Terry.

The road was busy, and they walked against the traffic along the sandy pavement. With fewer people wandering about, they were able to find a table out the front of a reasonable-looking pub. A blackboard outside advertised Ploughman's lunches, scampi and chicken in a basket.

'Can we go in the arcades?' said Alma when they'd finished their drinks.

'Here's one for you, Terry,' said Pat, stopping at a stall outside the second arcade. 'You've got to burst the balloons; you get a prize if you get three the same colour.'

Terry dug in his pocket and handed fifty pence to the man, who passed Terry three darts in return. 'I'll be lucky to hit anything with these,' said Terry.

'Go for the yellows,' said Martin.

Terry weighed the darts for a second in his hand and then leant over the edge of the stall, his thigh pressed against the wooden surround. The first two balloons burst with a bang, their ragged yellow skins left pinned to the baize backboard.

Terry took a step to his right and set himself again. The others cheered as the third balloon exploded under the dart's metal tip.

'Anything off the bottom two shelves,' said the man, turning to the display of sun-faded prizes.

'I'll have the bear,' said Terry, pointing to a honey-coloured soft toy with a chocolate brown nose and matching circles on its palms and the soles of its feet. The man took the bear from the shelf and passed it over to Terry, who turned and handed it to Alma. 'Here you go – it's for you.'

'Oh thanks, Terry, I love him.' Alma hugged the bear to her chest and then kissed it on the nose. 'Thanks,' she said again and kissed Terry on the cheek.

There were fewer cars on the site when they got back. Many of those that remained were parked with their boots open while the owners moved in and out of the chalets with boxes and bags and suitcases. Someone had cut the grass during the day, and the square in front of their chalet, sheltered from the breeze, was thick with the scent of it. Terry helped himself to a beer from the fridge and sat out the front in a deckchair. Pat came out and sat down next to him.

'I thought we could have that pie tonight, and I'll do some mash with it. What do you think?'

'Sounds good,' said Terry.

'Did you put any sun lotion on today?' said Pat. 'You look like a lobster.'

Terry looked down at his pink belly. 'I thought I was tanning up nicely,' he said.

It was hot inside the chalet, and they ate their tea with the doors and all the windows open. Pat had insisted that Terry put a shirt on at the table, and this trapped the heat coming off his sunburnt body, making him hotter still. Sweat beaded on the top of his head and ran down his face, or the back of his neck, pooling in the folds of flesh at his shirt collar. It was cooler outside, and they sat for a while after the meal listening to the birds calling back and forth from the trees.

'Shall we go to the club for one?' said Terry. 'The band aren't on I promise.'

'I think I'll go to bed early if you don't mind,' said Alma. 'I'm not feeling that great.'

'I'll stay with you?' said Martin.

'No, you go,' said Alma. 'I'll be fine, honest.'

'I think I might give it a miss as well,' said Pat. 'I fancy just reading my book. You and Martin go though.'

Terry looked across at Martin who took a swig of his beer but said nothing. Terry could feel Pat's eyes on him. 'Well, I guess it's just the two of us, kidda,' he said.

Though the club was less crowded than the night before, many of the tables were occupied, and a handful of people stood at the bar. Terry got the drinks, and they found a free table in the centre of what was normally the dance floor. The people around them were older: couples in their sixties or seventies in smart clothes fifteen years out of date, smoking cheap cigarettes. A medley of songs from the fifties and sixties rolled around the room.

'I think I preferred the band,' said Martin, taking the top off his pint.

'You're joking,' said Terry, as Peggy Sue faded into the Everly Brothers, 'this is a classic.'

The lead singer and the keyboard player from the band were leaning on the end of the bar smoking thin cigars, chatting to the barman. Terry could see why they favoured the stetsons on stage since both were completely bald, their wrinkled scalps dotted with liver spots.

When Martin had lived at home, he and Terry had fallen into a routine of going out for a pint together on a Tuesday night, when there was nothing decent on the telly. Then they'd had the row over Martin deciding not to go to college, and the tradition had stopped. That was when Martin had begun shutting himself away in his room, and, with Pat at work, Terry had spent his evenings stretched out on the sofa watching episodes of *Minder* or *Juliet Bravo*.

'I'm glad you came,' said Terry.

Martin was looking around the room but turned back and picked up his pint when Terry spoke.

'Yeah,' he took a sip of his beer, 'I'm sure Alma'll be fine, probably just a stomach ache or something.'

'Yeah. No, I meant this weekend. I'm glad you both came – it's been nice.'

'Oh,' said Martin, 'yeah.'

Terry picked up his own glass and took a long drink from it. Over the funereal hush of conversation, Elvis warbled "Are You Lonesome Tonight?".

'Alma's a nice girl.'

'Jesus,' said Martin, 'are they trying to clear the place or what? It's like a morgue in here.'

'I might need you for the round again Wednesday, Thursday, if that's alright. I've got my treatment this week.'

'Yeah, no problem. I told you, whenever. I quite enjoy it.'

'Yeah, your mum said.'

Martin was looking around the room. A scar, a pale nick barely visible, cut into the pink of his upper lip. Terry remembered the freezing January afternoon when Martin had got it, falling off his sledge at the park and sliding face first down the icy slope. Martin had always been accident prone; Terry seemed to have spent years carrying him in and out of A & E.

'Have you thought any more about college?' Terry asked.

Martin looked at him. His shoulders sagged. 'I can't, Dad. I need to get a job, start earning some money. For the baby.'

Terry glanced down at the table and then towards the bar. The third band member had joined the others. He had about as much hair as the other two.

'And anyway, you're probably gonna need me on the round over the next few months.'

'Well, you can't do that if you've got a job. And I can't pay you.'

'What if we made it bigger, took on more streets? Then we could do it together.'

Terry shook his head. 'It's not as easy as that. Besides, you don't wanna be a milkman.'

'Why not?' said Martin, sounding irritated. 'I like it, Dad. I like meeting the customers, chatting to them, I like feeling they're relying on me. I've even got used to the mornings.'

'That I find hard to believe,' said Terry.

Martin made no reply. He finished his pint and picked up Terry's empty glass. 'I'll get us another.'

Terry watched him walk to the bar. An old man in a shirt and tie at the next table was mouthing along to "Eleanor Rigby", his wife deadpan in the seat opposite.

Though the sun had set over an hour ago, it was not yet fully dark when Martin and Terry walked back to the chalet. The air was warm and the campsite quiet. The soft crunch of their feet on the gravel path close under the vast sky. Terry could smell the sea. He could feel the size of it, as though he were on a small island floating freely at its centre, great depths beneath.

Pat was awake when Terry came in. She put her book down on the bedcover and smiled up at him. 'Did you have a nice evening?'

Terry heard the other bedroom door slide shut. He unbuckled his trousers and sat down on the bed to slide them off. 'Yeah,' he said, 'yeah, it was really nice.'

It was raining the following morning. Terry heard it patting against the felt roof of the chalet when he woke and so turned over to go back to sleep. When he woke again later, the rain had increased in intensity. Pat was not beside him, but he could hear voices and the creaking of floorboards over the pounding of the rain.

Pat had the lights on in the living room when Terry came through. Martin was stood by the front window looking out at the rain slanting across the grass. The cloud was so low, clumps of it seemed to creep between the chalets, cutting off each from its neighbour.

Pat made sausage sandwiches for breakfast, and Alma ate hers tucked into the corner of the sofa in her pyjamas, a blanket drawn over her knees. Sometime during the course of the morning, the rain transformed into a fine, wet mist that sheathed the chalet, coating the windows and turning the chalets around them into blurred black boxes on a grey, white canvas. With no television, Terry was restless. He moved continually between the chairs and the sofa and the window while Pat provided endless cups of tea, requiring him to make constant visits to the toilet.

Eventually, rooting around in a drawer, he found a pack of playing cards, miraculously complete. After a couple of hands of clock patience, he managed to persuade the others to play Sevens and then Newmarket for sweets.

By mid-afternoon, it was clear that the weather was not going to improve, so they cleaned up, packed the car and set off for home. It was almost 6pm when they pulled up in front of Alma's house.

'Thanks for a lovely weekend – I had a great time,' said Alma, as Terry passed her her bag. 'I'll show you the photos when I get them developed.'

Pat got out of the car and gave Alma a hug. 'Bye, love, see you soon.'

Terry handed Martin his rucksack. He had Alma's bear in his other hand.

'I'll see you, kidda.'

'Yeah, see ya.'

Pat hugged Martin, and he set off towards the house. He was

halfway down the path when Terry called out, 'I'll put the float keys under the visor – for Wednesday.'

Martin stopped and turned. He nodded. 'OK, Dad. Take care.'

Phil's car was parked up outside the caravan when they arrived back. As Terry pulled up behind it, Phil appeared around the side and began walking towards them, followed by Dennis, the cat.

'Where have you two been? I thought you'd done a Mark Thatcher on us; I've been looking for you all weekend.'

'We went away for a couple of days,' said Terry, popping the boot. He handed Phil a box of food. 'Here, make yourself useful. Why, what's up?'

Phil glanced down at the box and then around as if he were searching for somewhere to put it. 'We're through,' he said, 'in the darts, they put us through to the next round. The Cross Keys got disqualified. Apparently, one of them snapped a pool cue across the back of some bloke's head and then tried to shove it up his nose – ungentlemanly conduct they said.'

'Oh I dunno,' said Terry. 'I could think of more ungentlemanly places he could've tried to shove it.'

Phil laughed.

'Seriously though,' said Terry, 'this is it now; I can feel it. As soon as we get the dates through, I need to organise my chemo sessions around the darts; I can't afford to feel like last time. As the great man almost said, "darts is not a matter of life and death, it's far more important than that".'

'Bill Shankly,' said Phil.

TWENTY-SIX

In a purely practical sense, the Mablethorpe weekend, as it was referred to later, changed nothing. Terry was still very ill. He continued to feel dreadful during and after the chemotherapy sessions, taking longer each time to recover his strength. Pat arranged with her supervisor to take every Wednesday off to accompany Terry to the hospital and look after him when they got home. If Terry felt well enough, he would join Martin on the round on Saturday and then take over again the following week. Often this arrangement was extended by a couple of days.

Psychologically, however, things were not as they were. Terry told no one, but he thought of his future grandchild all the time. Now when he practised his darts, he imagined he was throwing for him – he always pictured the child as a boy – and would try to do well to gain his admiration. On the round, he felt the child as a presence in the cab alongside him, and Terry would answer his imaginary questions about the float or certain customers. For a while, until the nausea washed in like a fast tide over his thoughts, when he sat in the chair at the hospital with the tube in his arm filling him with poison, he felt heroic. As though, in his suffering, he grew in the eyes of the not-yet-born boy looking on.

The days were long and warm, and Terry's vision of the future was clear. He would survive the cancer, and they would win the darts. Anything seemed possible.

Opening day of the course fishing season was 14 June, and Terry and Phil had not missed one for twenty years; it was tradition. The sun had blazed all afternoon, and now, as evening approached, the river bank had taken on that lazy serenity of early summer.

Terry watched Phil bend to pull his keep-net to the surface and turn it inside out to release the two small roach he had caught. The fish held still for a moment, as if to show off the vibrant orange of their fins and then pushed out into deeper water and were lost from sight. Beyond the opposite bank, the sun had dipped below the horizon, colouring the base of the lowest clouds a vivid pink. Clusters of midges rose and dipped erratically a few feet above the river.

'I'm ready for a pint,' said Phil.

'I might just give it another five minutes,' said Terry, standing up. 'I'm sure there's a big one under that tree.' He ambled upstream and stepped carefully into the water, knee deep in his waist-high waders. He flicked his float out into a pool of slack water close to the bank under the low branches of the overhanging tree and fixed his attention on the bright orange tip. Nothing moved. After a few minutes, he scooped out the last handful of maggots from a pouch around his waist and tossed them towards the float, pitting the water with dozens of tiny holes that broadened and combined into rings, rippling the glassy surface.

'I don't know why you like that spot so much,' said Phil, arriving behind him, 'you never seem to catch there.'

Terry made no reply but raised his rod and began reeling in the line, before turning to wade ashore and set about packing up his gear. He was aware of Phil watching him as he shook out his empty net and dismantled his rod, splitting it into three sections and then sliding it into its cloth case. He put away his reel, hook and float in their designated places in the tackle box and threw away his shot. He placed the box inside his wicker basket, closed the lid and then sat down on it next to Phil.

'That's where I put my old man,' he said. He nodded towards the river as Phil turned to him.

'What do you mean?'

'That's why I like that spot,' said Terry. 'I chucked my dad's ashes in the water under that tree.'

Phil looked at the thick, dark water beneath the tree's overhanging branches but said nothing, waiting for Terry to go on.

'My mum was going to scatter them all on his allotment, but this was where he first brought me fishing, so I nicked a couple of handfuls out of the jar when she was at work and brought them down here in his old bait box. I sat here for ages just watching the river, thinking, and then I remember just after I'd thrown them in, a kingfisher swooped in from nowhere and landed on that lowest branch over there. I was sure it was him.' Terry was looking at the river but felt Phil's eyes on him. Swallows dived into the clouds of midges and took off again like spitfires into the fading light.

'You're not going to die,' said Phil.

'It's not dying I'm worried about,' said Terry. 'Well, it wasn't at first. It was lying in hospital for years like him, wasting away. People coming to see you, looking at you like they know you're not coming out but trying to be jolly, pretending everything'll be OK. Now, I just want to be around for Martin's baby.'

They strolled back to the car in silence. Wildflowers pushed through the long grass alongside the track, and butterflies flitted among them. In the church car park, Terry stopped alongside Phil as he loaded his boot. 'What's going on with Julie?'

Phil closed the boot and leaned back against the car. 'I don't know, nothing much. She's still at her mother's.'

'Did she say why she left? Other than the Bowie fan I mean.'

Phil shrugged. 'She said she was bored. Bored of the curtains, bored of the carpets, bored of me I suppose.'

'Well, you need to do something. Apart from changing the carpets I mean. Sort it out. You can't carry on like this.'

'Yeah, but what?'

'You said yourself it felt somehow linked to the darts, well we're still in it. Go and see her. Or him. Take the bull by the horns. Surprise her.'

Phil nodded. 'You're right. I will. Cheers.'

Terry smiled and took a step towards his car. 'I'd still change the curtains though if I was you,' he said, 'they're awful.'

TWENTY-SEVEN

Phil turned off the car engine and slipped down in his seat, sinking his chin into his chest. He was parked at the far end of the playground, furthest from the school entrance, between a Ford Cortina and a red, soft-top MG with the roof down. Julie's Metro was over by the door. Phil pictured its neat little interior; its beige seats infused with Julie's sweet perfume.

Through the car next to him, he could see her in her classroom, moving about with an easy purpose, carrying large sheets of paper back and forth between her desk and the walls. Phil had hoped that she might look a little less content, perhaps even a touch melancholic, but that didn't appear to be the case. She was taking down a display of some kind, children's pictures of gingerbread men and houses, and replacing them with new ones in the shape of flowers and birds and butterflies. She was side on to him, and the gentle curve of her throat, and the way her hair settled on her neck as she tipped her head to pin the pictures to the wall, made his heart ache.

His attention was caught by a movement in the doorway behind her. It was him, Keith. Julie turned, the light through the window flashing through her hair. Keith took two steps into the classroom towards her. Phil slunk lower in his seat, dread at what he might be about to see rising through him. Keith was saying something, using his hands to emphasise whatever point, or suggestion, he was trying to make, but Julie looked at him impassively and shook her head. She turned back to the wall to straighten a final drawing, while Keith continued to talk, and then lifted her bag from the back of her chair and walked past him, flicking off the classroom light on her way out. Keith followed.

He had caught up with her by the time the two of them emerged into the afternoon sunlight and walked alongside her to her car, gesticulating and talking urgently, his head craned towards her. Julie opened the car door, said something to Keith which appeared to shut him up definitively, got in and drove away.

Phil had wanted to speak to her. He thought about following her home to her mother's but realised that that would look ridiculous. With horror, he saw that Keith was walking slowly across the playground towards him. Of course, he thought, glancing at the MG next to him, it had to be his – all leather seats and walnut dash – had to be. Phil suddenly hoped it would rain.

Keith had spotted him, and as their eyes met, Phil made his decision to get out of the car. Sort it out, Terry had said.

'Oh, hi there, Phil. I didn't expect to see you here.' Keith grinned at him awkwardly, pulling down the knot of his tie an inch further from his unbuttoned shirt collar. Phil took him in. Soft brown shoes with a dark suit. To think this man had been in his house, rifling through his record collection.

'Don't you "hi there, Phil" me, you creep. Just stay the hell away from my wife.'

Keith placed a hand on the door jamb of the MG. 'That might be difficult,' he said, 'since we work together.'

Heat flushed up through Phil's body, balling in his chest. 'You know what I mean. She's not interested.'

Keith stood a touch taller, removing his hand from the car, and Phil noticed the slightest hint of a smirk in the corner of his mouth.

'Well,' he said, with a glint in his eye, 'she certainly was interested.'

Phil lunged forwards. He grabbed the lapels of Keith's suit jacket with both hands, bunching the shiny material into a tight ball at the deputy head's throat, and bent him backwards over the door of his car. Phil's moustache bristled against Keith's contorted face.

'Stay away from her,' he spat. 'If I hear you've so much as spoken to her, you'll be picking pieces of your precious Bowie LP collection out of your arse for the rest of your life. Do you understand?'

Keith tried to nod, but it was difficult with Phil's fists under his chin. Phil was panting with fury, and with a strength he was unaware he possessed, he lifted Keith and threw him backwards into the MG. Keith tumbled into the passenger seat, his legs dangling out over the car door, revealing a strip of hairy shin above his long grey socks. Phil peered over at him for a second, and then, for some reason unknown even to himself, he ripped off one of Keith's soft brown shoes and tossed it onto the stricken man's chest.

Then he turned, got back into his car and drove away, smiling to himself in the rear-view mirror as the first drop of rain splashed against the windscreen.

TWENTY-EIGHT

The triumphant announcement on the evening news of Argentinian surrender to British forces on the Falkland Islands appeared to confirm Terry's new-found conviction that anything seemed possible. A sentiment strengthened further the following day, when England swept aside a very good French team in their opening game of the World Cup, and the tabloids screamed that the long wait since 1966 was finally coming to an end.

A fortnight or so later, elimination in the second group stage following two goalless draws with West Germany and Spain was surely just a matter of team selection. If Ron Greenwood had only picked Margaret Thatcher at centre forward instead of Tony Woodcock, it was said, England would certainly have been World Champions.

As it was, inevitably, the Germans marched on to the final, in spite of goalkeeper Schumacher's assault on the French defender, Patrick Battiston in the semi. They took on Italy. Since Fiona was away at her sister's for the weekend, Tom invited Terry, Phil and Hans around to his place to watch the match on his new Hitachi television.

Terry was the first to arrive. Tom lived in a village, no more than four or five miles from the centre of town. It was definitely a village however, the locals insisted, in spite of the new estates encroaching to within a field of the nearest four-bedroom property. It had its own cricket team after all, three pubs and an independent butcher with certificates in the window.

Terry turned into the drive and parked up alongside Tom's black BMW. The house was detached, mock Georgian, in brick, with a pillared, sandstone portico framing the front door. Tom led Terry through a white hallway into a cream living room. The pale armchairs and sofa of a vast three-piece suite were angled to face an enormous dark wood unit against one wall containing the television.

'What do you think?' said Tom proudly.

'Looks like you'd have needed a crane to get it in,' said Terry.

Tom used the remote control to turn the television on. The sound came first, a rolling drone of thousands of indistinct voices, insect-like, and then the picture. A pitch as green as a child's painting. Tom looked at Terry and smiled.

'Wow,' said Terry.

Tom left the room and came back with two beers in dark bottles that were cold and wet to the touch.

Midway through the first half, towards the bottom of his third bottle of beer, Terry needed a pee. He left the others and followed Tom's directions up the stairs and along the thickly carpeted landing to the bathroom at the end of the hallway. The room was large, with a shower as well as a bath. It was also spotless. *Fiona's obviously a bit of a clean freak*, thought Terry. *Or maybe it's Tom.* He decided to sit down to avoid splashes, planting his feet on the shaggy little U-shaped rug around the base of the toilet. Sat down, he shuffled backwards and peered between his legs to see if there was any blood, but it was difficult to get a clear view.

Making his way back along the landing, Terry took a step into what he presumed had once been a spare bedroom but that Tom had transformed at some stage into a kind of office.

There was a desk with papers, a telephone and a filing cabinet. But Terry had been drawn in by the dartboard. A sheet of plywood protected the wallpaper behind the board, and what looked like the belt from a dressing gown was pinned to the carpet to mark the oche. Tom had half a dozen darts cases lined up on his desk, but three darts were already in the board. Terry couldn't resist.

Ten minutes later, Phil came in. 'That's where you are; we thought you'd fallen in.' He opened one of the dart cases. 'Fancy a game?'

'I definitely need to practise more,' said Phil, after Terry won the first game. 'I can't have you beating me every time. How are you feeling?'

'Yeah OK,' said Terry. 'I've got my last treatment on Wednesday, then I get a break for a month, and the same again. Six more sessions, every two weeks till the end of October.'

'Then what?'

Terry shrugged. 'Hopefully they've either got rid of it or reduced it enough for surgery.'

'How are you managing with the round?'

'Martin's helping – he's been brilliant. And the customers seem to love him.'

'Yeah, Julie said she'd seen him on her way to work.'

'How's things with you two?' asked Terry.

Phil nodded. 'OK,' he said. He smiled. 'It's just so good to have her home.'

'What exactly did you say to that prick?'

Phil laughed. 'I told him I'd stick his Bowie albums where the sun don't shine and then play 'em myself on a very long needle. Funny enough, he's got a new job in Dorking starting next term.'

'That's where you two are hiding,' said Tom, coming into the room. 'Make yourselves at home, why don't you?'

'Cheers,' said Terry. 'We have. How's the football going?'

'Half-time,' said Tom, 'nil-nil, they couldn't even score from a penalty.'

'Looks like you've been putting in a bit of practice yourself,' said Terry, peering out of the window. 'What's that goal doing in the garden?'

'Oh,' said Tom, fiddling with a set of darts on the desk, 'the, er, social services found us a boy, you know to maybe adopt, Adam. But it didn't really work out.' He moved back towards the door. 'I'll go and get some beers,' he said on his way out.

Tom came back with Hans as well as the beers. 'Might as well get some practice in,' said Tom, 'doesn't look like much is going to happen in the football.'

'Come on, Hans,' said Terry, 'how about a few tips. How do we get as good as you? Without growing six inches – ten in your case, Tom.'

'It is nothing to do with height,' said Hans. 'It is concentration and especially playing the right way for you. And practice, of course – you must repeat the same action over and over. So, Phil,' he said, putting his hands on Phil's shoulders as he was about to throw, 'you are the weakest player because you don't concentrate properly; you don't pay enough attention. And you throw too fast, not enough care.' He turned Phil slightly more sideways on. 'See your elbow moves too much. It is not the same every time, so the dart does not fly the same. Slow down a little bit; really feel the dart in your fingers, like a paintbrush, and try to make the throw the same. Your head perfectly still, your shoulders as well still. And your eyes never moving off the target.

'For you, Tom, sometimes you try too hard, think too much and play too slow. You are a good player when you play like your personality I think. You are fidgety, yes, but precise also. When you play a bit faster, you are good, without thinking too much.'

'That shouldn't be too difficult,' said Terry. 'What about me?' He stepped forwards to the oche.

'Ah,' said Hans, tapping the side of his head, 'for you, Terry, it is all in here I think.'

'First time anyone's ever said that,' said Phil. 'We thought there wasn't anything in there.'

'You are very determined, and your action is good, and your concentration is very good. It is just confidence that you need. You need to believe, that is all.'

Terry was secretly delighted with this assessment. And for the rest of the evening, he threw as well as he had ever done. At the oche, the thick carpet seemed to envelop his feet so that he felt no contact with it, and yet the pads of his thumb and index finger were sensitive to each of the millimetre grooves machined into the barrel of the darts. As soon as he stood poised to throw, he became detached from the others, as though a bubble had formed, stretched between him and the board, which loomed large at the other end. The others were outside, their voices distorted as if through water. At school he had been no good at maths until his teacher, Mr Williams, had said he could do it. Prior to that, the simple stuff was OK, but fractions and percentages and equations made no sense. Mr Williams had assured him he was clever enough. He said he had faith in Terry and that Terry just needed to have faith in himself. Soon, his exercise book was no longer covered in red corrections, and from then on, Terry was first into the classroom for each lesson and sat near the front.

Phil and Tom played well also. They had all improved for Hans's little tips, and just having him around watching them seemed to make a difference. He was calm and didn't say much, but they took encouragement from his understated congratulations. If they threw well, they might get a "good" from him; a nice finish or a treble would earn a "very good"; and for a really high score, Hans would add your name, so when Terry hit a one-forty, Hans nodded, pushed out his lips a fraction and said, 'Very good, Terry.'

'We need to make this a regular thing,' said Terry. 'All practise as much as we can at home but then try and get together a couple of times a week. We've got to win this competition; I need the dough.'

'I thought you said I had more chance of marrying Princess Di,' said Phil.

'Only cos she's already married,' said Terry, 'otherwise I'm sure you'd be in with a chance. Looks like she's into skinny blokes, though I'm not sure about the 'tache.'

'I got the dates through – the next round's in about three weeks,' said Phil.

'That's good,' said Terry. 'I'll be on a break from the chemo.'

'Yeah,' Phil went on, 'then there's the Midlands round sometime in September, and the semi for the whole of the North in November. Win that, and we're in the final – live from Jollees.'

'Imagine that,' said Tom. 'I'd be a nervous wreck.'

'If you are nervous, you will not play so good,' said Hans with a straight face.

'I'll get some more beers,' said Tom.

'How's the football going?' said Phil, when Tom came back.

'It's finished – Italy won 3-1. I guess we missed a decent second half.'

'Oh well,' said Terry, 'at least the Germans didn't win.'

TWENTY-NINE

Doctor Harvey was talking to him; he could see her mouth moving. Her lips were plump and pink, a fondant fancy. The thought of this sweet cake increased his nausea. He could hear the individual words the doctor was saying, but they were in the wrong order, or else some were missing, because he couldn't work out what she was saying. And then when he went to reply, it was Pat's voice he heard, not his own.

Pat was smiling at Doctor Harvey; that closed mouth smile with her head tilted slightly to one side that she used when he told her he'd been fishing all day and caught nothing. Or when Martin was little and he came to her crying over a broken toy. Her eyes were narrowed a little and red around the edges. Doctor Harvey held out her hand and Pat took it in hers but then stepped forwards and curled her arms around the doctor. The long white coat like a cloud obscuring the blue of Pat's blouse.

On the way home, they had to stop twice so that Terry could open the car door and lean out over the gutter. Pat appeared on the pavement on his side, and Terry wondered vaguely where she had managed to pull the damp flannel from that she was using to wipe his face. She was talking to him, but her voice was drowned out, dissolved in the rolling *swush* of tyres over tarmac, like waves breaking on a gravel beach.

Back at the caravan, Pat helped him into bed and wiped his face again. When she bent further to kiss him on his damp forehead, the smell of her perfume crawled up his nostrils like a fog seeping through a crack in the wall, filling his head with its cloying sweetness. He heaved, retching up a grey bile that burned his throat and fell heavily onto the bed sheet.

Though the curtains were drawn, it was still light when he woke later. He wondered what time it was but didn't have the energy, or will, to turn his head to the bedside clock. His hands and feet fizzed, and he imagined them glowing green under the covers. Strange snapshots and weird dreams had fractured his sleep. In one he was in the river, and Phil was fishing for him. Each time Phil cast, Terry would slip under the surface to avoid being caught to find the river full of others like him, floating around in their hospital gowns.

By Friday evening, he was able to keep down more than just water and dry crackers or toast. He spent the whole weekend lying on the sofa watching westerns, game shows and wrestling on *World of Sport*. On Sunday night, Pat brought fish and chips home from work to celebrate the end of his first course of chemo. Terry swung his legs to the floor and walked through to the kitchen when he heard her come in.

'How are you feeling?' she said to him, unwrapping the fish and chips and transferring the food onto plates.

Terry picked up the polystyrene cup of mushy peas and emptied the blob of bright green onto his chips. 'Yeah fine. Still don't feel like running a marathon, but I'll be better after these.'

Pat exhaled a small laugh. 'Shall we take them through? We can watch that wildlife programme on BBC2.'

The food was delicious: the fish firm but silky beneath the crisp batter and the chips soft and fat and salty, sweetened just enough by the peas. There was a period, Terry had noticed, a few days after his chemo sessions, once he was able to eat normal food again, when every mouthful was a delight. When his tongue and tastebuds seemed sensitive to every nuance of the flavour of his food, as though his palate was a receiver cranked up to detect signals it had never previously captured.

Neither of them spoke while they ate. Pat had drawn one curtain across to shade the television from the sun and was sat forwards in the armchair, her plate resting on a newspaper spread across the footstool to protect it from spillages. A shaft of sunlight streaked across the carpet, blanching it, so that the washed-out orange and yellow squares looked like markings on the hide of a sleeping animal. Terry caught Pat's eye as she ate, her mouth full of food, and she raised her eyebrows at him in a quick smile.

He thought again of this expression on Pat's face later when they were in bed. The way her eyes had softened and shone, a wordless transmission of love and solidarity. You and me. Terry was lying on his back with his eyes open, his right arm curled around Pat's shoulders. She had her head on his chest, her right leg bent and settled on his.

'I can hear your heart beating,' she said.

'Let me know if it stops.'

He felt her smile. She moved her hand up from his belly and placed it flat on his chest. 'Never.'

They lay for a while without speaking, Terry absently caressing the edge of Pat's ear between his thumb and index finger as though he were rolling tobacco. A car moved slowly along the track outside, its headlights briefly illuminating the room before it fell back into darkness.

'Mablethorpe was nice, wasn't it?' said Pat, into his chest.

Terry pictured Alma's smile when he handed her the soft toy, and Martin walking back from the bar in the club with a pint in each hand. 'Yeah,' he said.

'We should do something with them while you're on your

break from treatment. Make the most of it. Maybe go to the stepping stones at Dovedale for the day, take a picnic.'

Terry woke before his alarm in the morning. Though still dark, it was the dark of a summer night, shallow and soft around the edges, so that, as he lay with his eyes open, shapes emerged from the shadow, as though the room itself was slowly waking: the ceiling light, the wardrobe, the outline of the door frame at the foot of the bed.

He gave himself a mental check-up. No tingling or numbness in his hands and feet, no nausea. He didn't even feel tired. Sometimes it didn't seem possible to him that he was seriously ill. How was he able to feel so normal so much of the time? He knew the cancer was in him, but why couldn't he feel it there all of the time? When he tried to picture the battle going on inside his body, he got only the absurd image of his own cells as soldiers in fatigues leaping off landing craft at Goose Green to take on the invading forces. Did the chemo weaken the enemy, like precursory shelling, or pump up his own side?

Pat stirred beside him. 'You OK?' she muffled into her pillow.

'Yeah, I'm fine,' he replied, finally moving to turn off the alarm before it went off. 'Don't get up.'

In the kitchen, while he waited for the kettle to boil, he lifted the front page of the calendar tacked to the wall above the worktop, to mark the date of the next round of the cup. They'd been drawn against Skisby, an ex-mining village on the outskirts of Nottingham. Terry knew it vaguely as a place of potholes and pebbledash and kids kicking round the streets chucking stones at mangy cats and three-legged dogs. The picture for August was of a yellow dahlia, a small sun of tight, overlapping petals. Below it, the calendar was blank but for two identical entries. In the bottom right-hand corner of the squares for Monday the 16th and Monday the 30th, in pencil, Pat had written: "Terry". Terry looked at his own name for a second or two, puzzled. He lifted the page to September and saw the same two entries, Monday the 13th and Monday the 27th. There were two more in October. On the last one, Terry's name was underlined – the last session. He turned the page again. November was blank. The picture showed a small deer, its head swivelled ninety degrees to look directly at the camera. Terry let the pages drop back to August and wrote the word "Darts" in the space for Saturday the 7th.

It was almost a week since he'd done the milk round, and he was happy to be back at it. When he'd started in January, the cold had dragged the lads at the dairy deep into their thick winter coats, numbing their tongues, each concerned only with getting the work done as quickly as possible and returning to a warm bed. With the mild nights, they talked and joked more as they loaded their floats, teasing Terry about the amount of time he'd had off.

'Where've you been anyway?' shouted across one of the men. 'You moonlighting somewhere? We tried to get it out of that kid of yours, but he was giving nothing away.'

'I've heard he might be giving something away to that darkie on Tennyson Avenue,' said another of the men.

Terry stopped what he was doing and looked across at the man, who was smiling at his own joke, showing an uneven line of misshapen and missing teeth.

'Stick a cork in it, Fred; you don't know what you're talking about.'

Terry turned his head to the stairs to see Paul, one of the owners of the dairy, making his way down. 'Take no notice of that prick,' he said to Terry as he approached. 'It's good to see you, Terry, how are you feeling?'

'Yeah, I'm well, Paul, cheers. Her name's Alma,' he went on, 'they're a couple, her and Martin. She's really nice.'

'That's great. He's a good lad; the customers seem to love him – and not just the pretty ones. You should be proud.'

'I am,' said Terry.

It was light quickly, and by 7am, Terry was able to take off his jumper and enjoy the sun on his arms and the back of his neck. Without the school run, the roads and pavements were quieter. In the neat rows of bungalows and semis along Kings Drive, the clipped borders of the little front gardens were busy with trim pensioners watering the lawns and deadheading the roses.

'Morning, Terry,' said one old lady, who had a pair of secateurs in one hand but looked like she was struggling to find anything that needed pruning. 'Martin not with you today?' She wore an apron over her clothes with two large front pockets. She put away the secateurs in one and pulled a white handkerchief from the other, embroidered in one corner with a flower, or perhaps initials that Terry couldn't quite make out.

'He's such a lovely boy. Did he tell you he fixed my hose last week? Brian used to do all of those types of jobs; I've never been very mechanically minded. I was getting soaked just giving the delphiniums a quick drink, but your Martin said he'd have it fixed in a jiffy – and he did too, bless him.'

Terry pushed open the woman's gate. The paving blocks forming the path split the small front lawn in two, a neat three-foot-wide border encircling the twin squares of grass. There was not a weed in sight. The soil was the colour of marmite and looked like it had been strained through a flour sieve.

'Yes,' said Terry, exchanging the empty on the step for a bottle of full fat milk, 'he's pretty good with his hands, Martin. He's busy for a couple of weeks helping his mate with some removals; you'll just have to make do with me, Mrs H.'

'Oh, you'll do just fine, Terry,' she said, with a hint of a smile in her clear blue eyes, 'better than that so-and-so we had before, Mike, he was too slick for his own good. Brian used to say he didn't need to open the gate, that one, he could probably just slip right under.' She used her hand to demonstrate, and Terry laughed.

'I'm surprised he didn't leave a trail on the path,' she said.

Terry shook his head. 'I'll see you tomorrow, Mrs H,' he said.

He was laughing as he pulled away in the float and still chuckling away to himself two streets later, picturing Mike as an enormous slug with tentacles poking through a milkman's peaked cap.

For the next three weeks, Terry settled into a happy routine of work, sleep and darts. He took his time with the round, deliberately slowing things down to allow his customers to tell him about their lilies or petunias, or what their grandchildren had been up to. Martin had made a big impression apparently. Frequently, Terry was asked where he was or what he was doing, before being told of some occasion when Martin had helped them with something or other, or just taken a moment to ask after their well-being. A lovely lad, they all seemed to agree, so polite.

At first, Terry had been surprised at these little anecdotes, at the compliments he received on Martin's behalf, but he soon came to appreciate them. When he'd lived at home, Martin had never lifted a finger to help around the house. Right up until last year, Pat was still going into his room, when he finally emerged from his pit, to open the curtains, make the bed and gather dirty washing from the floor. Terry had chastised himself for being too soft on Martin when he was growing up and had blamed himself for his son's laziness. Maybe, though, Pat had been right all along. Perhaps it had been "just his age". Maybe he had grown out of it and was a good kid after all.

After a few days, Terry actually found himself fishing for these little stories. If the opportunity arose for him to chat to a customer he'd not spoken to for a while, he would grab it and then casually ask if everything was OK and if everything had gone alright when Martin was covering for him. He was even a touch disappointed if the person replied with a simple "fine" or "yes thanks" or some other equally neutral response.

Each day when he got home, Terry turned on the television and snoozed on and off flat out on the sofa. One morning, he watched as HMS *Hermes* returned to Portsmouth to a hero's welcome. The vast grey ship looked impossibly huge so close to shore and the men leaning over the rail waving and tossing their hats in the air comically small. The cameraman zoomed in on the flags and the faces of weeping mothers and girlfriends squeezed together on the dock. Terry had watched a similar group of women the day before, crowded behind a police cordon staring shell-shocked into the rubble of bombed-out buildings in London. As he slept, and then woke, and then slept again, the two events merged, the images scrambling with one another in his mind so that the mob on the quay in Portsmouth was sombre, dressed in black, while the grieving widows and children in London leaped and laughed and waved Union Jacks.

In the afternoons, after a lunch of beans on toast or a bacon sandwich, he practised. From one o'clock until four each day, he threw dart after dart at his board hung on the outside wall of the caravan, until the grass grew pale under his feet and turned eventually to dust. He practised his doubles, went round the clock and then back the other way, and set himself dozens of other little challenges to keep things interesting. One of the toughest was an impossible clockwise circuit of green trebles followed by an outer bull and then the red trebles in the other direction with a bullseye finish. Three misses and he had to start again. When he finally managed it, a couple of days before the next match, he screamed out in delight and dropped to his knees, startling his only spectator, a female blackbird grubbing about at the foot of a hawthorn bush for something to eat.

He stuck to this practice routine even when Pat was on nights and around during the day. Though lunch would be better if she was around. She'd make a toad in the hole or a macaroni cheese which they ate together at the small kitchen table with the caravan door open. While he played darts in the afternoon, she'd have a nap on the sofa in front of *Crown Court* or repeats of *The Cedar Tree*, seemingly unperturbed by the continual triptych of thuds against the caravan wall.

Two nights a week, Terry met up with the rest of the darts team to practise together. Linda at the pub had agreed to block off the board for them on Tuesday nights, and it gave Terry a thrill to see the "RESERVED" sign hanging across the dark cabinet doors in the corner of the bar. Fridays, the idea was to rotate between houses so that, each week, they took it turns to host. But if the weather was good, they all preferred to play outside at Terry's, racking up empty cans of beer until the sun went down. Tom had been unable to relax when they'd played at his house, constantly popping in and out to restock bowls of crisps and nuts and tidying up the empties almost before the last dregs had been drunk. And it was awkward with Fiona. At Phil's, Terry thought, it had been too quiet. Julie was lovely, and welcomed them all with her usual good humour, but she liked to watch *The Gentle Touch* on Fridays, so as soon as they made their way upstairs, she closed the lounge door and shut herself away with the television. The board was in a spare room at the back of the house. A room with heavy curtains and a thick carpet and that smell of never having been used. The narrow twin beds had been pushed together to make space for the board, the matching bedcovers pulled tightly over the pillows and dropping to within an inch of the floor. A dark wood dressing table with a lace doily on top sat beneath the window, a bowl of potpourri plumb centre.

Hans was in a flat provided by work, sharing with another Dutchman who he said hated darts, so they'd never bothered going there.

When they played at Terry's, he pulled the kitchen chairs out onto the grass. If Pat was not working, or out with the girls, she'd sit around with them chatting, drinking pale ale straight out of the bottle. The lads were at ease around her and spoke freely. She listened.

One Friday night in late July, they played on until the board was barely visible in the failing light. No one seemed in a rush to get home, and when darkness fell completely, they sat talking in the spilled glow from the windows and open doorway, their faces half shadowed. Bats wheeled in the blackness above their heads. Pat sat on the top step, her features invisible to Terry. Tom was perched forwards on his chair, telling her how he and Fiona had always wanted children but that they had not been able. It was him, he said, he had had the tests and apparently his fleet was carrying no cargo. The others had gone quiet, and Tom glanced around and shrugged as he said this and then took a long pull on his beer. Terry had heard this story before, years ago at one of Martin's birthday parties, and Tom had used the exact same expression. It was probably easier like that, he thought, less personal. He didn't have to think up some new way of saying it each time. Terry remembered on the previous occasion Tom had suggested, through a mouthful of birthday cake, that he and Fiona were considering adoption. He wondered why nothing had come of that idea then and why it had been revived now.

'Julie and I decided not to have kids,' said Phil. 'She said she saw enough of them at work. I suppose it's given us a bit more freedom to do things together – holidays and stuff – but still...'

Though spoken softly, these last words hung in the short silence that followed. The air, thick and close, appeared to wrap around them, preventing their escape into the night. Phil turned his head towards Terry, but Terry was unable to make out his expression.

'What about you, Hans?' asked Pat. 'Any kids?'

'Two boys,' Hans replied, 'aged seven and five. They live with their mother in Antwerp. She is from Belgium – a very kind woman but with no sense of humour at all.' They all laughed. 'Even with your Benny Hill, she did not find it funny.'

'That is serious,' said Terry, 'not amused by the comic genius that is Benny Hill – definite grounds for divorce.'

'We are only separated,' said Hans, not recognising Terry's sarcasm. 'I hope we can get back together one day. I miss the boys.'

Later, in bed, Terry snuggled into Pat, his belly against her spine, his hot thighs against the back of her legs. 'I love you,' he said.

'Why?' said Pat.

Terry smiled and kissed the back of her neck. 'Cos you've got a sense of humour,' he said and pinched her bottom.

'I still don't find Benny Hill funny,' Pat said, turning over.

THIRTY

By the time the next match came around, it was clear that the practice was paying off. Hans continued to give them each little pointers to improve their games so that they were all throwing with much more consistency than they had done previously. Now, when he stepped up to the oche, Terry was confident of where the dart was going rather than merely hopeful. His action felt smooth, his shoulder steady and his arm travelled back and forth along the same plane like the pendulum of a grandfather clock tapping out time.

They were back to playing a single opponent and won the match easily; a "demolition job" Terry called it in the pub later.

Out of politeness, they stayed for a pint after the match, but they were all keen to get back to The White Hart to celebrate properly. Linda had promised to put on a little spread "win, lose or draw", and while they would have liked to think word of their win had got around, it was no doubt the promise of free food that meant the bar was packed when they eventually got back.

'How did you get on, Terry?' shouted someone, as he led the others into the smoke-filled room. When Terry raised both arms above his head in reply, like a footballer who's just scored the winning goal in the cup final, the pub cheered, and Linda pulled out another platter of egg sandwiches from beneath the bar.

'First pint's on me, lads,' she said to more cheers. 'You've done us proud. Not you lot,' she said, as some of the men crowded at the bar drained their pints and pushed them hopefully forwards across the sticky surface.

'Cheers, Linda, you're a diamond,' said Tom, picking up his pint and scooping a pickled onion from an enormous jar alongside a tray of miniature sausage rolls.

Terry grabbed a cheese sandwich and folded the whole triangle into his mouth. 'Fantastic,' he managed to get out, losing a couple of shavings of grated cheese onto the floor as he reached for his glass.

He drank the first pint quickly and ordered four more. He and the rest of the team, as well as the plates of food, had attracted a bit of a crowd at the bar. Linda's heavy cleavage, resting snug against a bowl of salted nuts as she leaned over to listen to the boys recount the match, was doing no harm either. Tom and Terry were doing most of the talking, butting in and speaking over one another when they felt the story was flagging. Phil chipped in with corrections as to the score at a specific moment in the match or the double that had been hit to close out a leg. Hans leaned on the bar, taking great open-mouthed swallows from his pint and hoovering up pieces of pork pie.

'I thought you said they were a decent team, Phil,' said Bill, an old regular nursing a half of mild.

'They were meant to be,' cut in Terry before Phil could reply, 'but two of their fellas had gone to Skeggy for a stag do Friday night and ended up getting arrested for disturbance of the peace. Apparently, they're still in the cells trying to explain how they got the big wheel going at three in the morning. I reckon the blokes that replaced them only got in the team cos they watched *Bullseye*.'

Everyone laughed as Terry finished his pint and picked up another that Hans had lined up on the bar. 'And you should've seen the place,' said Tom, 'I saw one fella wiping his feet on the way out.'

'We'll have to come and give you some support next time,' said Charlie, a bookmaker in his sixties in shiny shoes and an ill-fitting suit worn thin at the seat and elbows. 'I could do a book.'

'Two more rounds and we're on the telly,' said Phil. 'Final's 8 January.'

'I think that's when Alma's due,' said Terry.

'We'll put a minibus on if you get to the final,' said Linda. 'I could ask Tony if we could use his.'

'A minibus?' said the old boy with the half of mild. 'You'll need a couple of coaches – we're all coming.'

Terry took a pull on his pint and placed it on the towel on the bar. 'Just nipping to the gents,' he said.

When he got back, a new head had appeared in the crowd that he recognised.

'Hey, Terry, look what the cat's dragged in,' said Tom, taking a short, fat cigar from his mouth and tilting back his head to release a thick cloud of smoke. Alongside him, waving his own cigar Groucho style in front of his grinning face, was Dave.

'Now then, Terry,' he said, 'what's this I hear about you turning into John Lowe while I've been away?'

'More like Arthur Lowe,' laughed Phil.

'Flippin 'eck,' said Terry, 'what are you doing here? I thought you weren't back for another month or so.'

'I missed you too,' said Dave. 'Come on, I couldn't let you have all the glory, could I. Phil's been keeping me up to date with the darts. Only two more wins and we're in the final, eh? I've been practising like mad, two, three hours a day. Fuck all else to do in Dudley of an evening. Or during the day for that matter. Felt like I was doing time in that bedsit.'

'Dudley?' said Terry. 'Looks like you've been locked up on the Costa del Sol with Ronnie Biggs.'

'Oh yeah,' said Dave, glancing down at the deep tan on his forearm, 'there was a fella down there renting out sun beds, so I had one off him for a few weeks, but the controls were a bit dodgy. You should've seen me before – I looked like Bob Monkhouse.'

'More like Bob Marley,' said Bill, finally finishing his drink and putting his glass down on the bar.

'What's he doing back?' Terry asked Phil later when Dave had gone to the toilet.

'Karen ran off with some bloke while he was away. I think he's hoping he can persuade her to come back. Some bloke with a jag apparently – a dentist.'

Terry took a sip from his pint and glanced in the direction of the toilets. 'Well, I hope he doesn't think he can walk back into the team; it wouldn't be fair on Hans. Besides, we need him if we want to try and win this thing; he's our best player.'

Phil made no reply but flicked his head to indicate that Dave was on his way back. Terry half turned, but Dave had stopped to talk to a man and his wife sat at a table by the fruit machine.

'Right, back at it next week, boys. We'll see what the weather's doing Friday. Are we OK to have the board Tuesday Linda, as usual?'

'Yep, no problem, Terry – I'll reserve it for you.'

'Oh, I can't make it this week,' said Tom. 'We're away, Tenby. We went the same week last year.'

'I'm struggling as well,' said Phil. 'I promised Julie I'd book something. Managed to find us a little place in the lakes; we're driving up in the morning. In fact,' he said, looking at his watch, 'I should get off.'

'You didn't say anything,' said Terry.

'Yeah, I know, it was a last-minute thing. I'm trying to be more spontaneous.'

'Bloody hell, what am I supposed to do? Hans, are you about?'

'Actually,' said Hans, 'I go to Holland on Tuesday for a few days. My wife is bringing me the boys.'

'I'm around,' said Dave, arriving into the circle. 'I'll play with you, Terry – so to speak – as long as you don't mind losing, that is.'

THIRTY-ONE

Tom's excitement at winning through to the next round of the darts, along with pride at his own part in the victory, was such that they were past Birmingham before he realised that Fiona was not listening to him. Or if she was, she pretended otherwise. Either way, she made it clear she was not interested.

Fortunately, the further south and west they travelled, the better the scenery became, and Tom was able to ignore the silence inside the car via a concerted perusal and appreciation of the landscape on the other side of the glass. The Severn was indeed magnificent, but the Wye, with the sun glinting off its silken surface as it laced between the hedges and trees, was simply sublime. They crossed into Wales at Monmouth, and guiding the BMW along the narrow lanes beneath the Black Mountains, Tom resolved to call Sandy.

Fiona's apparent indifference, and Tom's lack of a better idea, meant that he had booked the same hotel as the previous year. Which was unfortunate, because the food left a lot to be desired. When the owner greeted them warmly and told them proudly that she had also put them in the same room, Tom recalled the grubby bath and sagging mattress.

As soon as they were upstairs, Fiona changed her blouse and shoes and announced that she was going for a walk on the beach.

Tom thought about asking if she would like some company, but something about the way she pulled on her plimsolls told him that she probably did not.

When the door shut behind her, Tom flopped onto the bed. The mattress was worse than he had remembered; he had to swing his legs to the floor in order to sit up again. He dug in his pocket for Sandy's number, picked up the receiver of the phone on the bedside table and dialled zero for an outside line as instructed on the sheet of paper tacked to the back of the bedroom door. The dial whirred back into place and the tone changed in Tom's ear.

Listening to the ring at the other end of the line, Tom thought at first that Sandy was not going to answer. Eventually though, she did, breathing heavily, and Tom pictured her settling into her chair behind her enormous desk, beads of sweat breaking through the flushed skin at the top of her chest.

'Hi, Sandy, it's Tom Richards.'

He waited for Sandy to place the name. The bed appeared to be sucking him towards the centre, so he shuffled forwards to perch on the edge.

'Oh, yes, Tom, how are you, and Fiona?'

'We're fine, thanks, really well in fact. Just having a week in Wales actually.' A seagull flapped past the window, splashing a stream of white mess against the pane. Tom watched it dribble towards the bottom. 'Er, but we've been chatting – a lot. And we're both really keen to get things moving, and—'

'Hmm, good,' said Sandy.

'Yes, and I wanted to call you to say that I got that loan, the business grant I was telling you about, so that should sort out the cash flow – and I've had a couple of really good orders come in, so…' Tom shifted again on the bed, unsure how far to go with the lie.

'That's excellent news, Tom. Our finance chaps were a bit concerned, I don't mind telling you. But that's great, because I think I have the perfect match for you, a delightful little girl, just turned four. Rosemary is her name.'

Tom stood up, pulling the phone off the bedside table. He scrambled to replace it. 'Hello? Oh, sorry, I thought we'd been cut off. Rosemary? OK, fantastic, well we'll be back at the weekend, or we can come back sooner if necessary…'

'No, you two enjoy your holiday. I'll arrange for you to meet her next week. You'll be smitten – she's adorable.'

Tom was shaking when he put the phone down. He jumped to his feet and skipped across the carpet to the window. Fiona was crossing the street towards him, her long yellow skirt catching the sun as it swished around her legs in the onshore breeze. She looked up, and Tom smiled broadly at her and waved.

THIRTY-TWO

'Dave's back,' said Terry through a mouthful of bacon sandwich. He placed the sandwich down on the plate in front of him, peeled back the top layer and dolloped on more brown sauce. 'Apparently, Karen ran off with some bloke while he was away. A dentist.'

'She always did have good teeth,' said Pat, bending to toss bed sheets into the washing machine. She turned the dial and pressed the start button. The sound of water trickling into the tray was followed by a deep rumbling as the drum shook slowly into life. 'Still,' she said, 'it'll give you someone to practise with while the others are away.'

'Hmm,' said Terry, taking another bite from his sandwich, 'no, I think he's busy. I'll be fine on my own.'

Pat picked up a mug from the table and took a swig from it. She grimaced. 'Ugh, cold,' she said. 'Right, I'd better get off. I should be back just after six; don't forget to put the dinner in at half-five – but warm the oven first – I've left you a reminder.' She showed him a slip a paper she had placed next to the kettle. 'What do you think about next Sunday then? If the weather's still good.'

Terry looked up from the newspaper spread across the kitchen table.

'What I was saying last night, doing something with Martin and Alma, before your treatment starts again.'

'Oh, yeah, yeah good idea.'

'OK perfect, I'll sort it out. I'll see you later. Don't do too much.'

She kissed him on the side of the head with a loud smack, as he bit into his bacon sandwich. When she'd gone, Dennis, who had been sleeping on Terry's unmade side of the bed, appeared in the doorway. He stretched, had a sniff at his bowl, half covered by one of Terry's discarded shoes, and padded softly through into the living room. By the time Terry had made himself another mug of tea and, with the newspaper under his arm, followed Dennis, the cat was already asleep, tucked into the corner of the armchair, his front paw over his head as though shielding his eyes from the light.

The weather the following week was hot and sticky again. Terry wore shorts to work, and the float's vinyl seat squelched and squeaked every time he slid in or out of the cab. On Wednesday he brought a towel to sit on. By the end of the round, it was damp under his thighs, clinging to him momentarily as he got up to deliver the milk. Mrs Harrison asked after Martin again, and Terry told her that he would be doing the round again next week.

'Are you on holiday again then, Terry?' she asked. 'You're doing the right thing; you never know what's round the corner – I've learned that myself over the years. Brian always used to say to live each day as if it was your last. Every day above ground is a good day – that was his favourite expression.'

'Quite right,' said Terry. 'I'll see you tomorrow – all being well.' He closed the gate. Mrs Harrison had already turned back to her garden and was busy counting the unopened buds on a magnificent rose bush alongside her front door.

When he reached Alma's house, he thought about knocking but couldn't come up with a reason he could give for doing so.

Martin was probably working anyway, but it would be nice to see Alma; she'd be showing now. At times, it still felt unreal to him that Martin was going to be a dad, and he a grandfather. Alma's delicately swollen belly would be the physical proof of this hitherto intangible, unreachable truth.

As it turned out, the front door opened before he brought the float to a stop at the kerb outside.

'Mornin', Terry,' said Mrs Johnson, stood in the doorway in a tabard-style apron over the same orange skirt and mustard jumper she'd been wearing the first time Terry had met her. 'Come in for a cup of tea,' she said.

Before he had a chance to reply, she turned and went back into the house. Terry put the bottle carrier down on the front step, took out a pint of full fat and carried it with him into the house. It was dark in the hallway, and it took a second for his eyes to adjust to the change in light. The walls were papered in stripes of blue that were almost black, the patterned carpet predominantly a deep, dull green. On a mat to one side of the front door was a pair of Martin's trainers. Terry took a few paces forwards towards the light from the kitchen at the back of the house but then stopped and turned into the lounge. A large bay window overlooked the garden so that entering the room from the gloomy hallway felt like passing through a tunnel into an illuminated chamber. Mrs Johnson, tiny, was sat in an armchair facing the window, the saucer and handle of her tea cup pinched between her fingers, her eyes magnified behind her oversized glasses. She looked like a dormouse. She set down her teacup on a small table and poured Terry one from a china pot. 'Two sugars, Martin, tell me,' she said, 'sit down and take the weight off your feet.'

Terry took the cup and sat down on the end of a very soft sofa. 'Thanks,' he said.

'So, it appears that we are going to be family,' said Mrs Johnson, in a rolling timbre that seemed to furnish the statement with more syllables than it naturally possessed.

'Er, yeah, I suppose so,' said Terry, after a moment's pause. 'And how do you feel about it?'

Only Mrs Johnson's mouth moved when she spoke. When she finished, she sat perfectly still, her dark eyes fixed on Terry as though she would be quite content to wait all day for his response. He was unsure whether she was asking how he felt about the baby or the fact that he and her would be in some way related once it was born. He hadn't really thought about the latter.

'Erm, I was a bit concerned at first – about the baby I mean, not Alma – but now, yeah, I'm happy, looking forward to it. It's a bit strange thinking about being a granddad, but I'm sure I'll get used to it.'

Mrs Johnson said nothing for a moment, waiting, apparently, to see if Terry would continue. He smiled and took a sip of tea to indicate that he had finished speaking.

'Well, I think it is absolutely wonderful,' said Mrs Johnson. She put down her teacup carefully on the table in front of her, leaned further forwards in her chair and placed her left hand on his knee. Wearing shorts, this gesture felt more intimate than it might have done otherwise, and Terry felt uncomfortably self-conscious about his bare legs. Mrs Johnson's touch was cool on his exposed thigh; the skin on the back of her hand creased like old leather, puckered and loose over her knuckles.

She was watching him with not quite a smile but an expression of calm, of wisdom, on her delicate face. Terry had the impression that she was somehow looking inside him, that her hand on his leg was picking up a current of his thoughts and emotions. She took her hand back, and Terry glanced around the room. On a bookcase, in a nook to the side of the fireplace, were black-and-white photographs in frames. There were more on the mantlepiece. In the centre, larger than the others, was a picture of Martin and Terry and Pat on the beach at Mablethorpe. In the photograph, Pat was looking up from her book while Martin, laughing, had his hand outstretched towards the camera, his mouth open in some form of half-hearted protest. Between them, Terry was the only one not looking into the lens. He was turned towards Martin, holding a frisbee over his son's head. Terry remembered the photograph being taken. A moment later, Martin had posed for a second with the frisbee as a hat, before removing it and tossing it playfully at Alma.

'I remember that photograph – when it was taken I mean,' said Terry. 'She's really good, isn't she?'

'Martin is a lovely young man,' said Mrs Johnson, 'and Alma tell me she had a marvellous time with you on that holiday – a good family.'

'How is she?' asked Terry.

'She is very well,' said Mrs Johnson, nodding almost imperceptibly. 'Martin look after her.'

Terry finished his tea and reached forwards to put his cup and saucer down on the table. 'I'd better get off, finish the round, the customers will be wondering what's happened to me.' He stood up and glanced through the window at the milk float parked up outside. 'Thanks for the tea.'

Mrs Johnson moved only her head to look up at him. 'And how are you?' she said.

Terry sat back down. 'Oh, I'm fine, I feel OK – considering. Thanks.'

'Martin tell me you go back to the hospital next week.'

'Er, yeah, he's going to do the round for me.'

Terry picked up the milk bottle from the table and got back to his feet. 'I'll take this through to the kitchen for you, thanks again for the tea.'

When he got back to the front door, Mrs Johnson had opened it and was stood on the threshold waiting for him. She slid her hand into the front pocket of her apron and removed something from it.

'Take this,' she said, opening her fist to him. A crucifix on a thin gold chain lay cupped in the soft brown skin of her palm. Terry looked at it and then up into Mrs Johnson's eyes, bright behind the lenses of her spectacles.

'I is praying for you,' she said.

Terry took the crucifix and then curled his hand around it. 'Thank you,' he said.

THIRTY-THREE

Though the forecast was for a break in what had been a long spell of good weather, there was no sign of it on Sunday morning. The sky was entirely free of clouds, and, if anything, the temperature seemed to have increased another degree or two.

'It must be seventy out there already,' said Pat, putting the empty washing basket down on the kitchen work surface. Terry glanced up from the newspaper. Pat unclipped the cotton peg bag from around her waist and tossed it into the basket. Her mother had made the bag herself from one of Pat's old gym vests and given it to Pat, along with various other "useful" items, when she and Terry had first moved in together. Terry remembered Pat showing him the name tag still sewn into the collar of the vest: Patricia Fisher. Another of the gifts had been a wooden rolling pin. Pat's mother had claimed to have two and therefore no need for this one, but Pat had joked with Terry that it was a tradition for Fisher women to receive such a weapon in order to keep their future husbands on the straight and narrow.

'You not practising this morning? We'll be out all afternoon.'

'No,' said Terry, looking back down at the newspaper, 'it's too hot. Anyway, I've got a session planned with the lads next week; I'll get back to it then.'

'If you're up to it,' said Pat.

Terry had been trying not to think too much about restarting the chemotherapy the following day, or, at least, he had been pretending not to think about it. In truth, as the last week had gone by, it had been increasingly at the front of his mind. And for the last couple of days, he'd thought of little else. He'd contemplated going fishing, but with Phil away, he would have had to go alone and didn't relish having so much time to think. It had even been difficult to motivate himself to play darts. Instead, for the last few days, he'd spent hours on the sofa, hoping that the banalities of daytime television would be a distraction from his impending appointment with tubes, needles and mind-numbing nausea. The outing with Martin and Alma this afternoon would be a break from all of that, from his thoughts about the hospital and the treatment and how he would feel after it.

It was like an oven in the car. The first thing both Terry and Pat did when they got in was to wind the windows all the way down. When they reached Alma's house, Terry got out, but by the time he made it to the gate, she and Martin were already coming up the path. Alma was walking ahead of Martin in a yellow sleeveless dress, the hem of which was raised slightly at the front by the definite bump in her belly.

'I don't reckon much to your new float, Terry,' said a neighbour over the garden wall. 'You won't get much milk in that. You got a new helper 'n' all?'

'Alright, Stan, that's my missus Pat.'

Pat smiled at the neighbour and then raised her hand to wave at Mrs Johnson who had appeared in the doorway.

'We brought a blanket to sit on,' said Martin, 'and a bit of leftover chicken from lunch. Rose thought we might get hungry.'

'You going somewhere nice?' said the neighbour. 'It's supposed to rain later.'

'Just a little run out to Dovedale,' said Terry, with a glance up at the brilliantly blue sky. 'We'll keep our fingers crossed. I'll see you tomorr... soon, Stan.'

Pat was turned in her seat when Terry got in the car. 'You look lovely, Alma,' she said. 'You alright, love?'

'I'm good thanks, Pat. I was a bit sick at the start, but I'm much better now.'

'How's your nan?'

'Oh, she's absolutely fine, tough as old boots.'

'Sharp as a tack too,' said Terry.

'God, it's boiling in here,' said Martin, winding down his window.

Terry loved the countryside north of the city. The new estates extended further out than when he was a kid, but it really didn't take long to get beyond them and for the scenery to change. As the roads narrowed to lanes lined with hedges of holly and hawthorn, drystone walls replaced brick, and patches of lawn stretched into fields, cut by streams and grazed by cows and flocks of sheep.

Terry manoeuvred the car down a short, steep incline and over a narrow humpbacked bridge.

'Wow, it's really pretty out here,' said Alma, 'so rural. I feel like I'm in a Constable painting.'

'There's Thorpe Cloud,' said Martin. 'Looks busy.'

Terry glanced across at the familiar flat-topped hill to his right. Dozens of small figures were milling around on the summit and making their way up and down the paths on the hill's flanks, the bright colours of their clothing marking them out against the grass and the dark rock higher up. As Terry negotiated the next tight bend in the road, he braked at the line of traffic in front of him.

'Must be a queue for the car park,' he said, bringing the car to a stop.

'Mmm, nice countryside smell,' said Pat, as a thick waft

of manure invaded the car. 'Still, better than petrol fumes I suppose.'

'Might get those as well if we sit here for long,' said Terry.

By the time they reached the car park, they were all sweating. Terry could feel the back of his shirt stuck to the car seat. Pat was fanning herself with a water bill from their old house that she'd found stuffed in the back of the glovebox. An attendant in a hat, with a leather satchel across his shoulder, stopped them.

'Pound.'

'A pound?' said Terry. 'We're only here for the afternoon – a couple of hours. Don't we get a discount?'

'We're not a charity.'

'I thought you were: National Trust.'

'Car park's private – pound please.'

Terry turned to Pat who was already fishing in her bag for her purse. She handed him a one-pound note.

'It used to be free,' said Terry, passing the note through the window.

'So did the Yorkshire Ripper,' said the attendant and moved on to the next car.

Even the little gift shop had a queue on the steps waiting to go in, and the line of people at the ice-cream van snaked halfway across the car park.

'We'll get one later,' said Terry, 'might be less people.'

'Hey, Mum,' said Martin, 'do you remember when you bought me that ruler from the shop? I pestered you for ages and then couldn't decide whether I wanted the one with the hedgehog or the squirrel on it.'

'Yeah, I remember,' said Pat, smiling.

'Which one did you choose?' said Alma.

Martin thought for a moment. 'I can't remember,' he said. 'The squirrel I think. I only had it a few days, then James McCready broke it first day back at school.'

'It's alright,' said Terry, laughing, 'I'll buy you another one.'

They crossed the bridge and walked upstream, the river on their left, the grassy lower slopes of Thorpe Cloud rising away from them to the right. The river ran quickly over the pebbly bottom, low and clear as gin. Terry swiped his forearm over his brow, but within seconds, the sweat was running into his eyes again. He couldn't remember heat like this since '76. The air was unmoving and thick, with the weight of a winter coat. Breathing through his nose seemed impossible, so Terry sucked in each hot breath with a gaping mouth, drying out his throat and tongue.

'Bloody hell,' he said, turning to the others, 'I could kill a pint; my mouth's like sandpaper.'

'We've only just got here,' said Pat. 'Are you OK, love?' she said to Alma.

At the stepping stones, there were people everywhere. Each of the dozen or so square blocks traversing the river had at least one person balanced on it; most had two or even three. A line of people on either bank waited for someone to complete the crossing so that they could have a go. Aunts and mothers and grandmothers sat, with their shoes and stockings beside them, dipping their pale feet in the water while kids splashed in the shallows. A man in a white hat with a floppy brim lounged with his back against one of the stones in the middle of the river, the water to the centre of his chest, as though he were in a bathtub.

'He's brave,' said Martin, 'that water must be freezing.'

'Or stupid,' said Terry.

Blankets and foldable chairs covered the grass. Families sprawled in the hot sun eating home-made sandwiches and passing around packets of bourbon biscuits, or custard creams, their exposed skin steadily reddening. Occasionally, someone would turn to wave at a friend or family member making their way, in a stream of the most unlikely looking mountaineers, up and down the slopes of Thorpe Cloud.

'What about over there?' said Pat.

'I'm going to put my feet in the water,' said Alma, once they'd put the blanket and bags down.

'I'll come with you,' said Martin.

'You OK, love?' said Pat, when the others had gone.

'Yeah, I'm fine,' said Terry, 'just hot.'

'Do you want a bit of cake?'

'No thanks, I'll have some later.'

Terry picked up Pat's cardigan from the blanket and draped it over his head and neck like a shawl. Martin and Alma were paddling in the shallow water where the bank had eroded to form a small shingle beach. Returning to shore, Alma took hold of Martin's hand, walking gingerly over the loose pebbles on the river bed. Martin was saying something to her and she nodded, looking down at where best to place her feet. They sat down to put their trainers and sandals back on and then took their place in line to cross the stepping stones. Martin went first, turning on each stone to hold Alma as she stepped across to join him. On the way back, they stopped on the middle stone, and Alma looked up to wave at Pat and Terry. They both raised a hand in return.

'She's so sweet,' said Pat.

'She is,' agreed Terry, 'but don't worry, she'll keep Martin in line.'

'How was the water?' said Pat, when they got back to the blanket.

'Lovely,' said Alma.

'Freezing,' said Martin.

Terry folded Pat's cardigan under his head and lay back on the blanket. The earth beneath it was warm, the short grass, grazed for centuries by gritstone sheep, soft under his back.

When he woke sometime later, the sun had crossed the river, and a light breeze was blowing upstream from the south, rippling the surface of the water. Though a steady flow of people still hopped across the stepping stones, the river bank was quieter, and families around them were packing up to leave.

'I'm going to go up,' said Martin. 'Anyone else coming?'

'I will,' said Alma, making to get up.

Pat put her hand on Alma's arm. 'I'm not sure that's a good idea in your condition, love, it's quite steep – and further than you think.'

'Dad?'

'No, I'll leave you to it,' said Terry, 'but don't be too long. Give us a wave from the top.'

The three of them watched Martin go, but the path bent around the hillside, and he was quickly out of sight. Terry cast his eyes higher to where the path came back into view. The route was choked with people, all of them, it appeared, making their way downhill. A cloud passed suddenly in front of the sun, casting the group on the hillside into shadow.

'I hope the ice-cream van's still there by the time he gets down,' said Terry.

With the sun covered, it felt like the temperature had dropped ten degrees in a matter of seconds. Terry turned to look across the river where not one but a bank of white cloud had appeared over the trees to conceal the sun. To the south, in the direction of the car park, the sky was no longer blue but grey, washed out and grubby nearby but darker and more menacing in the distance. Pat was looking downstream also.

'Maybe your mate Stan was right,' she said. 'I hope Martin makes it down before that gets here.'

As she said this, the sun broke through a gap in the clouds as they shifted quickly northwards. On the far bank, the slenderest of the branches on the trees arced upstream, and the leaves flapped like bunting at a summer fete as the wind lifted.

The first drop of rain fell out of a clear sky. At least, that was the impression Terry had when he felt it land on his forehead and opened his eyes to a patch of blue above him. Pat, though, was already putting things in her bag, and she retrieved her cardigan from under Terry's head as he sat up. Behind them, Thorpe Cloud was in deep shadow. The sky over the summit was soot black, and the keyhole of blue Terry had seen a moment earlier had disappeared. He shivered. It was no longer warm.

'Where's Alma?' he said, looking around.

'She's over there, by the river,' said Pat. 'Come on, let's get this blanket away.'

When they reached her, Alma was crouching, taking pictures of a peloton of ducks. Three babies in a line behind their mother were battling upstream to take shelter in some slack water under a tree on the far bank. Alma stood up and turned, craning back her head to look towards the summit of Thorpe Cloud, exposing her throat like a small bird calling for its supper.

'I can't even see the top anymore,' she said.

'Here, put this on,' said Pat, pulling her cardigan from her bag and draping it around Alma's bare shoulders. For now, the raindrops fell sporadically, creating separate, individual craters in the surface of the river. But it was obvious that this would not be the case for long. The light had been snuffed out, and the leaden sky was swollen with a burden it looked desperate to shed. Terry took the car keys from his shorts pocket.

'You two get back to the car; I'll wait here for him.'

'You sure?' said Pat. 'You've got your chemo tomorrow; I can wait.'

'I'll be fine,' said Terry. 'Go on.'

Pat took the keys. 'OK,' she said, 'but promise me you'll wait for him at the bottom, you won't go up.'

Terry smiled at her. 'I'm not that daft,' he said.

He watched them go and then looked up at the hillside, but he could make out little of the higher slopes. *Hopefully he's further down than that anyway*, he thought.

The grass along the river bank was now empty. Pat and Alma had disappeared from view along the track to the car park, on which only two people, a couple in matching waterproof jackets with the hoods up, were still visible. They looked perfectly kitted out for the weather and were marching away from Terry with a purposeful stride. Unsure of what to do, Terry began walking towards the start of the path up the hillside. The thought struck him that perhaps Martin had taken a different way down. He knew there were at least another couple of routes, including one that traversed the summit and came down on the far side of the car park next to the road. What if Martin had gone that way? As Terry got closer to the base of the path, a figure came briefly into view above him but was then hidden once more around the flank of the hillside. Terry quickened his pace. Was that Martin? When the man reappeared still forty yards or so above Terry, he saw that it was not. He watched the man pick his way down the last section of the path and realised as he got closer that the man was wet through, his cotton T-shirt deformed with the weight of water in it, his hair flat to his skull. The man stopped at the bottom of the hill.

'Hope you're not thinking about going up there,' he said to Terry, 'it's pissing down.' He pulled the T-shirt away from his skin and shook his head like a dog drying off after a swim.

'I'm waiting for my son,' said Terry.

The man rubbed his head with both hands, flicking the water off them afterwards. 'No one else up there now,' he said, 'not that I've seen at least. He probably went down another way.' The man turned and set off at a jog towards the car park.

The rain was falling more steadily now. Terry bent his head against the fat drops that exploded on his shoulders. Why hadn't he brought a jacket? He looked around for shelter. It would be no good if he couldn't see the bottom of the path; he could miss Martin.

He ran, hunched like a soldier in no man's land, to a large ash tree standing alone in a dip between Thorpe Cloud and the hillside opposite. Further upstream, Terry remembered, were thick woods, and this tree appeared to have escaped from them in a dash down the valley.

Though he had the spot to himself now, he was clearly not the first to have used the tree's impressive canopy as a place to hide from the rain. The ground around the base of the trunk was worn clear of grass and covered in sheep droppings. It served its purpose well though. For the moment, the chalky soil beneath the tree was dry, and from here, Terry had a decent view not only of the first few yards of the path up Thorpe Cloud but also of a section a little higher that had been out of sight earlier. He looked at his watch. *How long should I give him?* he thought. Ten minutes later, Terry wondered whether it might not have been more sensible to go back with the others and wait for Martin in the car. Though the tree offered decent protection against the rain, the wind had got up. It whipped beneath the lower branches. Terry was cold. How could that be? It had been the hottest day for years only a few hours ago. *I guess I'll give that ice cream a miss*, he thought. He pictured Pat and Alma sitting in the car in the car park, the rain lashing against the windows. Would they be the only ones there? No, surely the attendant wouldn't have left. He tried to think whether there'd been some kind of hut for him. There must be – this is England – it rains all the time.

Terry remembered his mum telling him it had poured on the day he was born. He had heard the story often. The roads had turned to rivers, she had said, and the buses couldn't get through. She and little Terry had had to spend an extra night in hospital.

He'd be back there tomorrow. In that treatment room with its clean white surfaces, its hard edges, the bed with the throwaway sheet and that heartless machine pumping poison into his veins. He'd have preferred to stay here. Fortunately, he was unable to recall exactly how bad the treatment made him feel. Maybe it was like childbirth, he thought, you forget the pain.

It was gloomy under the tree and getting darker. As the wind lifted further and the rain increased in its intensity, Terry realised he could no longer make out the path. He strained his eyes, but it was no use. The rain fell in sheets, creating a screen around the tree, closing him in. He could hear it slapping the leaves above his head and drumming on the ground outside. He knew he would have to leave this refuge but hesitated. There was something comforting about the protection it gave him from the chaos beyond the branches' reach. As a child, he liked to sit under the workbench in the garden shed, listening to the rain pound the tin roof. He could still smell the damp wood mixed with petrol fumes from the old lawnmower in the corner.

When he crept out into the open, it was like stepping under a shower. In less than a minute, he was soaked, water running off his head and down his face. The noise was louder too, as though he'd moved from one room and opened a door to another. The river seethed and churned, and the sound of it bouncing over the rocks echoed through the valley.

Terry thought about going back to the car. Surely Martin couldn't still be out in this. He must have gone down another way. At the base of Thorpe Cloud, water was running off the hillside, coursing down the trenches worn into the slope like streams sprung from an underground source. Terry lifted his face to the deluge and called out Martin's name. The panic in his voice startled him. The sound cut through the drone of the river and the rain, alien, and then was gone. From the foot of the climb, he could see little of the route higher up. Forty or fifty yards above him, the path disappeared behind a bulge in the hillside below an overhanging rock. *If I just went up that far,* Terry reasoned, *I might be able to see further round the corner.*

Thousands of pairs of feet over the years had worn ruts into the hillside that scarred the slope like tributaries to the central path. But it was no use following any of these. Each was ankle deep in water, feeding the main channel. Terry walked above them, on the grass, which was short and slick. He slipped almost immediately but managed to get his hand down before his backside hit the ground. When he fell again a few steps further on, he cracked his knee against a rock half buried in the hillside. 'Oh, you bastard,' he shouted, his face scrunched in pain. He hobbled up the last few yards to the overhang, cursing. His knee throbbed and his hands were caked in dirt and sheep shit. He bent beneath the rock, wiped his hands in the wet grass and examined his knee. A line of blood from a half-inch gash below his kneecap mixed with the rain water to form a pinkish trail down his leg. He washed some mud from the cut and looked up the hill, but his view was obscured. He stood up to move out from under the rock and banged his head. 'For fuck's sake,' he said. Out in the open, he scanned the ground above him, but there was nothing but dark cloud and rain. The absence of colour was absolute. The washed-out hillside a monochrome in shades of grey, like the photographs on Alma's mantelpiece. *Don't let anything have happened to him*, he said to himself.

He stood for a minute or two, searching the hillside for a snatch of colour. What was Martin wearing? He thought about calling out again but didn't want to hear his own voice in the emptiness. He shivered. He was wet through, even his socks. His feet squelched inside his trainers. He dropped down a few steps and squeezed back under the rock, but it hurt his knee to crouch, so he sat down, unconcerned about the dirt and the sheep droppings. The skin around the cut was red and pulled tight, swelling nicely.

He thought again of Pat and Alma in the car, peering into the rain through the smeared glass. He pictured Alma in the back, her face up against the window, one hand resting protectively on her gently rounded tummy. *Oh don't be so dramatic*, he said to himself. They would be worried, but neither Alma nor Pat was the type to fall apart.

Sometimes, during his chemo, Terry would look across at Pat, searching her face for a sign of fear or panic but would find none. If needs be, her demeanour appeared to suggest, *I'll just sit here for as long as it takes*. It was him who was scared. Not so much of dying, that was too strange to get his head around, too abstract, but scared of being ill for too long. Scared of months or years of treatment, of lying in a hospital bed steadily declining while family and friends sat stoically around him in hard chairs, watching his slow demise. *Like Dad*, he thought.

He struggled to his feet, desperate to do something, placing his hand on the rock to prevent hitting his head again. As he stepped out from the shelter, he realised that the rain had eased a little. The sky immediately above him was definitely less dark, the worst of the clouds now further north, moving up the valley towards Buxton. Terry was looking in this direction when Martin came around the corner.

'Dad, what are you doing up here?'

Terry turned and felt a surge of relief wash through him. 'I'm waiting for a bloody bus – what do you think?'

'You're bleeding,' said Martin.

'I know,' said Terry, bending to look at his knee. 'It's nothing. Where've you been? I was worried – we all were.'

'No, your head,' said Martin, stepping closer to have a look. 'Your head's bleeding; it might need a stitch.'

Terry lifted his hand to his scalp but could feel nothing but wetness. 'I'll be fine,' he said, wiping his blood-streaked fingertips on the leg of his shorts.

'I lost the path,' said Martin. 'One minute I was OK, then the next I couldn't see a thing. I was wandering about trying to find the way down, and then I just had this weird feeling that I was about to step off the mountain. That there was a big drop in front of me. So I just stopped and waited. I got soaked. I thought I was going to be up there all night. I kept thinking about Alma – and the baby.' He paused, looking down at Terry's knee. 'When the cloud cleared, I was around the other side of the hill above some rocks, right near the edge.'

Martin turned away as if to look for the spot he was talking about, but Terry could see that he was shaken. How many times had he seen that look, that fight to contain his emotions? Even as a small child, Martin had done all he could not to cry in front of Terry. Terry took a step towards him, and for the first time in years, he wrapped his arms around his son and pulled him close. Martin was almost five inches taller than him, and soon to be a father himself, but for now, he hugged Terry as he had done as a boy.

'God,' said Terry, 'we're as wet as each other. Come on, let's get down. Careful, the grass is really slippy.'

'Yeah, I know,' said Martin.

Terry, walking in front, slipped twice on the way down, the second time landing flat on his backside on the wet grass.

'You OK, Dad?' said Martin from behind.

'I'm fine,' said Terry, scrambling to his feet. 'I just fancied a quick sit-down.'

Including theirs, there were three cars in the car park. *We're not the only fools still out in this then*, thought Terry.

'The ice-cream van's gone,' said Martin.

'Never mind,' said Terry, 'the gift shop might still be open; I can still get you that ruler if you like.'

Apart from two patches cleared from the inside on the passenger's window and one at the rear, the car was fogged up. The engine was running, and a cloud of warm, damp air escaped from the car as Terry opened the door.

'You're soaked,' said Alma.

'Yeah, it's raining,' said Terry, before he could stop himself.

'Are you both OK?' asked Pat, twisting in her seat to look at Martin and then turning back to check on Terry. 'You've cut yourself,' she said, leaning towards him to inspect his head. She pulled back a few inches, 'and you stink.'

'Yeah,' said Terry, 'I had a little roll around in some rabbit shit, or it might be sheep, I can't really tell the difference.' He pulled a rag from the tray in the door and began wiping the windscreen. 'What have you two been talking about anyway?'

Pat cast a quick glance at Alma in the back seat and smiled conspiratorially. 'Oh, I dunno,' she said, 'you two idiots mainly.'

Back in town, Alma and Martin turned at the doorstep and waved.

'You don't mind the caravan too much, do you?' said Terry.

Pat turned to look at him. 'Course not, why? I like it – it's cosy.'

'Tom was telling me about this law they've just passed, right to buy or something, for council houses. You get like a seventy per cent discount. If we win the darts, I'll pay off the round, but I want to use the rest of the money to help them buy that place.'

Pat put her hand on his knee. 'I think that's a lovely idea,' she said.

THIRTY-FOUR

Phil glanced up from the recipe book open on the kitchen worktop to the clock on the wall. Julie would be home any minute. A simple supper for two Hamlyn had it down as, but Phil felt as though he'd been flailing around with pans and ingredients all afternoon.

Outside, the storm had moved away to the north, but flashes of lightning continued to illuminate the prematurely dark sky, and the rain tore the petals from the perennials in the garden, scattering them on the black soil like pieces of crepe paper.

Phil, happy for the moment that dinner was under control, nipped into the living room and began flicking through his record collection. The two Bowie albums, one of which he missed already, had long since been smashed to pieces and consigned to the dustbin. Joni Mitchell? No, too obviously sentimental. Kate Bush? Too whiney. He settled on Fleetwood Mac, *Rumours*; Julie loved that one.

The dining table was laid already, but he looked it over again anyway. Strictly speaking, white wine was the only sensible option, and there was a bottle chilling in the fridge, but he would let Julie choose. If she wanted red, so be it.

When he heard, and then saw, Julie's car pull onto the drive, Phil hurried back through into the kitchen to check on the oven. He quickly scanned the recipe book to make sure he hadn't forgotten anything and then closed it and returned it to the shelf between Prue Leith and the Good Housekeeping Cookery Book.

'Mmm,' said Julie from the doorway, 'something smells good.'

'You go through, love,' said Phil, pushing his hands into a pair of flowery oven gloves, 'it won't be long. You didn't get too wet?'

'No,' said Julie, over her shoulder, 'but it's still chucking it down out there.'

Carrying the food through, Phil smiled to himself as he heard the music turned up a touch in the living room. *Good choice*, he thought.

'Fish pie,' he announced, setting the hot dish down on a placemat in the centre of the table.

'Looks lovely,' said Julie, sitting down.

'Wine?'

'Of course,' said Julie, 'we should have white, shouldn't we?'

'I don't mind,' said Phil. 'I thought I'd let you decide.'

'White then,' said Julie, smiling up at him.

'Great,' said Phil.

'It's so nice not having to cook for a change,' said Julie, when Phil came back with the wine, 'and not having a roast for once.'

'Yes,' said Phil, spooning a portion of steaming fish pie onto Julie's plate, 'I thought I'd try something different, just something simple. It was quite easy actually.'

The pie was too hot for either of them to attempt a mouthful, so they each took a sip of wine and pushed at the food with their forks to release the heat.

'How's your mother?' asked Phil.

'Oh, fine,' said Julie, 'you know – chatty. She said to say hello.'

Phil nodded and blew on his fork.

'I'm going in to school tomorrow,' said Julie, lifting food to her lips gingerly, 'just to start getting my classroom ready, sort through the cupboards. There's loads of stuff I need to get rid of.'

'That's early,' said Phil, 'you don't go back for another two weeks.'

Julie was moving hot food around her mouth and said nothing.

'Do you know much about the new deputy head?' Phil asked. 'What he's like I mean.'

Julie swallowed. 'She,' she said, 'it's a woman. No, I've not heard anything.'

Phil nodded.

'This is lovely,' said Julie, indicating her plate and taking another sip of wine. 'The wine's good too.'

'Reisling,' said Phil, 'goes well with fish.'

'I love this one,' said Julie, as the opening piano bars of "Songbird" broke the silence between them.

'I was thinking about shaving my moustache off,' said Phil, smoothing it down between his finger and thumb. 'I wondered if it was a bit too seventies – what do you think?'

'Oh God,' said Julie, laughing, 'I don't know, I can't remember what you look like without it. I've only just got used to the new curtains.'

'Actually,' said Phil, 'I thought we should get rid of that old three-piece suite as well; I've seen a really nice one in that shop at the top of St. Peter's Street.'

'Blimey, Phil, steady on; I'll think I've come home to the wrong house. Your moustache is fine – I like it, and the sofa.'

'Not too boring?'

'No,' said Julie, pouring them both some more wine, 'not too boring.'

'There's cheesecake for afters,' said Phil, 'only bought I'm afraid.'

'Lovely,' said Julie.

Phil cleared the plates and brought the cheesecake through from the kitchen. As he was slicing it, he said, 'Have you thought any more about what you said on holiday? About, you know, maybe trying for a baby?'

Julie cut the point of her portion of cheesecake with her fork but then looked up at Phil without lifting it to her mouth.

'Yeah, well, sort of. I don't know; I think I got a bit carried away. Maybe all that fresh air went to my head, that or the Old Peculiar.' She put the food into her mouth, and Phil looked down at his own plate. 'That's not a no though,' she said. 'Let's just see how it goes over the next few weeks, and we'll take it from there, OK?'

Phil nodded and smiled. 'OK, great,' he said.

THIRTY-FIVE

After his drenching the day before, Terry woke up with a stinking cold, feeling as though he'd been in a fight. And if he'd imagined that the first series of treatment had toughened him up, that perhaps his body might have become in some way more accustomed to the chemotherapy drugs, more resilient, then he realised now that he was wrong. Not only that, but the dosage had been increased also. Now, it felt like his veins must be full of the stuff, and the side effects rendered him mute, a lump of anesthetised flesh incapable of coherant thought.

Everyone was so friendly when he arrived at the hospital, calling him by his first name and asking about the bump on his head. It was almost like being among old friends. Even Pat, who had been quiet in the car on the way, exchanged news and snippets of gossip with the nurses. On the way out, things were decidedly less convivial. It was late. Terry had not been up to leaving immediately after the treatment, so they'd remained at the hospital all day. Now he was in a wheelchair, too weak to walk.

When they got home, Pat tucked him into bed. By the time she got back with a hot water bottle, and a bowl for the floor, Terry was already asleep.

One evening the following week, Terry was flat out on the settee watching a rerun of *Porridge*, when there was a rap on the caravan door followed by the sound of it opening.

'Anyone in?' It was Phil, so Terry stayed where he was. 'Alright, matey,' said Phil, coming through into the living room, 'hard at it?'

'I'm just taking five minutes before my next aerobics routine,' said Terry. 'What brings you here?'

'Julie's got a couple of mates round, so I thought I'd escape for an hour or so.'

'And there was me thinking it was my sparkling company you were after.' Terry adjusted the cushion under his head. 'Do you want a cup of tea?'

'No, don't get up,' said Phil, as Terry settled back into the sofa, 'wouldn't want you overdoing it.' He laughed and moved back towards the kitchen. 'Actually,' he shouted over his shoulder, 'I'll have a beer if you've got one.'

'By the fridge,' shouted Terry. 'Grab me one while you're there.'

Terry pushed himself up on the settee as Phil returned with two cans of Stones.

'How you doing?' asked Phil, dropping into the armchair.

Terry cracked his can and took a long swig. He belched. 'Been better,' he said. He watched Phil pour some of his beer into a glass and then set the can down on the floor beside the armchair. 'The first few days are pretty rough – good for the diet though.' He patted his stomach.

'Yeah, Pat said they'd upped your drugs. Hopefully that means they're killing it.'

'Or me,' said Terry. 'You've seen her?'

'Yeah, I popped by a couple of times last week, but you were out for the count.'

'Oh,' said Terry, 'she never said. Have you got a date for the quarter final yet?'

'Yeah, that was one of the reasons I came round. 25 September – month today – somewhere near Sheffield.'

'We'd better get practising again then,' said Terry, 'get ourselves organised.'

Phil leaned over the arm of his chair to pick up the can. He poured the rest of the beer into his glass and replaced the can on the floor.

'Actually, we had a session last night – and a couple last week.' He lifted his glass and took a mouthful of beer.

'Eh? What without me?'

Phil's eyes flicked towards the television before he looked back at Terry, his face pinched into a semi-frown as if to say that the decision had been a difficult one to make. 'We didn't think you'd be up to it.' He paused. 'Dave filled in.'

'Dave?' Terry put his can down on the coffee table. 'Filled in? You mean he took my place.'

'Just 'til you're feeling better,' said Phil, ''til you get your strength back.'

'I'm fine,' said Terry, reaching for his can again. 'I'm playing in that quarter-final, not Dave. He can't just come and go as he pleases.'

'Yeah, of course,' said Phil, 'we've told him that. We just thought we'd better have a contingency plan in place, just in case.'

'Contingency my arse,' said Terry. 'When's the next practice?'

'The lads are coming round mine on Friday night,' said Phil, 'you're—'

'Right, I'll be there,' said Terry. 'Tell Dave he's got the night off.'

In the end, the practice session two nights later took place in the pub. Phil claimed it was to make it more like a match environment, but Terry suspected the real reason was so that it would be less awkward for Dave to be there. From the amount of people who asked him how he was, and especially from the way they asked him, Terry understood that everyone knew just how ill he was. Even Linda's latest lodger boyfriend, who ordinarily had trouble stringing more than two words together, made a point of removing the cigarette from his mouth long enough to enquire after Terry's health. Nobody mentioned the word cancer though. Or chemotherapy. Or even hospital. There was just a slightly different look in their eye or a softening in the tone of voice that gave away the genuine concern behind the usually rhetorical, "alright, Terry?". One or two people said how well he was looking, but it was clear that what they meant was, "considering". Either that, or they'd subconsciously noticed his weight loss and mistakenly taken it as a good thing. Terry didn't actually think it showed in his face yet, but he'd had to tighten his belt a notch, and his shirts were definitely less tight around the shoulders.

Two weeks on from his last treatment though, he didn't feel too bad. Maybe he was quicker to lean on the bar than usual, or even steal a sit-down on an available bar stool, but he'd always done those things. And he played OK, considering. Dave, though, had improved massively. He wasn't yet in Hans's league, but he was better than the rest of them.

'Bloody hell, Dave,' said Tom, after another big score, 'are you sure you went down to Dudley for work?'

'I told you,' said Dave, 'there was nothing else to do. At least some good came out of it though, eh?'

'What as well as Karen leaving you?' said Terry.

Dave pulled his darts from the board and turned back to the others. 'I'm still working on that one, Terry,' he said.

'I'll get the drinks in,' said Phil, into the silence that followed.

'Sorry,' said Terry, 'it was meant to be a joke – a bad one. I wasn't thinking.'

'Nothing new there,' said Dave. 'Don't worry about it; it's

my own fault she left. I only called her twice the whole time I was away.'

'You called me more than that,' said Phil, passing Dave a pint.

'Yeah, but you're better looking,' said Terry. 'Joke, joke,' he added quickly, laughing.

At the end of the evening, no one mentioned meeting up again the following week. Though he felt OK now, Terry knew that with his next chemo session on Monday, the days following would be a write-off. The others were just being tactful.

As it turned out, it was more than two months before Terry picked up another dart. With each successive treatment, the time it took for him to recover grew longer. And the "recovery" less pronounced. The nausea went on long after there was anything left in Terry's stomach to expel, and the fatigue, the crippling weariness, left him pinned to the sofa for days on end. At times he was too weak to change the channel, gazing blindly at programme after programme without the strength even to shift his position to ease the ache in his hip, or back, or both.

As with the first course of treatment, Terry had arranged with Martin for him to cover the milk round on the day he went into hospital and for one or two days afterwards. Previously, this had stretched to the best part of a week. This time, it was soon clear that Martin would have to take over completely. Just until he gets his strength back, Terry had heard Pat explain.

Pat continued to accompany him to the hospital on Mondays, but now she stayed with him on the following two days as well, not returning to work until Thursday. Her boss had been very understanding when she'd asked him about it, she told Terry, and the girls in her team had been great, fiddling with the rotas so that Pat worked a day shift every second Sunday and a night the following Thursday. That way, she had almost five full days with him around the time of the treatment.

In the other weeks, those prior to his next appointment, when Terry at least spent more time awake than asleep, Alma came round most afternoons. The first time this happened, Terry assumed it was a one-off, that she had just popped in on her way to or from somewhere else, a courtesy call. He was embarrassed that she'd found him lounging on the settee in the middle of the afternoon. When she came again the next day with a rice pudding that her nan had made, claiming that she was bored sitting around at home and was happy to spend the afternoon watching TV with him, Terry understood that conversations were taking place without his knowledge: agreements to keep an eye on him, to look after him even. But he didn't have the energy, or the will, to object. In fact, once he realised that Alma, as good as her word, was content to sit for long periods in silence while he dozed through chat shows and old black-and-white films, he found he was glad of her company.

One afternoon, in early September, Terry had hauled himself up into a sitting position to drink his tea that Alma had just made him, when he glanced across at her and was struck, in that instant, as though some outside party had declared it to him, by just how much he cared for her. The strength of the sentiment came as a shock to him. He liked her of course, and had come to appreciate her calm, and kindness, and her playful sense of humour, but it was more than that. It was as if, suddenly, in that moment, he realised that Alma was part of his family now, just as her nan had said.

When, with one hand clutching her mug of tea, and the other absently caressing the soft swell of her tummy through her pullover, she looked across at Terry and caught his eye, it was as though she could read his thoughts. She smiled, and Terry felt self-conscious at the depth of his emotions.

'Er, what's happening with your college course?' Terry asked.

Alma took a sip of her tea. 'It starts in a couple of weeks. I'm going to go in two days a week until Christmas, then finish off the course after the baby.'

Terry looked again at Alma's belly and nodded. After a short silence he said,

'Do you think Martin would have gone if he didn't have to do the round?'

'It doesn't matter,' said Alma, 'he can go next year. Anyway, he loves the milk round. He's like you – he enjoys getting to know people, chatting to them.'

'I can't believe he can get up in the morning,' said Terry. 'We never used to see him before midday when he was at home.'

Alma smiled. 'He's grown up,' she said. She put her feet up onto the poof and stretched out, undoing the top button of her jeans.

'Are you looking forward to having the baby?' said Terry. 'I mean you're not nervous about being so young or anything?'

'I can't wait,' said Alma. 'Rose had my nan when she was sixteen, and look at her. She ended up looking after everybody; she did OK.'

The evening before the next darts match, Phil came round again. Pat had just left for work, and Terry, as usual, had taken up residence on the sofa.

'I thought you'd be at the pub getting some last-minute practice in,' said Terry.

'I'm on my way,' replied Phil. 'I just thought I'd nip in, see how you were.'

'I don't think I'm fit to play,' said Terry sarcastically. 'How's Dave been getting on?'

'Yeah, he's playing well,' said Phil. 'We'll see how it goes tomorrow.'

'Well you'd better win,' said Terry. 'I want my place back for the semi-final.'

'We'll do our best,' said Phil. 'I'll let you know how we get on.'

By the time Terry underwent the penultimate treatment in the second week of October, the doctors told Pat that they would have to put back the last session seven days to give Terry more time to recover. 'His immune system is just too weak,' he heard them tell her. 'He needs to regain some strength. We're happy that the drugs seem to be working, the tumour has definitely got much smaller, but his body just wouldn't be able to cope with another dose straight away.' They all looked at him.

'If he rests up an extra week,' Doctor Harvey said, 'and then comes out of the final session OK, we'll assess him again before Christmas. All being well, we'll be able to operate sometime in January.'

At home, Terry watched Pat cross out the entry for the last treatment on the calendar and turn the page to rewrite it in for 1 November. The rest of the month was blank but for the 28th, where Terry had written in the word "semi", followed by an exclamation mark. For the past month or so, the idea of getting well enough to play in the semi-final, however unlikely that had seemed at times, had kept him going. He'd dreamt about winning the final and handing over the prize money to Alma and Martin to buy the house. Now, he was too exhausted even to think about it. With an effort, he hoisted up the waistband of his trousers. The amount of weight he'd lost in the last few weeks was shocking. It scared him. His clothes no longer felt they belonged to him but to some former, fatter self. *Not really a problem*, he thought disconsolately, *seeing as though I spend most of my time in my pyjamas.*

On one of his good days, he and Pat had made vague plans to celebrate his final chemotherapy session. But when the day came, Terry was in no fit state, and as the next few slipped by, the sense was more one of relief, of liberation, than celebration.

Nevertheless, Terry did eventually begin to feel human again. By the middle of the month, his appetite was coming back, and he'd started playing darts again. But the days were shortening, and it was getting cold outside. Pat pestered him to come inside and rest. She was worried his immune system was low, she said. If he got ill now, he might struggle to recover.

Two weeks later, Terry and the rest of the team, including Dave, agreed that all five of them would travel up to the semi-final, and they'd see how it went when they got there.

THIRTY-SIX

'I'm really sorry I can't come,' said Pat, 'I've just had so much time off recently.' She placed a mug of tea down on Terry's bedside table and then bent to plant a kiss on his forehead. 'Good luck.'

Terry hauled himself into a sitting position, shoving a pillow behind his back. 'It's fine,' he said, reaching for the tea, 'thanks.'

'Do you want these open?' said Pat, opening the curtains.

'How did you guess?' said Terry, turning his head and scrunching his eyes against the sudden brightness. Pat edged back around the bed and leaned to give Terry another kiss. 'Look after yourself; don't try and do too much.' She smiled. 'I hope you win.'

The coach was already parked up outside the pub when Terry and Phil arrived. It was a damp, overcast morning, with a thin fog moving slowly between the branches of the bare trees. The houses, their dark roofs slick and dotted with lumps of moss, appeared to huddle together for warmth. A sign on the pub door said "Closed", but when Terry pulled it open, the smell of bacon cooking hit him before the hum of voices. A cluster of people stood at the bar in a cloud of cigarette smoke, each with a pint in their hand. Bottles of ketchup and brown sauce lined the counter behind them between plates of limp sandwiches. Hans and Dave were over by the dartboard with a few others. When he saw them, Hans tipped back the remains of his pint and, with his fingers, signalled to Linda for four more.

'Just a tomato juice for me,' said Terry.

'Yeah, and I'll just have a half for now,' said Phil.

'Save a seat for Tom,' said Phil to Dave, as they sat down on the coach, 'we're picking him up on the way through.'

'Or we could just leave him, then me and Terry could both play, eh, Terry?'

'Sounds good to me.' Terry sat down behind the driver.

'Some mates you two are,' said Phil.

Linda was the last to get on the coach. 'You can sit next to me if you like, Linda,' said Dave, patting the seat next to him. 'I'm sure Tom'll find somewhere else to sit.'

When the coach pulled up in front of Tom's house, Phil jumped out, but Tom was already on his way before Phil made it onto the drive. Tom was almost at the coach when his front door reopened and Fiona appeared and called something to him. Terry couldn't make out what she said, but he watched Tom turn at the sound of Fiona's voice and then spin back around to look up into the coach. It was Phil who stepped back on board to pass on the message.

'There's a phone call for you, Terry.'

'For me?' said Terry, standing up.

Tom shrugged as Terry passed him on the drive. The telephone lay off its cradle on a table in the hallway.

'It's Alma,' said Pat, her voice flat but urgent. 'They've brought her into hospital; she's bleeding. I can't get away for another couple of hours at least, and Rose doesn't know where Martin is.'

'He's at the football,' said Terry.

'Shit,' said Pat.

237

'But it's too early,' said Terry. He tried to think what the date was and when Alma was due. *Not 'til January*, he thought. 'Who's taken her in?'

'Rose called an ambulance,' said Pat. 'Shit.'

'I'll go,' said Terry. He could hear Pat breathing on the other end of the line. He was staring at a picture of Tom and a much thinner Fiona on their wedding day.

'But what about your match?' said Pat.

'Dave can play,' said Terry. 'I'm leaving now. I'll see you there later.'

Outside, he pulled the zip of his jacket to the collar and scurried across the drive, trying hard not to slip on the wet leaves stuck to the tarmac beneath his feet. The smell of a bonfire smoking in a neighbouring garden reminded Terry of his grandfather's allotment, raking the paths and turning the soil ready for winter. Phil and Tom were waiting for him by the door to the coach. Dave and some of the others from the pub were peering through the windows wondering what was going on.

'Everything OK?' asked Phil.

'It's Alma,' said Terry. 'She's gone into hospital. Can I borrow your car, Tom?'

Tom glanced at his BMW parked in front of the house. 'Er, yeah, of course. Keys are on the table next to the phone.'

Terry opened his palm. 'Yeah, got them.'

'What about the match?' said Phil.

Terry turned on his way to the car. 'Dave can play. I'll see you later.'

The roads were quiet on the way to the hospital and the pavements empty. The mist beneath the low, white cloud seemed to snuff out any signs of life. Even the crows hunched on the naked branches were unmoving.

The maternity ward was in a different block to where Terry had his chemotherapy treatment, in an older part of the hospital round the back. When it was built, an ash tree had been planted in the centre of a small patch of grass outside that was now fully grown. Terry had not been here since Martin was born. He waited for the lift with a man holding a bunch of flowers in front of his face as though it were an ice cream and rode with him to the third floor. A sign on the wall opposite pointed out the direction to the reception.

'Hello,' said the woman behind the desk.

'Er, I'm looking for a girl who was brought in this morning,' said Terry.

The woman smiled. 'OK, and does she have a name?'

'Oh, yes, Alma, er Johnson, Alma Johnson.'

The woman looked down and ran her finger along a list of names on a sheet of paper on her desk. The flesh either side of her wedding ring bulged, almost completely obscuring it. Terry wondered how she would ever get it off.

'Are you the father?' she said, looking up.

'No, er father-in-law.'

The woman nodded. 'OK. She's in emergency at the moment, you'll have to bide your time in the waiting room for now.' She pointed across and along the corridor. As Terry moved away, the man from the lift, still clutching his flowers, came out of one room, crossed the corridor and, without knocking, went into another.

Terry was alone in the waiting room. An internal window in the wall next to the door looked into the corridor. He picked a magazine from an untidy pile on a low table in the centre of the room but tossed it back down without looking at it. He walked a tour of the table and then stood at the window, gazing out at the brightly lit corridor. The glass appeared unnecessarily thick. He had the impression that he was hermetically sealed inside the room, like some kind of exhibit, a case study for examination. A porter pushed a trolley past the window and looked in, neither the trolley nor his soft-soled shoes making a sound on the polished floor. Terry watched him go and then sat down. Then he got back up again, went over to the door and opened it, looking up and down the corridor. The receptionist was gone from her desk. Where was everybody? Terry left the door open and sat down again. He glanced at his watch. There was no clock in the room and no natural light. *Like a casino*, thought Terry, *they don't want you to know how long you're in here for.*

He thought of Alma. The last time she had come to sit with him, they had watched an old Laurel and Hardy film together on BBC2 and laughed the whole way through. 'That lost, dopey look of Laurel's…' She giggled. '…When he scratches his head, reminds me of Martin when he can't find his socks in the morning.'

Terry had made her laugh with his Oliver Hardy impression. 'You should see us on the milk round,' he said. 'Well that's another fine mess you've got me into, Stanley.'

An hour or so later, he was sitting with his legs stretched out, his feet on the table, when he heard footsteps squeaking along the corridor towards the room. A woman appeared in the doorway, a similiar age to Pat and wearing the same uniform. Terry dropped his feet to the floor. She smiled at him without showing her teeth. Terry searched her eyes for news.

'Mr Fletcher?'

He stood up. 'Yes.'

The nurse took a breath, and her eyes softened. 'False alarm. Alma's fine.'

Terry exhaled. 'And the baby?'

'The baby's fine too – doing really well. Alma's just getting her things together, and you can take her home. She's a tough little cookie.'

Terry reached out a hand to the nurse. 'Thank you,' he said.

When Alma pushed open the swing doors from the ward, Terry was waiting for her in the corridor. She was wearing a pair of tracksuit bottoms and a baggy jumper two or three sizes too big so that her bump was barely visible. With her overnight bag slung over her shoulder, she looked like a student on her way to college rather than an expectant mother.

'I got a bit confused when they said my dad had come to pick me up,' she said. 'I thought there'd been some kind of mistake.'

Terry took a step towards Alma and put his arms around her, squeezing her shoulders against his own. 'No mistake,' he said.

Alma was chatty in the car, asking Terry about Tom and Phil and telling him about a brilliant film she'd seen with Alec Guinness playing about six parts.

'*Kind Hearts and Coronets*,' said Terry, 'a classic. I watched *Jaws* again last week. That scene on the boat where they're comparing scars is just genius – I love it.'

'That'll be me if I have a caesarean.' Alma laughed.

'Do you want to come in?' asked Alma, when they pulled up in front of her house. 'Nan'll be happy to see you.'

'No, I'll let you get some rest, say hello to her for me.'

'I will,' said Alma, going to open the car door. She turned, leaned across the car and gave Terry a kiss on the cheek. 'Thanks, Terry,' she said.

He watched her up the path. She turned at the door and gave him a wave. Rose was at the window but obviously didn't recognise the car and gave no sign of having seen him. He put the car in gear and pulled away.

The fog from the morning had lifted. Patches of blue sky punctured the white, expanding towards one another like ink stains on a paper towel. The BMW was a joy to drive. The suspension and fat tyres smoothed out the road, and the engine hummed with potential power that was realised immediately as Terry increased the pressure on the accelerator. The seat felt moulded to his exact frame. Even the knob of the gearstick appeared to cup his palm as though engineered to his own personal specifications. He turned on the radio. Tom had it tuned to Radio 2, and Neil Diamond's growling baritone filled the car.

He drove past the caravan site and on to Tom's house, thinking he would ask Fiona for a lift home. But her car was not on the drive. She was obviously out. He sat for a moment thinking. He could still smell the bonfire in the neighbour's garden. The low sun cut through the driver's side window, warm on his arm and the side of his face. He looked at his watch. The match didn't start for another five hours. He could still make it. He turned on the engine and steered the car back out onto the road, down the hill away from town, heading north.

THIRTY-SEVEN

He was making good time, so he stopped at a van in a lay-by on the A1, just outside Wetherby, for a sausage sandwich and a mug of tea. Before setting off again, he dug out a road atlas from the tray in the passenger door and worked out the rest of the route. He knew Whitley Bay was somewhere near Newcastle but wasn't sure which side of the estuary it was on. He was pleased to see that it was north-east of the city. He was a big fan of *The Likely Lads* and was looking forward to getting his first glimpse of the Tyne. *Maybe I'll cross it over that bridge from the opening credits*, he thought.

As it turned out, there was no bridge. At Jarrow, the road sunk into the earth, and Terry crossed the Tyne beneath it, in a tunnel that emerged into an industrial wasteland of concrete and weeds and rusted machinery. He pulled over to look at the map, alongside a vast, windswept tract of scrub that had probably once been a pit or shipyard. On a grassless football pitch across the road, a kid of around ten had a pigeon tied by the leg to a length of string with a chunk of wood attached to the other end. Each time the bird attempted to fly away, it would get twelve or fifteen feet into the air before being pulled back to the ground by the weight of the wood.

As he came into Whitley Bay, he stopped to ask an old man walking his dog the way to the working men's club.

'It's on the front, two doors down from the Spanish City,' said the man. 'Ye cannae miss that – it looks like the bloody Taj Mahal.'

The man was right; it stuck out like a sore thumb. As Terry got closer, the building's great white dome and twin minarets pierced the skyline above the rows of terraced houses and shabby arcades and burger bars. Cars and coaches were parked everywhere so that Terry was forced to find a spot down a side street.

Though the sky was still clear, an icy wind whipped off the sea, tossing around discarded crisp packets and old newspapers and kicking polystyrene chip trays along the gutters. A teenage couple, him in a T-shirt and her tugging at the hem of her skirt to keep her knickers from showing, walked awkwardly along the street arm in arm, apparently oblivious to the cold.

Inside the club, the temperature was somewhere in the nineties. The whole place – the floor, the walls, even the tables and chairs – seemed to be sweating. Music blasted from speakers in the ceiling but served only as backing to the drum of voices. A stage had been set up at one end of the room lit with red, blue and green disco lights. In the centre, in the glare of a light that looked like it might once have been used to search for ships in distress, was the dartboard. Practice boards dotted the walls to the side of the stage. Terry scanned the room for the others. From the scrum, it was obvious that the bar was at the other end of the room to the stage, running the entire length of the back wall. The haze of cigarette smoke reminded Terry of the fog from this morning. Though it was unlikely to clear as quickly.

He saw Hans first, a couple of rows back from the bar, and recognised Phil's head alongside him.

'Shouldn't you lot be practising?' said Terry, coming up behind Phil.

'Bloody hell,' said Tom, who had been hidden between Phil and Hans, 'what are you doing here?'

'I fancied a drive,' said Terry, with a grin.

'What about Alma?' asked Phil.

'She's fine. False alarm. Have I missed anything? It looked like the world and his wife were in here from the cars outside.'

'That's the bingo next door; apparently they come from miles around.' Phil nodded towards the stage. 'There's a local league match on first; we're not on until later. Are you – do you feel – up to playing?'

'Well, I'm not here for the sightseeing,' said Terry, 'and the amusement arcades are shut.'

'What about me?' said Dave, appearing through the crowd and taking his pint from Tom. 'Not that I'm not happy to see you, Terry, obviously.'

'Let's just see how it goes when we practise,' said Phil, looking at his watch. 'They said we could have one of the boards in half an hour. Maybe I'll drop out if needs be.'

When they got on the practice board forty minutes later, Dave threw terribly. The only problem for Terry was that he was worse. He had no feel. The darts were like wooden spoons in his hand and travelled through the air with the same grace. The more he tried to force it, the slower his action became and the tighter he pinched the barrel of the dart, neither of which did anything to improve his accuracy. Phil was struggling too. He was trying to encourage Terry and Dave, but Terry could see that worrying about them was affecting Phil's own game.

'OK, stop,' said Hans.

They all turned to look at him. The disco lights flashed through his hair, silhouetting him in a swirl of cigarette smoke like a genie from a lamp.

'Relax,' he said, 'you are all doing too much thinking; you are all good players now – stop thinking so much.'

'Shouldn't be too hard for you, Dave,' said Terry.

'Sod off,' said Dave.

'That is better,' said Hans. 'It is more normal when you are rude to each other.'

'I think I might have a pint,' said Terry, 'settle my nerves. I don't think I can drink any more tomato juice.'

'I'll get them,' said Phil.

Whether it was the beer or Hans's little pep talk, Terry's throwing began to improve. And with each dart that landed vaguely where he was aiming, his confidence grew. Then he relaxed and his game improved further. Soon he was enjoying himself enough to look around the room between throws. He spotted Linda, with her long red hair, on one side of the room in the centre of a group from The White Hart.

Their opponents were practising on the board next to them, each in a loose red and white striped shirt that looked like they'd been cut from a deckchair or beach hut. Over the left breast was a picture of a man wearing a pork pie hat with the pub name "The King's Head" beneath it. "STOKOE" was printed across the shoulders on the back above a large number "73".

'You know you're not allowed subs,' said one of the men.

'We thought you might not notice,' said Terry.

'This must be like a home match for you,' said Phil.

'You're joking, man,' said another of the men, with a head like a bowling ball, 'it's like a foreign country this side of the river. We had to get wor passports stamped coming in.'

'Aye,' chipped in one of his teammates, lowering his pint glass to reveal a thick moustache tipped with the froth off his pint, 'and they speak another language. We cannae understand a word they're saying.'

Eventually, the match on the competition board finished. A small man with grey hair tinged nicotine yellow at the front and combed slick to his head in a side parting, came over to the two teams. He held a cigarette between his thumb and index finger which he used to emphasise his speech. He wore a suit that looked as old as he was, with wide lapels and dandruff across the shoulders.

'Right, fellas,' he said, his Adam's apple sticking out sharply above his shirt collar, 'we'll start in forty-five minutes, give everyone time to get a drink. We've got a bit of a surprise for youse – a special guest MC. So you'll come on over there,' he pointed to the side of the stage with his cigarette, 'and you'll need to give us a walk-on song for each of youse. I'll be over there.' Ash fell from his cigarette as he flicked it in the direction of the bar. 'Have a think about it.' He tapped the now non-existent ash from his cigarette and took a drag, then used it to point at Terry.

'What's going on with youse lot? I've only had three pints, but I could swear there's five of youse.' Terry looked at Dave, who turned his head to look at Terry. Then they both looked at Phil.

'I'm not playing,' said Phil. 'I'm just here for the beer.'

'OK,' said the man, 'well bring us over your playing order and your songs, and I'll pass 'em on to Sid and Tony.'

He set off across the stage, walking with a slight roll, his legs bowed and the heels of his shoes worn low on the outside.

'Couldn't stop a pig in an alley that one,' said Dave.

'Cheers, Phil,' said Terry.

'Yeah, thanks,' said Dave.

'I was playing rubbish anyway,' said Phil. 'Anyone got any ideas for the walk-on music?'

'I've got a good one for Hans,' said Terry. 'I heard it on the way up – it's perfect.'

'Ladies and gentlemen.'

Terry and the rest of the team stood with their opponents at the foot of the stairs in the corner of the stage. The coachload from the pub, along with at least twice that number of supporters from The King's Head, crowded the floor, glasses glinting in the lights, their heads tipped back to focus on the man with the mike in the centre of the stage.

'It's the one you've all been waiting for. For a place in the final at Jollees in January. Will The White Hart get theirs broken, or will the King lose his head? It's that age-old battle, the head versus the heart…'

In the spotlight, in a dark suit and tie, his curly hair receding at the temples to form an unruly quiff at the front, stood Sid Waddell. Like he'd never been anywhere else. Like Tom Jones at the London Palladium. The crowd cheered and chanted the names of the two pubs. Sid smiled broadly, his teeth flashing, and then raised his palm to quieten them, like Canute trying to stop the tide. Except the mob fell silent, and Sid continued.

'First up, for The White Hart…' Behind Terry, the crowd from the pub cheered. Sid paused for a second to allow the noise to settle. '…He's the most famous Hans since Christian Andersen, but will he have a tale to tell tonight? Give a special north-east welcome to Hans "Dutchie" Boogman.' Sid took half a step back and swung his arm to the side of the stage, taking the spotlight with it. As it fell on Hans making his way up the steps, music filled the room, and for the second time that day, Terry smiled at the deep, unmistakeable voice of Neil Diamond.

Tom turned to Terry with a puzzled look on his face. Terry indicated for him to be patient. 'Wait,' he mouthed with a broad grin.

Hans reached the centre of the stage right on cue, and Terry, unable to contain himself, belted out, 'Hans, touching Hans…'

Tom, Phil and Dave were laughing and singing and slapping Terry on the back all at the same time.

'Brilliant,' shouted Tom. 'Genius.'

As the song built to the chorus, the entire room lifted their arms to the ceiling, sloshing beer onto the floor, and sung along to "Sweet Caroline".

By the time Terry and the pair from The King's Head had been introduced, the crowd was really enjoying itself. But Sid, like the conductor of the world's worst orchestra, had them in the palm of his hand and brought the racket to near silence with a slash of his microphone baton. Terry looked out at the crowd below. With so many King's Head fans in replica red and white shirts, the room resembled a Roker Park terrace on a Saturday afternoon, with The White Hart supporters grouped together to one side in the away end. Terry had taken Martin to his first match at the Baseball Ground when he was six. He remembered him clutching his hand in silence as they dodged through the masses in the narrow streets before kick-off. Then the look on his face, the big eyes, the soft little mouth agape in wonder at the sheer size of the space, at the scarves and the grown men singing.

From the start, Hans was unstoppable. Neither the crowd, nor the lights, or the fact that they were playing for a place in the final seemed to bother him at all. He waddled awkwardly to the oche and threw his darts as if no one was watching. As if he was at home in his garage or spare room, or down The White Hart on a Friday night. Terry did OK, and he was delighted, and relieved, to have regained some of his form, but it would scarcely have mattered if he'd missed the board completely. Hans was that good.

Dave was in his element as Sid introduced him to the crowd, walking on to Rod Stewart belting out "Tonight I'm Yours". He took his time, milking the cheers from The White Hart crew but also the boos and whistles from the rest of the room. Tom, though, was uncomfortable with the attention and didn't play well. Both of their games were close, but they lost them nevertheless, and the score was 2-2 after the doubles.

As Tom and Dave were shaking hands with their opponents, the grey-haired man in the threadbare suit who had spoken to them earlier, another cigarette burning between his fingers, announced that there would be a fifteen-minute break. 'To get yousselves a refill from the bar.' Not that the bar had been noticeably any quieter during play as far as Terry had noticed. However, the room clearly considered it wise to take the announcer's advice, as there followed a broadly general movement in that direction. Sid, and the announcer himself, stepped off the stage to join the migration to the other end of the room. Tom and Dave followed them down the steps.

'I can't believe I missed that double six in the last leg,' said Tom, re-enacting the shot, 'felt like I snatched at it. What do you think, Hans?'

'You just got a bit unlucky,' said Phil. 'You played OK. There was nothing in it.'

Hans, who had beaten the rush to the bar and, as a result, Terry thought, had probably missed the shot in question, took a slug from his pint. 'Don't worry so much,' he said. 'You are too tight I think. It must be natural – like van Gogh with his paintbrush.'

'Just don't go chopping your ear off,' said Dave.

'Are you OK, Terry?' asked Phil.

'Yeah, yeah, I'm fine,' said Terry, glancing around. 'I wouldn't mind a sit-down for five minutes though; it's like a sauna in here.'

Linda, who was sat to one side of them at a huge round table with a load of White Hart regulars, pulled out the chair next to her. 'Here you go, Terry,' she said, patting the chair. 'Come and sit next to me.' When he was seated, she pulled a tissue from her handbag under the table and leaned over to wipe the sweat from Terry's head and neck. Phil and Dave sat down in a couple of spare seats on the other side of the table, the surface of which was littered with beer glasses and Linda's vodka tonics.

'You're doing great, Terry,' said Linda, tossing the tissue onto the table and handing him another. 'You all are. We're really proud of you.'

Terry wiped his eyes and face with the tissue. The middle of his back was aching, and it felt good to sit down. He leaned heavily against his seat.

Other than the odd shouted comment, and the cheers at the end of each leg, the crowd had been surprisingly well behaved, respecting each player's turn at the oche with a dignified silence. Or close enough anyway. It was as if someone was controlling the noise in the room with a dial, regulating the volume. Up between throws, and down again as each player settled into his stance. Since the break, the volume control had been cranked up a notch. Across the table, Phil was saying something to him, but Terry couldn't make it out. Tom appeared from behind Linda and put a pint of water down in front of him.

'Here you go, Terry, get that down you. You look like you're burning up.'

Terry picked up the water and drained half the glass. 'I'll be alright in a minute,' he said. 'It's these pills I'm on; they give me hot flushes.'

'You're not pregnant, are you?' shouted Dave across the table.

'If I was, I think I've lost the baby,' said Terry, patting his diminished stomach.

'Shouldn't we be practising?' said Tom. 'Keep our eye in.'

At the far end of the stage, their opponents occupied both training boards.

'Just give me a minute,' said Terry.

Before they could move, however, Sid Waddell strolled into the spotlight on stage, turned on his microphone and brought the crowd to attention with a couple of sharp taps on its fuzzy head. The sound rasped around the room like shots from a pellet gun.

Hans was introduced first to cheers from The White Hart supporters, but they were flattened by the roar from The King's Head fans as their man was announced onto the stage. Clearly,

251

he was their star player. Not that it made any difference to Hans. He appeared oblivious to what was going on around him and threw with the same metronomic accuracy as he had done in the doubles.

'That man was born to play darts,' said Tom. 'I reckon he could be a pro.'

When Hans, with no hesitation or calculation, hit the treble fifteen to leave himself double fourteen at the next visit, even The King's Head crowd seemed to let out a collective gasp of admiration. Hans gathered his darts without expression. Terry watched him take a gulp from his pint, check his flights and then calmly reposition himself at the oche. The first dart landed in the centre of the bed.

'Three-two,' said Phil into Terry's ear. 'Three more points for the win.'

As Hans came off the stage, he looked surprised to be mobbed by the locals from The White Hart, many of whom, taking into account the cans on the coach on the way up, had now been drinking for the best part of eight hours. Terry saw Hans say something to Tom over the heads of the melee, as he made his way onto the stage.

Tom's opponent, somewhere in his sixties, was the oldest player on the other team. He was no taller than Tom and without an ounce of fat, his skinny arms dark from years of exposure to the sun, lean muscle over bone. He had a full head of hair, neatly combed, but his face betrayed a lifetime of hard work – or hardship. The skin was lined and weathered, drawn tight over prominent cheekbones and loose in his hollowed-out cheeks. His whole body appeared taut; tripwired for fight or flight.

Tom threw first. His first dart landed in the one but was only a fraction of an inch from the trebles, and he recovered with his next two shots, hitting the single and then the treble twenty. While his opponent was at the oche, Tom never stopped moving, shifting his weight from one leg to the other, tightening his barrels and constantly checking that his flights were properly inserted. Terry took this as a good sign. It was when Tom stopped fidgeting and fiddling, when he stopped his non-stop shuffling and tried to force himself to concentrate, that things went badly. Then, he would lose his natural action and slow his throw to such an extent that it was almost as if he had trouble letting go of the darts altogether. Over the last few months, Hans had continually encouraged Tom to throw at a tempo that matched his personality. 'You do everything fast,' he said. 'Why is darts different?' Tom's opponent was clearly of the same philosophy, so Sid had scarcely the chance to announce one player's score before the first dart of the other thumped into the board.

'They're like a couple of squirrels nipping in to pinch a nut off a bird table,' said Phil.

'Perfect opponent for Tom,' replied Terry. 'Let's him play quickly.'

Terry was right, but he realised that this was also true for the player from The King's Head. The match was tight, with neither player able to take a definitive edge over the other, and the first two legs went with the darts. Fortunately, Tom threw first in the decider and managed to hold his lead to reach a double first, in spite of the raucous encouragement his opponent received from his striped supporters. When he hit the double with his second dart to secure victory, he threw up his arms and skipped into the air as though hurdling a low fence. The crowd from The White Hart roared as Tom turned to salute them with a clenched fist and an enormous smile.

Terry felt better for the sit-down and the water, but when he climbed the steps onto the stage, the heat was horrific, like a lead cloak thrown across his shoulders. His opponent was the man with the frothy moustache from earlier. He had long, wide sideburns to go with it and a thick cap of dark, wavy hair to his collar. Terry wondered whether this was better or worse than his own bald head in this heat.

Whichever was the case, his opponent threw coolly and without fuss. With his flared trousers and strong chin, his mane glossy under the lights, he looked like a pop star: the David Essex of darts. For some reason, when he took the first leg, his fans in the crowd began singing a hit by the Bay City Rollers, banging out the chorus like they were at a concert. Sid indulged them for a few moments and then called the unholy choir to order to allow Terry to start the next leg.

Terry tried hard to pretend the crowd was not there and to ignore the fact that the temperature in the room was approaching that of the surface of the sun. But it was impossible. Sweat and smoke stung his eyes and the board seemed to shimmer in the heat haze. His opponent, on the other hand, appeared quite unperturbed. On the contrary, the hotter it became and the more vocal the crowd, the better he played.

In the circumstances, Terry threw okay, but he never felt in the match, never really got going enough to give himself a chance of winning. When he came off stage afterwards to commiserations from his teammates and The White Hart supporters, it was as though it had happened to someone else. As though he had not taken part but, like them, had merely been a spectator looking on.

'I need some fresh air,' he said.

Stepping outside was like unzipping himself from a hot sleeping bag and sticking his head out of the tent flap. He lifted his face to the sky and inhaled an enormous breath of air. It was damp and salty and cleared his senses almost immediately. Closing the door behind him snuffed out the noise from inside to a background rumble, replaced by that of the sea breaking over pebbles on the beach. He walked across the road towards the sound, the dark sky unbroken ahead of him. Once beyond the glare from the lights of the Spanish City, and the glow of the street lamps, Terry had the impression that he was standing on the edge of the world, with endless nothing ahead of him.

He couldn't make out where the sea finished and the sky began and imagined himself out there somewhere in a boat, floating between the two. He thought of Pat at home in the caravan beneath the same black sky. He hadn't told her he was coming here, though she must have worked it out by now. All of a sudden, he wanted to be home, to be holding her, telling her they'd won.

Walking back up the beach, he heard his name called out. Phil was in the middle of the road. 'What are you doing down there? Are you alright?'

'Just watching the sea. What's going on?'

'Dave lost – it's four all. One of you has to drop out, then the last three singles are drawn randomly.'

Terry thought for a moment. A blast of arctic air blew in off the sea, sending a ripple of cold through his body, making him shiver. He pushed his hands into his jacket pockets. One of his fingers touched something tucked tight into a corner. He pulled it out. It was the crucifix that Rose had given him when she'd asked him in for a cup of tea. Terry looked up at Phil. 'I'll play,' he said.

Going back into the club, the heat, the lights, the noise, was like opening the door into another world. The scrum at the bar showed no sign of thinning, and The King's Head supporters were still celebrating their man's win over Dave with another rendition of the Bay City Rollers song, which they appeared to have now adopted as their official anthem. Terry shrugged off his jacket, folded it carefully onto the chair next to Linda and climbed up on stage to join Tom, who was already there practising.

'How are you feeling?' said Tom.

'Yeah, better thanks,' Terry replied.

After a couple of minutes, Dave came over. 'Good luck, fellas,' he said, slapping Terry on the back. 'No pressure, but you'd better win.'

'You alright with me playing?' asked Terry.

'Yeah course,' said Dave. 'I was playing rubbish anyway. Now you can't blame me if we lose.'

'Cheers for the confidence,' said Terry.

Terry was drawn against Tom's first opponent, and if anything, he played even quicker against Terry than he had in his previous game. The first leg seemed to go in a flash, and Terry was 1-0 down. He looked into the crowd, and Hans shouted something to him, but he was unable to make out the words. *I need to play at my own pace*, thought Terry, *not get dragged into his.*

In the next leg, he took a deliberate pause each time before coming to the oche and another after throwing his third dart. This second deliberation, prior to retrieving his darts, meant that his hand had scarcely moved away from the board before his opponents first dart smacked into it. It hadn't been Terry's intention to annoy him, but slowing down the game was clearly having that effect.

'Your milk must be fucking cheese if you deliver it at that speed,' he said after Terry took the leg.

Terry took a sip of his water. 'No rush,' he said. He looked into the crowd to where The White Hart were congregated. They were cheering and clapping and pumping their fists at him. Hans, a head taller than most of them, gave Terry a thumbs up.

In the deciding leg, Terry's opponent had the darts and pushed the first to the right. His next two were straight but missed the treble. Forty-one. Terry waited for him to collect his darts and then took a sip of water. Walking to the oche, he heard Phil's voice over the hum of the crowd. 'Come on, Terry.' His first dart landed just below the treble twenty, his second a fraction above it, blocking his view. He lowered his eyes to the bottom of the board but could only hit the single nineteen.

'Fifty-nine,' announced Sid, his deep voice somehow managing to express both disappointment and hope in three short syllables. Terry pulled his darts from the board and felt a rush of air close to his ear as his opponent's dart flashed past him.

'One hundred and forty,' cried Sid, to huge cheers from the crowd.

Terry wiped his hand on his trousers and settled himself, the little toe of his right foot against the block of wood on the floor. Again his first two darts flew straight but obscured his path to the treble. He took half a step to his left and tried to squeeze the last dart through a gap that was not really there. It ricocheted off another barrel and into the treble five.

'Fifty-five,' commiserated Sid.

A dart whistled past his head as he turned from retrieving his darts. He had barely made it back to the table before the crowd cheered and Sid called out, 'One hundred.'

Terry inhaled deeply. A trickle of sweat slipped inside his shirt collar and ran down his back. His first dart dropped marginally below the treble, and his second slammed into the board alongside it. This time, his view was clear and the first two darts perfectly positioned as markers for the third. He aimed a hair's width higher, and the dart pinged against the wire and bounced out of the board. It stuck upright in the floorboards of the stage no more than twelve inches from his feet. He lifted his eyes to the ceiling. The paint was cracked and yellowed from exhaled nicotine. He took his time extracting his dart from the floor, checking the tip and flight for damage. His opponent was already at the oche, impatient to throw, so Terry strolled slowly to the board to make him wait. The scoreboard showed he was over a hundred behind.

When his opponent drilled his first dart into the treble twenty, Terry's heart sank. His second, though, drifted left into the five, and he overcompensated with his third, pushing it into the single one. Sixty-six. Even so, his opponent was already on a finish. Terry was still in the three hundreds. He tightened the

257

barrels of his darts and stepped forwards into the spotlight. Thud, treble twenty, thump, treble twenty. Terry picked the third dart from his other hand without moving his head or eyes a millimetre. As the dart landed, nestled alongside the other two in the treble, Phil and the others, and the coachload from The White Hart, screamed.

'One hundred and eighty,' bellowed Sid, stretching out each word so that the call outlasted the cheers from the crowd.

Terry punched his fist. But it was probably too late; Sid was already calling his opponent's out shot.

'Barry, you require one hundred and fifty-four.'

Difficult but definitely possible. For some reason, Barry chose to attempt the treble eighteen first. Terry flinched as he narrowly missed, hitting only the single. He was still alive. Barry jerked his head in frustration and switched his attention to the twenty. But again hit only the single. His third dart was on its way to the board almost before the second had landed, and Terry groaned inwardly as it crept into the corner of the treble. The King's Head fans erupted.

'Ninety-eight.'

Terry stepped forwards as Sid announced the score to the room. One-six-seven, the second highest possible checkout. Terry had never made this in his life. He waited for the noise of the crowd to drop and then sent his opening dart towards the board. Treble nineteen. He tried not to think about it, keeping his eyes on the exact same spot. His next dart looked good all the way but thudded into the board the wrong side of the wire. Terry's shoulders sagged, and the whole room appeared to release a collective gasp, as though the dart had pierced some invisible bubble that had been holding the audience within it. He took a moment to collect himself and sent his final dart into the single twenty. His opponent was already behind him at the oche. Sid, perhaps anticipating that this was the last act, waited for Terry to retrieve his darts before making his announcement.

'Barry, you require fifty-six.'

Terry looked into the crowd. Smoke played in the down glow from the ceiling lights. Hans stood alongside Linda with a pint in his hand, Tom in front, twitchy as a schoolboy outside the head's office. Phil caught Terry's eye and gave him a smile that seemed to convey hard luck and encouragement in equal measure.

Barry's first dart landed in the treble sixteen, which seemed to throw him for a split second. He had been aiming for the single. Eight left. Double four. Terry felt bad for Tom. He would have to win to keep them in the match. He thought of Martin, and Alma, and the money for the house. *Please let him miss*, he thought. The second dart was an inch off target. It landed smack in the centre of the single four. Double two. Terry held his breath, his eyes glued to the double as if it were he that needed to hit it. And suddenly, the dart was there. In the board but low. Terry had another chance. Seventy-one left, which way to go?

He took aim for the treble seventeen and hit the single. Fifty-four. Fourteen tops, or eighteen double eighteen. He exhaled and reset himself, focused on the eighteen in the top-right quadrant of the board. As the dart left his hand, he felt sick. He gasped, 'No,' as it missed the eighteen entirely and dropped into its neighbour, four. The room was silent; Terry had the weird feeling that if he turned around, there would be nobody there, that they'd have all gone home. He looked at the scoreboard. Fifty. He still had a dart. He'd been here before. This time, though, the red dot in the centre of the board looked no more than a pinprick. At home he'd finished almost every practice session with a bull. He'd hit hundreds over the last few months. Rarely, though, at the first attempt.

Terry drew his arm back for the final time and released the dart. It travelled the seven feet nine and a quarter inches in less than half a second so that when it struck the board, Terry had not moved. And he remained in that same position, leaning forwards over his right leg, elbow cocked, his head perfectly still, even as the crowd erupted behind him and Sid Waddell screeched into the microphone. Terry turned around. Phil, Tom and Dave were bouncing up and down, hugging one another in the middle of a jubilant scrum of White Hart supporters. Even Hans had put his pint down to applaud.

Linda was the first to him as Terry came off stage, squeezing him in a tight bear hug and lifting him off his feet as the others crowded in, clapping him on the shoulders and back and trying to shake his hand.

'Brilliant,' said Phil. 'Unbelievable! Where did that come from?'

Terry glanced down at his jacket, folded on the chair. 'I don't know,' he said. 'Maybe that walk on the beach did me good.'

Phil was about to make some reply when Sid called the room to order for the next game.

'Come on, Tom', shouted Terry. 'I've set you up – finish 'em off.'

Tom's opponent had been introduced first and was laughing and joking with Sid as if they were old friends when Tom reached the centre of the stage. He was a big man, more wide than tall, with a great shiny head that appeared to sit directly upon his vast, rounded shoulders. His thick arms were heavily tattooed in dark ink, though such was the quality, the only thing Terry could actually make out was "Mam" and "Dad" scrawled across the back of his hands. When Tom got to him, rather than shake hands, he wrapped Tom in an embrace that enveloped him almost entirely, smashing him on the back as though trying to dislodge a piece of apple from his windpipe. Tom coughed as he was released.

'I think he might have broken a rib,' said Dave.

The first two legs were tight but went with the darts, both players hitting good doubles before their opponent had the chance to nip in and steal. Halfway through the final leg, two of The King's Head player's darts bounced out, with the other left stranded in the one. He turned to his supporters, his arms outstretched in a gesture of helplessness.

'Come on, Tom,' said Terry.

Two visits later and Tom should have been able to throw down to a double, but he missed the eleven with his final dart, hitting the fourteen instead, to leave twenty-nine. But he was well in front. Tom walked quickly back from the board fiddling with his darts, his sharp face creased in concentration.

Though Terry was a few years older, he had known Tom since school. Like him, Tom was not a natural sportsman or scholar, but whereas Terry had a tendency towards laziness, preferring to hide at the back of class in lessons and to treat cross-country as an excuse for a walk and a chat, Tom was a tryer. Yes, he was sometimes low in confidence and gave the appearance of being beaten, resigned perhaps to his fate, but nothing could be further from the truth. Tom was a grafter, not a quitter.

He moved busily to the oche and threw his first dart. Thirteen. Yes. Sixteen left. Tom's second dart was too far left. Still double eight. Terry fixed his eyes on the tiny red rectangle on the left of the board, as Tom's final dart landed in it.

Someone behind him was the first to react, a roar that was quickly lost in the din. Beer splashed against Terry's neck and ran down inside his shirt collar. Phil grabbed him and planted a kiss on his forehead. Linda was on a chair, her head thrown back, hair loose over her shoulders, whistling through her fingers.

The White Hart supporters went bananas, engulfing the players. Through the tangle of hot bodies, Terry caught a glimpse of Tom on stage. His opponent had him under the armpits, his feet off the ground, showing him to the crowd as though he were the cup itself. When Tom finally managed to get off stage, straightening his hair and shirt, he was beaming.

'Such a nice guy,' he said, 'he wants us to have a drink with them at the bar.'

By the time last orders were called, Tom and his opponent were new best pals. At some point in the evening, they had decided it would be a good idea to swap shirts, like footballers, failing, in their enthusiasm at this new friendship, to take into account the difference in size. As a result, Tom stood at the bar dressed in what looked like the big top from a circus, while his opponent, who had been unable even to pull Tom's shirt over his massive head, leaned alongside him topless, his vast, sweating torso shimmering under the overhead lights.

'We're going next door for one,' said Phil, as Terry returned from the toilet. 'Apparently there's a band on, Beatles tribute.'

'I'm knackered,' said Terry, 'I'm going to have a lie-down on the bus.'

The driver was asleep across two of the front seats, and Terry tapped on the glass to wake him. On board, he made his way to the back of the coach and sprawled out. He stirred with the noise of the others getting on later, and someone shifted his feet so that they could sit down, but he soon dropped off again as the beer and the rhythm of the coach sent everyone to sleep.

When he woke later, he was dying for a pee. The coach was stopped with the engine running. He sat up. Phil was helping Tom off the coach. Terry walked to the front, grabbing at the seats on his way forwards, groggy with sleep and booze. Phil had an arm around Tom's shoulders and was trying to guide him towards his front door. Terry took the other side. He would have to empty his bladder once Tom was inside, he thought.

'Who brought Tom's car back?' he said.

'What?' said Phil.

'Tom's car?'

'Wha?' slurred Tom.

Terry put his hand in his jacket pocket. 'Shit,' he said. He pulled out Tom's car keys and looked across at Phil. 'I've left Tom's car in Whitley Bay.'

THIRTY-EIGHT

When Terry woke the next day feeling dreadful, he put it down to a hangover. Worth it though, he thought, running through the match and picturing himself on stage in the final receiving the trophy from John Lowe or Eric Bristow. He staggered to the toilet, head thumping, his limbs and lower back aching like he'd spent the night on a park bench.

'I'll bring you a cup of tea through,' shouted Pat, as he fell back into bed.

She got in alongside him and listened as Terry ran through the events of the previous day: Alma, the drive north, his bullseye checkout. She was still dressed for work, and as Terry spoke, she rubbed her stockinged foot up and down against his ankle. When he got to the part about Tom's car she howled, causing Terry to spill tea over his bare chest. He flinched and tipped more onto the bedcovers.

'Sorry,' laughed Pat, 'are you feeling a bit delicate this morning?'

Terry had arranged with Martin to do the milk round, so when Pat told him she was going to pop over to see Alma, Terry set up shop on the settee and spent the day watching telly. When she came back later and asked him how he was feeling, he lied and told her much better.

Dragging himself out of bed on Tuesday morning required a massive effort. To make it worse, it was freezing outside and had snowed overnight, coating the ground, the car and the bare trees in an inch of soft, white powder. He brushed the windscreen clear and jammed the car's heater on full. But it was scarcely any warmer by the time he reached the dairy.

In the first few streets, the snow was unspoilt: a white carpet between the dark houses. The tyres of Terry's float cut parallel tracks in it, like those of a ghostly tram, his boot prints to each front door those of the alighting passengers. At first, the cold took his mind off the ache in his back, the dull squeeze of his brain against the inside of his skull. But soon the three combined, taking strength, it seemed, from one another to weaken their exhausted host. It was usually quiet at this time in the morning, but the snow deepened the silence around him so that Terry felt he could hear his own heart racing.

When he finally got back to the caravan, he went straight to bed and, in spite of his aches, slept on until Pat came in from work at six. He stood under the shower for an age, directing the hot water at his neck and kidneys, but the jet was too weak to offer much relief. He swallowed two paracetamol with a glass of water.

'You're not going out, surely?' said Pat.

'Practice night,' said Terry. 'I'll see how I get on. If I'm not feeling up to it, I'll come home early, I promise.'

He kissed Pat and took his jacket off the back of a chair.

'Take a hat,' said Pat. 'It's freezing.'

The snow had melted. The branches and trunks of the trees were black, bark dripping, the streets a mess of murky slush. Linda, wearing baubles for earings, had Christmas songs on the jukebox and was hanging tinsel from the bar.

'Hi, Terry,' she said. 'I've reserved the board permanently until the final. You can come and play whenever you like.'

'It's a bit early for decorations, isn't it? It's not even December yet.'

'The snow got me in the mood,' she said. 'I love it when it's all white outside.'

Terry took his lemonade over to the dartboard where Tom and Phil were playing.

'Not drinking?' asked Phil.

'No,' said Terry, sitting down at a nearby table, 'alcohol doesn't seem to mix well with my medication. I've been feeling pretty rough since Sunday. Sorry about the car, Tom.'

'Don't be,' said Tom. 'It worked out a treat. I went up on the train yesterday and met Geoff, the big bloke from The King's Head. He's president of the Sunderland supporters club; he wants me to do a thousand T-shirts for him. It's a massive order. And he says there'll be more. Seems like he's involved in loads of stuff up there.'

'I'll bet he is,' said Terry, 'and not all of it legal I'd imagine. Where's the others?'

'Hans couldn't make it, and Dave's out with Karen,' said Phil. 'He's hoping they'll get back together.'

Terry sat and watched for a while, sipping his lemonade. As the pub filled up, people came over to congratulate the three of them and offer to buy them a drink. Linda had already booked a coach for the final, and it appeared that everyone was looking forward to another day out. Terry made an effort to get into the spirit of the evening, but the paracetamol had done nothing to ease his headache and, despite having slept for most of the day, he was still shattered. And he knew he had to get up at 3am.

'I'm gonna get off,' he said. 'I'm knackered, and I'm playing rubbish anyway.'

'Thursday, same time,' said Phil. 'We're going to try to make it four nights a week up until the final.'

Terry said his goodbyes to some of the regulars and waved at Linda.

'Don't forget your car,' shouted Phil.

On Thursday morning, a letter came from the hospital. Terry was to come in the following week for tests, and, if all was well, he would have surgery to remove what was left of the tumour on the 5th of January.

'Bloody hell,' said Terry to Pat, 'that's only three days before the final. Do you think we can get it put back?'

'Let's see what they say next week,' said Pat. 'I'll try and come with you.'

Pat managed to persuade Terry not to go to the pub that night. Though, the truth was, it had not been that difficult. It was dark by 5pm and had been raining all day. The forecast was for the temperature to drop, turning the rain to sleet overnight, and Terry was not looking forward to the round. He was struggling to do anything for longer than a couple of minutes without having to stop to get his strength back, and the ache in his lower back and vice-like tightness across his skull were constant. That morning, he had fallen onto the bed while putting on his trousers and been unable to get back to his feet for a minute or so, such was the thumping in his brain. If he tried to move, he thought, he was going to throw up.

Some days were better than others, but when Pat suggested Martin take over the milk round until after the operation in January, Terry agreed that it might not be a bad idea.

'It'll give me a chance to practise with the boys,' he said, 'not having to get up in the morning.'

By the time of the hospital visit the following week, Terry had made only one of the scheduled practice sessions at the pub. He told himself he would make up for this by playing at home, but it was miserable outside at this time of the year, and his fingers were quickly too numb to feel the darts properly. Besides which, he just had no energy. He was eating nothing. Most days, he moved only from bed to settee and back again, with the odd stop in the kitchen in between to make mugs of tea. And even that was an effort.

Pat drove them to the hospital, and while Terry gazed only at the road ahead, he was aware of her flicking glances at him all the way there. Walking across the car park, she had to stop twice and then slow her pace to allow him to catch up. She wore a satin scarf knotted close at her throat, her shoulders drawn tight in her dark winter coat. Terry felt saddened, and somehow guilty, at the concern etched in Pat's face, at the pinch of her mouth and the sharp crease between her eyes.

When they left the hospital later, it was raining. The black outside was a shock after the harsh white lights of the corridors and consulting rooms. Pat had her arm through Terry's, but he knew that it was more for his benefit than hers.

Traffic through town was busy on the drive back. The shops were just closing and people were making their way home from work and from Christmas shopping. The brake lights of the cars in front blurred red through the damp windscreen. Terry ran through again in his head what the doctor had said. That his numbers were not as good as they had hoped. He was not well enough to have surgery next month. He gazed out of his side window, at the shoppers hunched against the rain, at the glow from the shopfronts and the Christmas lights reflected in the puddles on the pavement. The car stopped, and he felt Pat's hand on his knee.

'You OK, love?'

He turned to face her and nodded. 'Yeah,' he said. 'At least not having the operation might give me more chance of playing in the final.'

One positive that did come out of the hospital visit over the next couple of weeks, was that Terry was released from the terrible skull-splitting headaches he'd endured since the semi-final. The doctors had agreed to change the tablets he was taking, so now he was actually able to move around a little without feeling as though he was about to be sick. Not that he was inclined to move much anyway however. He was as weak as a kitten. Sometimes even a trip to the toilet would require a stop en route in the kitchen to lean on the back of a chair or sit down.

His trousers no longer fitted him. In spite of Pat making extra holes in his belt, the waistband flapped loose when he walked, threatening to slip over his hip bones to land in a crumpled pile at his feet. Looking in the mirror in the bathroom, Terry saw his father's face reflected back. Soft, wispy hairs sprouted pathetically from his scalp, and the skin sagged below his eyes and in the hollows of his sunken cheeks. Even his eyelids appeared to have lost weight.

When Pat wasn't working, she would sit watching TV with him, making mugs of sweet tea and bowls of tomato soup. Phil and Tom came over on a couple of evenings, and they filled him in on what they had been doing at work and news from the pub. It was Terry who had to ask how practice was going. He told them he was hoping to make at least one or two of the sessions that week, but they all knew that was not going to happen.

On the days Pat worked, Alma came round. They hadn't said as much, but Terry suspected that this was another arrangement the two of them had cooked up together. Occasionally, Martin would come too, but since he was covering the milk round, and slept most afternoons, Alma usually came alone. There was a show on the new channel that they liked to watch where the contestants had to make words from random letters and do sums against the clock. Alma always did better than Terry on the words round, but years of adding up dart scores and working out finishes meant that Terry got his revenge with the maths. At the end of each show, a nine-letter word was jumbled into a conundrum that the contestants competed to solve in less than thirty seconds. Alma never failed to beat Terry at this.

'I could be here 'til Christmas before I get one of these,' said Terry one afternoon, just before the letters were revealed.

'Christmas,' shouted Alma, as the jumbled word spun into view.

'Bloody hell,' laughed Terry, 'I might actually have got that one.'

'Sorry,' said Alma, 'I couldn't help myself.'

'Do you think you could get Pat a present from me?' said Terry. 'I'll give you the money obviously.'

Alma looked at him. 'Yeah sure, what do you want to get her?'

'I dunno. You got any ideas?'

Alma smiled. She had her feet up on the pouf, both hands resting on her bump. 'I'll have a think,' she said.

An advert came on after the programme finished showing Isaac Newton trying to solve a Rubik's Cube beneath an apple tree.

'Do you and Martin want to come here for Christmas?' said Terry. 'And Rose. I know it's a bit small, but we'd love to have you.'

'That would be really nice,' said Alma, 'but only if we can watch the Queen's speech. It's a tradition in our house.'

Terry pretended to tug the peak of a cap and bowed his head. 'Of course, ma'am,' he said.

THIRTY-NINE

Tom woke early, as usual. The house was quiet. He lay on his back, with Fiona sleeping alongside him, and ran through the day ahead in his mind. Last year, they had gone to Fiona's sister's and spent the afternoon surrounded by overexcited nieces and nephews, fuelled by chocolate, tearing through a living room knee-deep in wrapping paper. Fiona had cried all the way home.

Her sister had made it clear when she "happened to pop by" a month ago that she was expecting a return invitation, but Tom and Fiona had been in agreement that it would be too much at the moment. Next year, they said, when things have settled down.

Tom cast his mind forwards to the final in two weeks' time. With Geoff's order, and more to come, he wasn't desperate for the money anymore, but winning was still important; it would top everything off. And he wanted it for Terry too, though it looked unlikely he would be able to play. The semi was only a month ago, but he'd definitely gone downhill since then.

Fiona stirred next to him, and he thought she was just turning over in her sleep, but she placed a hand on his chest.

'Merry Christmas,' she whispered.

Tom put his own hand on hers. 'Do you want a cup of tea?' he said. 'I can't sleep anymore; I'm too excited.'

'Go on then,' said Fiona, 'but don't make too much noise.'

Tom paused outside the small bedroom, where a lamp on the floor shed a soft glow along the thick carpet. The door was cracked open a touch, but Tom could hear nothing from inside.

Waiting for the kettle to boil downstairs, he wandered into the living room. He'd gone a bit over the top with the tree this year, but he could tell that Fiona had been secretly happy about it. He looked at the presents piled around its base and smiled. Maybe he'd gone a bit over the top there as well.

When he got back with the tea, Fiona was sat up in bed with the light on. His spot was taken. Rosemary's beaming little face, framed by soft brown curls, gazed up at him over the top of a pillowcase bulging with toys.

'Look, Daddy,' she said, showing him a satsuma clutched in her fist, 'Santa's been.'

Tom put the teas down and lifted the bedcovers.

'Well, come on then,' he said, getting in next to her, 'make some space for me.'

Rosemary passed him the satsuma and dived into her sack. When half of the contents lay scattered across the bed, she stopped and lifted her head.

'Did Santa bring you presents as well, Mummy?' she said.

Fiona pulled Rosemary into her, kissing the top of the little girl's head. She lifted her eyes to Tom's. 'You're my present, sweetheart,' she said.

FORTY

A thin light bled through the bedroom curtains. Outside, the street was quiet. Phil lay on his back, listening to Julie's soft breathing alongside him. She had been tired a lot lately, some nights barely making it past 9pm. Still, term was over now – the break would do her good: recharge her batteries.

Phil eased back the covers and slipped out of bed. Julie stirred and turned over to his side, her face angled up at him on the pillow, the pale skin of her throat and forehead catching the half-light. In the silence of the bedroom, watching her sleeping, the thought of having almost lost her was grotesque. As though the shadow of death had passed close to him.

Downstairs, the day dawned overcast and grey through the kitchen window. The garden lay heavy with dew. A robin, pecking at damp seed on the bird table in the centre of the lawn, gave the only sign of life, or colour, to the drab scene. Phil thought about the darts final in two weeks' time, and about Terry. Pat seemed pretty sure that he would be unable to play, and Phil had already spoken to the others about giving him their share of the prize money if they won. They all knew how desperately Terry wanted to pay off the milk round and help Martin with the house. Sometimes, it seemed as though that was more important to him than surviving the cancer.

Julie opened her eyes and stretched as Phil pushed open the bedroom door with his foot. 'I brought you a cup of tea,' he said.

Julie shuffled herself upright and flicked on the bedside light. 'Thanks,' she said.

'It's a bit grey outside,' said Phil, knocking off his slippers and getting back into bed. 'Damp.'

Julie leaned away from him and dipped her hand beneath the bed. When she came back up, she was holding out a present. 'Merry Christmas,' she said.

'I thought we were taking them to your mother's?' said Phil. 'My ones for you are already in the car.'

Julie smiled. 'This is a special one,' she said, 'just for us two.'

Phil took the present and gave it a squeeze.

'No guessing,' laughed Julie.

Phil unwrapped the present and held it in both hands. It was a soft toy. A rabbit with a pink nose and long, floppy ears. He turned his head to Julie for an explanation. She was smiling at him, her eyes shiny with tears.

'I'm pregnant,' she said.

In the street outside, someone cried out, 'Ho ho ho!', and they both laughed.

'But what... when?' stuttered Phil.

'I went to the doctors on Tuesday,' said Julie. 'It's only early, so you mustn't tell anyone. It must have been after you won your semi-final.'

Phil laughed again. 'Crikey,' he said, 'and I didn't even play.'

FORTY-ONE

'Merry Christmas,' said Pat. Her arm came over and pressed against Terry's chest, and she shuffled up against him, kissing the back of his neck. He lay still for a moment, relishing the warmth of Pat's body against his. Then he rolled to face her, kissed her on the lips and pulled her in tight to him, throwing his leg over her hip.

'Merry Christmas, beautiful.'

'How do you feel?' said Pat, when Terry released her. Her hand was resting on his upper arm, her thumb moving back and forth over his bare skin. He did a quick self-assessment. No headache, no nausea – hungry if anything.

'OK,' he said.

'Good,' said Pat, kissing him again. 'I'll make us a cup of tea.'

Terry had often marvelled at Pat's ability to drink tea whilst it was still scalding hot. It was a skill she reckoned she'd developed when Martin was little, swallowing down cups between laundry, and nappy changes, and a thousand other domestic duties. At work, she'd perfected the art, grabbing a minute or two in the nurse's tea room before being buzzed to change a patient's sheets or catheter or, as was often the case, both. Either she drank it boiling hot, she said, or stone cold. Never anywhere in between.

So when Pat jumped out of bed to go and prep the vegetables, her mug empty, Terry had barely had a sip of his. She put the radio on in the kitchen, and Terry heard her clattering about, singing along to the usual playlist of Christmas classics.

When he came through into the kitchen, she was stood over the table in her apron, stuffing the turkey.

'He doesn't look like he's enjoying that too much,' said Terry.

'How do you know?' said Pat. 'You can't see his face.'

Terry sat down. 'Body language,' he said. 'I've been through it; I know exactly how he feels.'

Pat laughed and nodded towards the sprouts. 'You can peel those if you like, less traumatising for you.'

Terry pulled the bag of brussels towards him and began removing the outer leaves. He scored a cross in the bottom of each one and dropped them into the saucepan.

'You didn't mind not going out last night, did you?' he said.

'No, I was knackered when I got in anyway. It was nice – just the two of us. Reminded me of that one when I was pregnant with Martin, in that little house in Richardson Street, do you remember?'

'God, yeah, it was freezing. And the gas ran out before the turkey had cooked. We ended up eating your mum's mince pies for main course. We went to bed when it got dark just to get warm.'

At half past ten, Pat put the turkey in the oven and stood back to assess the preparations. The hobs and work surface alongside the cooker were stacked with pans of vegetables. Terry watched Pat peer in each one, marking off with her finger from a list in her head.

'Right,' she said, apparently satisfied that nothing had been forgotten, 'I'll go and pick up the others; we'll sort the table out

276

when they get here. We'll need that extra chair from the living room.' She untied her apron and hung it on the hook beside the door from which she took down her coat. 'You go and sit down for a bit; I won't be long.'

Terry went through into the living room and turned on the television. There was a Christmas service on BBC2 from a church in Lichfield. Terry had never been particularly religious, but he did enjoy a good carol sung properly, as opposed to the first three lines screeched tunelessly through the keyhole, before the percussion on the front door demanding money, that he was used to in the run-up to Christmas.

When Pat returned with Rose, Alma and Martin, Terry was asleep. He was in the front room of a small terraced house eating Christmas dinner with Pat. It was snowing inside the house so that the dining table, and even the fat turkey between them, was coated with a layer of crisp white crystals. Terry could make out each flake individually. A snowman in a school cap and tie sat at the end of the table with a plate of untouched food in front of him.

'Martin looks a bit chilly,' said Pat, pulling the small carrot nose from the snowman's face and biting into it.

Terry woke with a start. On the television, the choir sang, 'When the snow lay round about, deep and crisp and even.'

'You OK, love?' said Pat.

Terry looked up, confused and shaken from the dream. Martin appeared behind Pat, and Terry stared at him, half expecting his nose to be missing.

'Hi, Dad, Merry Christmas.' He pulled a couple of presents from a shopping bag and bent to place them under the tree. In doing so, he disturbed the wiring, and the lights went out.

'Still got this old thing,' he said, fiddling with the plug so that the lights came back on, 'I'm surprised it hasn't caught fire by now.'

Terry pushed himself up on the settee. 'Ayup, kidda,' he said.

'Hi, Terry, Merry Christmas,' said Alma, flopping down alongside him. 'Anything good on?'

'*The Two Ronnies* later,' said Terry.

Alma stretched her legs in front of her, her head against the back of the sofa turned towards the television. She wore wool stockings under a red woollen dress stretched tight across her enormous bump. Her hand lay on it like a dark leaf on some great swollen fruit. She turned her head towards Terry and slapped him playfully on the thigh.

'Big, isn't it,' she said, cupping her belly in both hands, 'and solid, feel.'

She took hold of Terry's wrist and placed his hand on her bump. He felt the ribbed pattern of the dress under his palm and then a tiny pressure.

'It kicked,' he said, smiling. 'I felt it kick.'

Alma laughed. 'Yeah, I felt it too. He's going to be a footballer.'

'Where's your nan?' Terry asked.

'She's helping Mum with the table,' said Martin.

'I can do that,' said Terry.

'Oh, don't worry,' said Alma, 'she enjoys it. And she'll be filling Pat in on all the gossip.'

'And what gossip would that be?' asked Rose, shuffling into the room and sitting down in the armchair.

'What does everyone want to drink?' said Pat, coming in behind her.

'I'll have a nice glass of sherry if you have one, Pat,' said Rose.

'There's beer on the floor by the fridge, Martin,' said Terry. 'Put them in glasses since it's Christmas.'

'Just an orange juice for me please, Pat, or squash is fine,' said Alma.

'Shall we open the presents now?' said Martin, coming back with the beers.

'We should have a toast,' said Terry, raising his glass, 'to the baby.'

'And family,' said Pat.

'And to good health,' said Rose, looking at Terry.

Pat, perched on the arm of the chair, clinked glasses with Rose.

Martin took a present from under the tree, turned it over to read the label and handed it to Pat.

'Oh, this is gorgeous, Terry,' she said. She stood up and held the coat against herself. It was a pale, dusty green like bleached grass, with a wide collar and thick belt. She unfastened the large round buttons and slipped it on.

'Probably better without the apron.' She laughed.

'I got a bit of help from Alma,' admitted Terry, as Pat bent to kiss him.

She leaned across and pecked Alma on the cheek too. 'Well, thank you both. I love it.'

'You can open this one, love,' said Pat. 'It's beautifully wrapped.'

'To Mum and Dad,' Terry read, 'Merry Christmas, love Alma and Martin. It's almost too nice to open,' he said, turning to Alma.

Inside was a framed black-and-white photograph of Terry, Pat and Martin on the beach at Mablethorpe. 'It's the one you've got on the mantlepiece at your house,' said Terry.

'Nan said you liked it,' said Alma.

For the first time, Terry noticed the title of the book Pat was holding in the photograph. How had he not seen that before?

'It's lovely,' said Pat, balancing herself on the arm of the sofa alongside Terry. 'Next time you'll have to get one of all of us.'

Though it was crowded around the table with five of them, dinner was a big success. Rose said grace and then sat throughout the meal in the gold crown from her cracker, as regal as genuine royalty. She ate her food slowly and with great care, her large spectacles straddled low on her flat nose. She spoke little but followed the conversation intently, revolving her head to look upon each speaker like a wise owl. Terry had no appetite but did his best to disguise it. Alma, on the other hand, demolished her first plate and then piled on another, stacking carrots, parsnips and sprouts in great heaps that she then doused in dark gravy. Extra turkey was an excuse for more cranberry sauce which she spread like jam on a slice of toast.

Terry sat back in his chair, hot, and took a sip of his beer. His paper hat slipped down over his forehead, and he adjusted it back above his ears. The room was damp with steam, the windows, though pushed open, running with it.

'Are you OK, love?' said Pat.

Terry felt Rose's eyes on him. 'That was delicious,' he said. 'I'm just saving myself some room for the pudding.'

Pat accepted Martin's offer to help clear and wash up with a conspiratorial smile at Terry but insisted that the others go through to the living room and leave them to it.

At 3pm, they were all together to watch the Queen; Rose in the armchair still wearing her crown. Halfway through, as Her Majesty quoted the poet John Donne, Alma groaned and clutched her stomach. She followed this up with a long, low guttural moan that drowned out entirely the Queen's clipped monologue.

'Sorry,' she said, with a strain, 'I think I need to lie down.'

'That'll be the sprouts,' said Terry.

Martin laughed nervously.

'Come on,' said Pat, 'you can stretch out in our room.'

For the next couple of hours, it was difficult to concentrate on the television. Even with the kitchen between them, and the bedroom door closed, Alma could be heard moaning and, on occasion, crying out in pain.

'She's not got food poisoning, has she?' said Terry.

'It's the baby, you idiot,' said Pat, who was rushing between rooms with wet flannels and water and cushions.

'But it's too early,' said Terry, 'it's not due for another two weeks. It's Christmas Day.'

'The baby doesn't know that.'

Eventually, Pat came into the living room pulling on her coat. 'I'm going to take her in,' she said. 'Come on, Martin. Rose, I'll drop you home on the way past.'

Terry watched the others gather up their things. A howl shook the walls of the caravan as though someone had dropped an enormously heavy object on their foot and was left pinned to the spot.

'When will you be back?' he said.

'I don't know,' said Pat, kissing him quickly on the forehead. 'I'll see you later.'

'Merry Christmas, Terry,' said Rose.

'Yeah, Merry Christmas, Dad,' said Martin.

With the others gone, the caravan seemed suddenly quiet. Martin's beer, half drunk, stood on the coffee table alongside the empty sherry glass. Pat's new coat was folded neatly in its wrapping paper on the floor, Rose's slight frame still visible in the sag of the armchair. Only the falsetto fakery of Paul Daniels on the television cut through the silence. 'Now that's magic,' he said.

The Two Ronnies didn't seem as funny watching it on his own, and even if he hadn't have slept through most of *Death on the Nile*, he wasn't sure he'd have followed it anyway. From what he could make out, everyone had a motive, almost all a weapon and few a decent alibi. Still, Poirot appeared to find the case straightforward enough and, as usual, was rather pleased with himself at solving it. Terry had always preferred Miss Marple.

At midnight, he took himself off to bed. He turned off the lights on the Christmas tree but left one on in the kitchen for Pat.

He didn't hear her come in but woke when she pressed up against him in the dark.

'It's a girl,' she whispered in his ear. 'Merry Christmas, Granddad.'

FORTY-TWO

Two days later, on the 27th, Terry woke with a pain so acute that he squealed as though run through with a sword. His knees were drawn up to his chest, and something sharp and hot was inside him trying to get out. His hand went instinctively to the spot below his waist where the pain was centred in a vain attempt to lessen the agony. But the stabbing only increased in intensity, and he was unable, unwilling even, to prevent himself from peeing into his pyjamas. He cried out again as the urine crept, like hot lava, down through his penis and spilled from the end in what felt like molten lumps onto his raw thighs.

He was only barely aware of Pat jumping out of bed and had no idea at all how long he lay there, scarcely daring to breathe for fear of increasing the torture, before the ambulance arrived.

For the next forty-eight hours, following emergency surgery, the doctors managed Terry's pain with a combination of drugs that kept him sedated for the majority of the time. Occasionally, he would open his eyes, and sometimes he was sufficiently conscious to recognise Pat, sitting in a chair alongside his bed.

Once he was awake for longer periods, they encouraged him to move around the ward a couple of times a day to prevent bed sores and to get his legs moving again. A nurse took him to the bathroom and showed him how to empty and reattach his stoma.

The doctor had told Terry when he came round after the operation that they had removed his bladder, but with the drugs and everything that was going on, he hadn't really taken it in. He was just relieved that the pain had gone away.

On New Year's Day, Pat pushed Terry on what had become their usual mid-morning spin through the hospital and out into the little garden behind the geriatric ward.

'I've got a little surprise for you,' she said, parking up the chair and pressing on the brake with her foot. She held open the door, and Terry walked slowly through it.

It was known as the garden, but in reality was little more than a small square patch of grass bordered by a staff car park on one side and the walls of the hospital on the other three. Benches, donated by relatives of those no longer able to enjoy the space, pressed into the thin gravel that ran around the outside of the square. After the stuffiness and artificial light of the ward, coming outside was like shedding a layer of dead skin. The air was damp and earthy, and the sun, which even at this time of the year streaked in low over the car park, made baubles of the dewdrops on the wet grass.

A family occupied the bench on which Terry and Pat usually sat. It took Terry a moment to realise that it was Martin, Alma and Amy. He walked over, placing his feet deliberately on the narrow path, and dipped his head to look into the pram. The baby was sleeping. A pink woollen blanket was pulled snug under her chin, a matching bonnet covering her round little head. Martin shuffled across to give Terry a seat.

'Hi, Dad,' he said, 'Happy New Year.'

The doctors were happy that Terry was well enough to go home on the 3rd of January. The truth was they needed the bed. But Terry had started eating again, albeit only some softish foods, and though the wound was still swollen and tender, it had at least stopped leaking. Pat was going to check on the stitches, and Terry had promised that he would get up and move about at least three times a day, but without overdoing it. No lifting, no pub, no darts.

On Wednesday evening, Phil came round while Terry was watching John Wayne slug his way around London as a New York cop frustrated by Scotland Yard's more restrained style of policing.

'I thought you were meant to get a bit of exercise now and then,' said Phil.

'I am,' replied Terry. 'Can't you see the track I've worn in the carpet between here and the kettle?'

'How you feeling?'

'Yeah, not too bad, been worse.'

Phil sat down. 'We've been chatting, me and the lads, we think you should play in the final on Saturday.'

Terry turned his head towards Phil, but there was no sign that he was joking.

'Me? I haven't picked up a dart for weeks. And Dave…'

'We all want you to play; we're not bothered if we lose.'

'I am – I need the money.'

'You know what I mean.'

Terry turned back to the television. He was a big fan of John Wayne, but he definitely made a better cowboy than cop.

'I don't even know if I could stand up for that long, never mind throw a dart.'

'Have a think about it,' said Phil. 'We've got a coach again, but I'll drive you if you like. And we'll try and remember the car this time.'

After Phil had left, Terry hauled himself up from the settee. He stood in the middle of the living-room carpet, one foot in front of the other as though he were at the oche, and threw an imaginary dart at the wall.

'Not too bad,' he said to himself.

FORTY-THREE

In the end, Pat said that if anyone was going to drive Terry, she would do it. That way, she could keep an eye on him, and if the others wanted to stay on after the final drinking, she could bring him home.

He had slept badly. He could still only lie on his back and had spent much of the night staring at a small patch of light on the ceiling above a crack in the curtains. He ran through the match in his head: throwing the winning dart, lifting the trophy. But mainly, he thought about Amy and Pat. He listened to her breathing next to him. He was so lucky.

'Are you sure this is it?' said Pat, stopping the car. Someone behind beeped their horn. Crowds of people filled the pavements and manoeuvred between the traffic.

'Yeah, it's on top of the bus station.' A huge banner hung over the side of the drab, concrete building advertising Embassy cigarettes. 'We have to go round the back. There's a special player's entrance.'

The special entrance turned out to be a lift, directly off the street, watched over by a pair of jobsworth security guards. They insisted that Pat would have to go back around to the front and go in by the friends and family door. Pat kissed him. 'Good luck,' she said.

Terry went up alone and came out backstage. Another security guard, in a clip-on tie that arced over his impressive gut, pointed him towards the players' lounge. The room was rammed and full of smoke. Packets of the sponsor's cigarettes lay scattered across every surface. Practice boards ran along one wall and a bar along another. Eric Bristow was stood with a pint in his hand, chatting to Sid Waddell. Terry spotted Phil and the others at one of the boards.

'Terry,' said Hans, who saw him first. 'It is so nice to see you again.'

'Can you believe all this?' said Tom. 'You seen Brissie over there? And the other bloke, Keith Deller.'

A couple of boards away, a kid in bright red trousers, and a haircut like his mum had done it, stood sipping an orange juice. He looked young enough to be still at school.

'He's got about as much chance as we have,' said Terry.

After an hour or so, one of the organisers took them and their opponents into a room across the corridor to run through how things would work. He held a cigarette in one hand and clutched a packet in the other. A second pack stuck out of his suit's top pocket. *Clearly a fan of the sponsor's product*, Terry thought.

'The telly calls the shots,' the man said, in a thick cloud of smoke, 'so it's one doubles and a singles match each, if needed. First team to three wins, wins. Try not to look at the camera. Sid'll announce you on, and we'll cue your music. You'll have to stay backstage when you're not playing, but you can watch it on the telly in the players' lounge.' He turned to Terry. 'Your man's told us about your little problem, so we've put a stool next to the drinks table in case you need to sit down.'

'I'll be fine,' said Terry, as everyone looked at him.

'These boys are on at three so you've got to be done by two-thirty latest.'

Terry and the others turned to see the two world finalists walk into the room.

'Good luck, fellas,' they said, going around the two teams, shaking hands.

'Be lucky,' said Bristow to Terry.

'You too,' said Terry.

'Right,' said the organiser, drawing on his cigarette and stubbing it out in one of the sponsor's ashtrays, 'follow me.'

At the end of the corridor, he pushed open a door with "STAGE" written on it, and the acoustics changed. It was dimly lit, and they were behind a makeshift wall with the joinery visible, wires and thick cables snaking across the floor. Terry could hear the noise of the crowd on the other side of the wall.

'I'll come and get you from the lounge, and you'll wait over there,' he said, pointing to a curtain at the end of the wall. 'Sid'll give you the build-up, then when the music starts, you're on. Try not to trip over the wires.' He looked at his watch. 'First game in thirty-five minutes.'

'Time for another pint,' said Hans.

If anything, the players' lounge had filled up further since they'd been gone. A bunch of people surrounded the pros warming up on the practice boards, and another crowd were over by a television watching horse racing. It was three deep at the bar.

'I'm going to the loo,' said Terry.

Phil followed him. 'How are you feeling?' he said. 'Nervous?'

'Nervous I'm going to make a prat of myself,' said Terry. 'I can't hit a barn door.'

There were three empty urinals in the toilet, but the only stall was occupied. Terry hesitated. Phil took the urinal closest to the far wall. After a second or two, he glanced around at Terry, who was still dawdling in the centre of the room. At that moment, the stall toilet flushed, and the door unlocked. Terry allowed the man out and then went in and slid the bolt across. He undid his belt and lifted his shirt. The bag was not full, but he emptied it anyway. When he came out, Phil was still there. Terry saw him waiting in the mirror while he washed his hands.

'The result's really not important,' said Phil, when Terry turned to face him. 'I'm just happy you made it.'

'Me too,' said Terry.

Back in the players' lounge, it was surreal watching Hans and Tom on the telly. Somehow, the difference in size and stature of the two of them appeared exaggerated on screen so that they looked comical on stage together: Pooh and Piglet in matching shirts.

Each time the camera scanned the crowd, Terry tried to pick out Pat but couldn't spot her.

'Look,' said Phil, 'there's Linda, and Dave, and Karen. How did he persuade her to come?'

Though they lost narrowly, Tom was like a kid at Christmas when he came back to the lounge, bouncing around, unsure which present to open next.

'It's amazing,' he said. 'I know we lost, sorry, but the crowd, and Hans is playing so well. He'll win his game, and I feel good – I can't wait to get back on.'

They turned back to the television as they heard Sid introduce Hans for his singles, and the opening bars of "Sweet Caroline" started up. Tom and Terry began to sing along, and by the chorus, the whole room had joined in.

Hans looked as relaxed as ever on stage and won his game comfortably to level the match. Then Tom, throwing quickly and as well as he'd ever done, played the game of his life to put them 2-1 up.

'I guess it's down to us,' said Phil. 'One of us wins, and we're champions.'

'If you win, I'll only need to go on stage to pick up the trophy,' said Terry.

Phil's opponent had the darts in the first leg and got down to the double first. But he looked nervous and missed five darts at it to give Phil a chance. Phil was miles out with his first dart but somehow managed to hit double eighteen with his second to take the leg. Tom threw his arms around Terry's shoulders. 'Come on, Phil,' he said, 'one more.'

When the noise from the crowd died down, Phil came back to the oche and threw twenty-six. His opponent took the lead and never surrendered it. In the decider, the occasion seemed to get to both players, and they limped down from 501, each seemingly doing their best to underscore the other. Eventually, Phil, and the others, watched on as his opponent put them both out of their misery by hitting double two at the fourth attempt.

'Oh well,' said Terry. 'I suppose this is it then.'

Standing behind the curtain in the semi-dark, Terry could hear the hum of the crowd on the other side: jumbled voices talking, shouting, laughing, beer glasses chinking, footsteps, chairs scraping across the wooden floor. And then silence. He lifted his hand to the crucifix around his neck.

'Ladies and gentlemen. For The White Hart – like Muhammad Ali, you can knock him down, but you can't knock him out, like Lazarus of Bethany, he's back – please put your hands together for The Milkman, Terry Fletcher.'

Terry took a breath and pushed through the curtain. In the split second before the spotlight fell upon him, casting the crowd into shadow, he saw Pat. She was on her feet in the centre of the room. Alma was next to her with her camera pointed at him. Martin stood on her other side waving, holding Amy to his chest. He thought of Rose in her living room at home, watching on telly, the Mablethorpe picture on the mantlepiece. His family. He had thrown thousands of darts over the last year; he could do this in his sleep. He would win it for them.

Music shook the room, and the crowd sang along. Terry walked towards the centre of the stage, where Sid Waddell waited for him in a haze of smoke and flashing lights, as though in a dream. *Like Saint Peter at the Pearly gates*, thought Terry.

He held out his hand. 'It's good to see you, Terry,' he said.

'Believe me,' said Terry, 'it's good to see you too, Sid.'

ACKNOWLEDGEMENTS

When I applied for a place at the Faber Academy, I told them that like many people I had always wanted to write, but that the reason I had never done so (out in the open at least) was that I was afraid to fail.

A couple of weeks later, submitting my first piece for the other members of the group to critique, it took me two days to press send. My coursemates replied, eventually, with kindness and encouragement, for which I can't thank them enough. Special thanks to Pip Creed, Deborah den Herder, Ali Milton, Rhee Joseph, Anna Chiara Brunetti and Susan Downer. Keep writing my friends.

The tutors at Faber were wonderful. Thank you to Helen Shipman and to Tom Bromley for their wisdom, insight and support.

Many thanks to Tim Lott, author of the Penguin Modern Classic The Scent of Dried Roses, and to Kitty Walker, editor, both of whom gave me terrific, honest and constructive feedback on my early drafts, as well as the assurance that what I had written was actually worth reading.

Thank you to Samar Hamman from Rocking Chair Books, who, though she didn't finally take me on, encouraged me enough to believe that one day this book might get published.

Thank you to the team at The Book Guild for making that dream a reality.

To Siân, Lily and Noah, for your love, thank you.

Finally, I would like to thank anyone who takes the time to read this book. If you laugh only once, feel empathy towards any of the characters, or are pleased in some small way by the rhythm of a single sentence, then I shall consider that I have not failed.